Dear Anni
Thank you for

SON OF INFLUENCE

A Novel

ERIK LEWIN

Jeffrey Park Press

Las Vegas

Jeffrey Park Press

jeffreyparkpress.com

Printed in the United States of America

First Printing, 2018

This book is a work of fiction. Names, characters, places and incidents
either are products of the author's imagination or are used fictitiously.
Any resemblance to actual events or locales or persons, living or dead,
is entirely coincidental.

ISBN 978-0-9991133-0-01 (paperback)
ISBN 978-0-9991133-1-8 (ebook)
ISBN 978-0-9991133-2-5 (audio downloadable file)
ISBN 978-0-999-1133-3-2 (ebook)

For my mother and father

Acknowledgments

The author would like to thank the following individuals: Joshua Adams, David Schneider, and Roy Faerber.

Chapter 1

M y father kicked his legs up onto the desk. He was wearing handmade-leather cowboy boots that matched the beige fedora on his head. A brown cigar hung from his mouth. The desk was thick oak and brimmed with stacks of papers and contracts of the city's power brokers.

"Tell me about the delivery," he said.

My father's eyes creased at the plume of smoke he blew at Monkey, his main shipment guy, sitting across from him. Monkey was bestowed this name because the man's upper body was powerful and broad, with giant swaths of black furry hair that poked out from his back. He was an industrious worker, but no doubt slowed by a crippled intellect. A flash of panic lit Monkey's eyes.

"Listen, Larry, them guys down at Riverside, they mistook the order for the shoes and coats, not us. We went down there with the rig, the whole damn load, and he said turn back with it. He said he didn't order that much."

Monkey struggled to shift his large frame in the chair. I sunk into the depth of the Italian leather couch, tapping a cigarette into an old-school glass ashtray, and braced for my father's reaction.

"You know what?" Larry Lowe started, his middle-aged limbs springing to life, quickly hovering over Monkey. "I'll have your balls!" His hand shot out like a claw and I swear, he grabbed a fistful of Monkey's potatoes in a vice grip until the man screeched. "You never leave a job without my say-so. Got it?"

"Yes, boss. I got it." Monkey's oblong head wobbled up and down.

"Good." The old man released his grip. "Now, how about a hit of cognac, before I hit the road?" He patted Monkey reassuringly on his hulking shoulders.

"Sure thing, Larry," he said, breathing out in sputtered coughs.

My father ambled over to the counter where he kept his bottles, right next to the couch. I nervously shifted and covered the title of a novel I'd just bought, The Weight of Love, fearing he'd belittle me in his familiar refrain of how delicate I was. He hadn't bothered to wipe off his black-smudged fingers, filthy from having opened several crates of garments in the adjacent, cavernous warehouse. He opened the seal on a sleek bottle that looked like it was once the treasure of a fifteenth-century French king. In his private office he coveted fine, unique pieces, including a pair of wood-carved elephants, their ivory tusks gleaming.

"I gotta take a leak," he announced, after pouring a glass for him and Monkey.

Monkey and I glanced at each other. He struck me as an oversized boy, yet one who perfected the tip-toe between awe and fear of my father.

"Larry! Assemblyman Norris on line-eight!" It was Betty, his longtime receptionist on speaker. In the late 1990s, before texts and the days of routine emails, she was the only person who could find him, wherever the hell he was.

Larry emerged and sat back in his giant chair. The leather seemed to groan with exasperation, as if asking its occupant to consider a lighter, gentler touch. "Put him through." He set the cigar down, leaving it to smolder in the ashtray, and lit a cigarette in its place. "Norris, how ya doin'?" He popped the phone off the hook. "I remember that. Yes. But the senate wants your vote to confirm the zoning, so stop blubbering about it. Look, this is a big day—my kid got into law school and I gotta run. I'll see you at the brunch tomorrow. Ciao." He stubbed out the smoke he inhaled and knocked back a shot of the exquisite cognac.

"Monkey, get outta here and fix that order. It can't wait. Let's go, little Lowe," he snapped. "Your mother can't wait either."

We always stopped at the office on the way out at night, leaving the shop, as he called it, and my mother always waited in the car. This time we were late to a dinner in my honor. I grabbed my book, stood up from the couch, and tried to smooth all the fresh creases on my suit slacks.

Earlier, I wouldn't even have made it out of the house if not for my mother. "Mom, what do I wear to this thing?" I asked, holding up a black suit for her examination.

"You going on a hit after dessert? How about a little color? Maybe your father's yellow tie?"

"The one I wore to my Bar Mitzvah?"

"You do still have the baby face."

She was right about that. At twenty-two, I still got carded for cigarettes and softcore porn. My slight frame did my face no favors. I closed the door to my bedroom and stripped off the towel. I took stock of my naked body in the mirror. I was relieved to find I had any torso at all.

"Let's go!" my father roared from downstairs.

I surveyed the mess of clothes and whipped up an ensemble: black suit, white shirt, black shoes. To hell with the Bar Mitzvah tie. I'd made it through puberty. I often wondered if manhood would be another story.

After we left the shop, my father slid behind the wheel of his big Caddie. My mother and I sat helplessly while he brought its nose to the back bumper of every car in his way.

"Larry, if I go through the windshield, you do not have permission to borrow my car," my mother said calmly, her small fingers gripping the seat handle. This prospect of a gruesome car wreck was so common over the years that my mother learned to tolerate it. She knew Larry liked to direct traffic. But this time, my father slowed the Caddie down.

We arrived at Carmine's late. The revelers were already there, drinking and chatting around the bar. There were no television sets, and Tony Bennett's rendition of Anything Goes played softly. Large antique lamps glowed warmly over round nightclub tables, and crushed velvet curtains provided privacy.

"Larry, Joanna, Delton, get in here!" Uncle Nate called.

He wasn't my real uncle, just an old friend of the Lowe family. A criminal defense attorney, he was often in the papers with his big-time clients. Growing up, I heard him talk about indictments and verdicts, and while I never understood what those things meant, I always wanted to be just like him someday.

"Hey Nate, do you really need another starch binge?" I jabbed at his paunch.

"Need that hand broken, kid?" Nate retorted, gesturing over his shoulder.

I took note of Nate's entourage, a collection of double-chinned wise guys talking quietly among themselves, probably debating the preferred means of body removal, be it land or water.

"How about a song, everybody?" A friend of Nate's, a retired judge, took a seat at an old grand piano. She was feeble and wrinkled, but in her prime had hammered guys so hard at sentencing, prisons closed from decay before their stretches were up.

"Once he finishes law school, he'll be ready for my office," I overheard my father say to Nate. "Then, there'll be a Lowe Family Shoe and Apparel business," he added, finishing another Scotch. "That's the reality. As a lawyer, he'll be dangerous enough to do his own deals."

We took our seats in the dining area set up specially for our party, and snappy busboys placed bottles of sparkling water, red wine, and antipasti platters on the table.

Nicky Denetti lit a cigar. He was Nate's client and the most reputed mobster in the city. He sat across from me, and I stuffed my jittering hands into my pockets. It was hard not to stare at the large divot on his forehead, a switchblade cut he famously took as a kid.

"Nicky, I'd like to introduce my nephew, Delton Lowe," Nate said. "And leave a little food, the kid's actually supposed to grow."

Nicky didn't register Nate's wise-crack, his eyes boring into me. There was no question Nicky made me nervous, though I hungered to know more about his life of nefarious activities.

"This kid ever kiss a girl?" he chuckled through a mouthful of stuffed peppers. Before I could react, those black eyes diverted elsewhere.

"Actually, I heard you had a girl over the house recently," Nate said, dabbing his chin with a napkin tucked at his collar.

"How'd you know that?"

"As a lawyer, you have to find things out for yourself," he said. After a couple bites of lasagna, he looked back at me.

"We talking wedding bells?"

"Ha. Not exactly."

"You just put accidental kids in the not-happening pile," Mom interjected, and went back to chatting with the retired judge.

"We just watched old episodes of Family Ties in my room," I said, winking at Nate.

"Appreciate the fact that you even have a bedroom," my father spat into my ear. His voice came out of nowhere. It often felt as if he were omnipresent.

"What do you mean?" I asked. My father leaned toward Nicky, ignoring my question, and whispered something.

"Your father and I slept in the street, coming up, so you wouldn't have to. You hear me, Delton?" Nate said.

"I do." Nate could cross-examine a corpse, I thought.

"And they often still do, by choice," my mother added, running a hand through her long hair. She never liked the world my father inhabited. "Delton, honey, you'll be different."

I didn't understand their language, what they were really saying. My father never shared his past, or his concerns, with me. I never knew what made him pace ruts into the floor late at night, when I was growing up. I was older, but as ignorant of his daily life as ever before.

"Hey Larry, that piece of shit assembly guy didn't clear this tenant out on Gun Hill Road. This guy doesn't do what he said he was gonna do, I'll have to do it my way," Nicky said, taking off his cream-and-gold-tinted glasses to put a cold eye on my father.

"Nicky, there's no need to be—" Nate interjected.

"Counselor, when something concerns you, with respect to my affairs, you'll be the first to know. I'm trying to have a conversation here," Nicky said.

"Nothing to worry about, Nicky," my father said. "This is a small thing. It's Jimmy K's property and I just took back his bank note, clearing the way to get his tenant out. I spoke with Assemblyman Norris, and he agreed to go along. The tenant will have no legal recourse in court. It's as good as done."

The velvet curtains of our private dining room opened, and snappy busboys returned to clear the table. Right behind them, Rollie, the longtime owner of Carmine's, leaned over and slung a tomato-stained arm around my shoulder. He then kissed me on the scalp and clapped sharply for a waiter, who brought a cake with candles, bearing my name in grey frosting. My father put his cigar down, stuck two fingers in his mouth and blew a sharp whistle. Everybody cheered and hollered, and the retired judge shouted, "To Delton! To his future!"

I looked at all the expectant faces. There was no turning back.

"Thank you, everybody!" I yelled, and blew out the candles.

Uncle Nate produced a gift, which I unwrapped right away. A large, leather-bound law dictionary. I flipped through the scuffed tome, its frayed margins filled with illegible written notes.

"That was my first law dictionary, kid. Keep it under your pillow every night for a year, and you'll be talking Latin in your sleep," Nate said, kissing my cheek.

I felt the weight of it in my arms. I immediately thought, this is the first ticket I ever had to Nate and my father's respect. I noticed my mother take a rare sip of wine and struggle to light a cigarette; perhaps she sensed the momentum of this train about to start on its track. She smiled at me in a way only I could see. She never drew attention. It occurred to me that unconditional love did not need to announce itself.

"You'll be in charge of it all one day, little Lowe. What a lucky kid. But don't forget," Larry Lowe took the Cuban cigar out of his mouth, and pointed its stub at me. "It's up to you. Do the right thing and put this education to good use."

The dictionary's alien language intimidated me. Did I belong in law school? I'd scarcely agreed to go in the first place. Yet I had no other plan, and my father could be very convincing. A part of me wanted to run away, but knew I wouldn't. This was my chance to belong in my father's world. Besides, how could I refuse to follow this path, painstakingly cut with his own sacrifices? These were my marching orders. But what had he gotten me into?

Chapter 2

The morning of orientation had arrived. I spit out my toothpaste and wiped clear a spot in the steamed mirror. I had new chin growth! What an affirmation of manhood! To see those black hairs sprout, wild as sunflowers, was to revel in a certain success. I'd worked the razor over those soft pores for years, and finally, the skin had ripened. I stroked the hairs while the edges of steam evaporated, and it was plain to see. Things came in their own time.

The orientation was billed as a necessary introduction to the school and its policies. I was running behind, and when I pushed open the large double-doors to the auditorium, they made an awful squeak that could raise the dead. The occupants all turned their heads at this interruption, and I shimmied down an aisle until finally slumping into a seat.

The place was packed with the first-year class, an ocean of khaki shorts and drab-colored t-shirts. I wondered if I had stumbled into a cattle-call for a Gap ad. A man in an ancient brown suit and bow tie, perhaps fashionable during the Civil War, took the podium and announced he was the dean.

"You are now 1Ls (first-year law students). The final important point to remain mindful of is that you must exercise and eat well over the course of the year."

What were the other important points? It also struck me as odd that this last one needed emphasis. Would we not naturally subsist?

"It is a common phenomenon for loved ones to have no idea what you will be experiencing. Try to be patient with them, for their concern is due to love," the dean continued, twiddling at his bow tie the way Charles Manson might have plucked an eerie guitar note to hypnotize his family.

As the dean wrapped up his remarks and ended the proceedings, the roomful of newbie, terror-stricken strangers trampled the aisles for the exit. On closer inspection, a couple of pretty girls emerged from the throng. Thank goodness! Attractive females were in the mix, if not as a fringe contingent. Outside the dimly lit auditorium, afternoon sunlight warmed the grounds and fresh-cut grass scented the air. A team of squirrels darted up a tree and I thought, how bad can this be?

A silver Mercedes parked in reverse at my feet. Its vanity plate read, EMPWR. The driver got out and I immediately noticed his meaty forearms and cropped hair. He only needed a sweater tied over his chest and he'd be ideal as an Alpha-Beta from Revenge of the Nerds. He brushed by me as if I were invisible. And yet, it was the plenitude of khakis and rimmed glasses that concerned me most. The nerdy-looking folks seemed to belong here.

The administration had rolled out beverage carts and a catered buffet on the lawn. I desperately wanted to hightail it home, but knew I couldn't run from the power-hungry and academics of the world forever. The new 1Ls scrambled to the food line, pushing and shoving for first place. You would have thought jobs at big firms were waiting to be snatched under trays of roast beef. I detested lines, but saw the bar cart beckon.

"I'd like a Scotch on the rocks, please."

The bartender moved quickly and handed over the drink. The first sip snuggled to my chest like a furry pet. People talk about comfort food, but the first taste of a strong drink is the real pacifier.

"You must be a thirsty 1L," I heard a voice say.

It was the dean! He ordered peach schnapps. His confederate jacket was off, and in the warm weather his slacks were hiked up, offering a view of pale calves and stringy black hairs.

"Delton Lowe. Scared shitless 1L," I said, shaking hands.

"Ah, an honest lawyer. We could use more of those." He drank oddly, lapping several sips with his tongue.

"Did you, or do you still practice law?" I asked casually, like I was at a bar.

"I worked for fifteen years in civil litigation. It was hectic, but I won cases that took down some big elephants. In fact, a couple set legal precedent. If you're lucky enough, you may get punished with them by your torts teacher."

I didn't even know what a legal precedent or a tort was, but it already sounded like punishment.

"Come, let me introduce you to a couple 1Ls. One other piece of advice, Delton, during your stay here, make love, not war, whenever possible," he said, with a little eyebrow raise that made me even more uncomfortable.

"Delton Lowe, this is Harry Marshall and Randy Miner. See you later, counselors." The dean took his peach cocktail and hiked up slacks elsewhere.

"Well, I guess we'll all be called counselors someday," Harry offered. He actually looked a little different from the crowd, with his woolly goatee, shaggy hair, and flannel shirt.

"You're an optimist, Harry, I like that. Where are you from?" I motioned to the barkeep for another Scotch and tossed a couple bucks in the tip jar. Harry stroked his chin, becoming quite excited.

"Originally, I'm from Bensonhurst, Brooklyn. I was going to pursue a career as a rabbi or Talmudic scholar, but then I realized this,"—he swept his arms about the grounds—"was part of that training."

He bent over to show me the yarmulke buried under that swath of twisty, unwashed hair. In my experience, he seemed to already have the hygienic part of rabbinical studies down. As a Hebrew man, I supported old Harry, but didn't actively observe the tenets of the faith.

"We're gonna get a minyan together tonight. You part of the tribe?" Randy asked.

He had a short boxy frame like a high school wrestler, but a high-pitched voice. I noticed the yarmulke on his head, too.

"I am."

"Great, you in?" he asked.

"You mean ten circumcised Jewish men for prayer?"

"Yes," they affirmed in unison.

"No, sorry."

I couldn't help but be cautious. Once, a friend of Nate's—a defense lawyer who represented Tupac or something—invited me to a Shabbat dinner at his temple to 'meet people' my age. Little did I know he was orthodox. I arrived to find the men and women separated during prayer. Afterward, at dinner, my host bailed and stuck me next to a single girl on the prowl. As if that wasn't awkward enough, the grown-ups at the table ganged up on me with questions about my Judaism and dating habits. It came out that I had been with Catholic girls, Shiksas! This revelation was more than they could bear. Wide-eyed with horror, they chastised me for this unseemly betrayal of my faith, until I fled the scene.

"Okay, Delton," Harry said, "We'll have a standing date by the library all year, so you're welcome to join us anytime."

"Okay, thanks fellas, next year in Jerusalem," I said, waving them off to wander the desert in solitude.

I walked across the lawn filled with makeshift tables and 1Ls seated with plates of food. The line had thinned. Approaching the back of the single-file, the girl in front of me looked a little familiar. She twirled brown curls and wore denim overalls that covered a tie-dyed t-shirt. She was busy yapping into a StarTAC cell phone. When she turned to the side, I recognized her.

She went to my college, a sorority girl, and while we didn't run in the same circles, our paths had crossed. If memory served, I once told her at a party in an alcohol- and drug-addled state, that our simultaneous arrival at a bathroom meant we were kindred spirits. She hadn't quite shared that interpretation. What was her name again? She shut her phone.

"You went to college at Albany, right?" I asked.

"I did," she confirmed.

"I'm Delton," I said, offering my hand. She shook it, seeming unable to place me.

"I don't suppose a long bathroom line rings any bells?" I asked, suddenly aware that I needed to stop talking or stop drinking, but as she studied me, the light of recognition dawned in her eyes.

"Oh, yeaaaah."

She opened her phone again, not taken with me or the memory.

"So, what do you make of all this so far?" I asked.

"Make of what, exactly?"

"Well, orientation. I actually just talked with the speaker from—"

"Who?"

The line moved forward.

"Oh, sorry, the dean. Anyway, that's not important," I hurriedly said, sensing this little reunion might be short-lived. "Would you like to hang out sometime this weekend? We could compare notes for battle. You are, after all, the only person I know here."

"I don't think there will be any time for that."

"Oh sure. This weekend doesn't work for me either."

She turned away with her plate of charcuterie and salad. I never did get her name.

My new home, presumably for the next three years, felt like a ghost town. A coastal summer getaway, it was left to a few locals to inhabit the rest of the year. A quick cigarette purchase and fill-up at the Last Stop by the Sea convenience mart offered an opportunity to interact with a local.

"Do you live in town, or just work here?" I asked the cashier.

"Oh honey, I've lived here since before you were born." Her face was deeply lined.

"That's a long time," I said.

"Well, one thing about the Point. Once people move here, they tend to stick around. You'll meet most of those folks at the Black Kettle."

"What's the Black Kettle?"

"That's where folks like to drink around here. Fresh pigs in a blanket on two-dollar Tuesdays! Come pay us a visit, darling."

"Okay, thanks!"

I gathered my provisions and headed to my new digs down the road. I hadn't moved so much as relocated, as the seaside bungalow came fully furnished, its motif a Victorian eyesore.

I cut the engine and sat quietly in the driveway. Tomorrow was the first day of classes. It occurred to me I'd never really studied in college. I'd just gotten by. In fact, I'd prided myself on being master of the so-called 'two-minute-drill.' Given enough high-grade hashish and chopped up ADD pills a friend generously gave of his prescription, there was no amount of work I could not complete between the hours of midnight and noon. This was the way I performed best, under acute pressure. I absorbed a whole semester's material during those hours. The results on papers and tests were always good enough to assure me that this method was effective. And yet, the dean's last words lingered in my mind . . . *no idea what you will be going through* . . . This would be a new ball game, its stakes higher, and my abilities tested. What if I actually failed?

As I unpacked duffle bags and linens from the trunk, I thought of wild times I'd shared with my buddies. There'd been many life-threatening adventures in this battle-tested Volvo. The auto-industry declares it a safe yet agile car, capable of withstanding stress and impact. After flooring it on slick highways, pulling out of tailspins, and smashing through a graveyard gate intact, I'd have to agree.

My friends were settling into their own new places in the city, with jobs in TV, ad companies, and startups. I didn't think I could land a job in a publishing house, even if that was what I wanted. That meant I would've been at home with my parents delivering pizzas. Unless I started selling off my organs, I couldn't afford to live anywhere else, or, by extension, do anything else. My father was covering a significant portion of this tab because he wanted me law school-educated, but I wondered how much of it was truly for me. After all, he attended a meager half-semester in college and never earned a degree. He hoped to have an attorney in the family.

Meanwhile, my friends were thrilled for their next chapter, with its youthful insulation from failure. They could screw up a job and plan their comeback amidst the camaraderie of friends, while I, on the other hand, was left to go mad in a shoddy bungalow at the edge of the world, with two-dollar pigs in a blanket from the Black Kettle to soothe my distress.

I shed these disabling thoughts and tried to focus on the matter at hand. After all, my new home was near the water and away from distractions, which, of course, was the problem. It was solemnly quiet on the street. The salty air tickled my nose. A seagull's squawk cracked the silence. I dragged my things inside in a few trips, then stepped back onto the porch to take a cigarette break.

"I vould help, dere, but no hands," a voice said.

A man stood at the foot of the driveway. The crevices in his face betrayed his middle-age, but his frame was lean and muscular in a spandex t-shirt. He smiled at me from under a glistening bald head, while holding a glass of wine and a paintbrush.

"Oh no, there's nothing more. But I'll tell you what. I'll help you with whatever you're drinking."

He threw his head back and spilled a little wine in the process.

"Ya, this is sure," he said.

Nothing like a cheery drunk next-door. He motioned for me to follow him to the front of the tri-level house, sleek with tall glass windows and high angular arches, and invited me inside. The interior was no disappointment, with a third-floor loft that overlooked a spacious living room. The most notable decorative touches, however, were large paintings that hung around the room. Easels, brushes and paint cans were stacked up in a corner on the cherrywood floor, between an American Indian sculpture and a glass console of ceramic figurines. A smooth jazz station drizzled synthesized saxophone.

"Red, ya?"

"Red sounds terrific. I'm Delton, by the way."

"Jaspr. I am new friend," he said, and gave a little wink. It didn't strike me as a come on, fortunately. After the dean, I'd reached my limit for unwelcome overtures.

"I think you mean neighbor, Jaspr, but yes," I said, swishing the wine, "new friends, too."

The paintings ranged from innocent to more questionable, even rather naughty and weird. There was a family portrait. He was probably in the portrait, a somewhat doughy boy with the same nose and eyes, Dalmatian at his side and slingshot in hand. When I view art, it often seems like a three-year-old sniffed glue and finger-painted the canvas, but that wasn't the case here. This fellow knew his lines and color.

What was an odd choice, I thought, was the pastel-colored ode to Don Johnson of Miami Vice, in a three-way kiss with Tubbs and a female suspect, or at least the conveniently placed handcuffs gave that impression. Another work featured a gaggle of Oompa Loompas covered in a purplish-brown paste, carrying on joyfully after having burned down the Wonka factory. I privately applauded them for breaking the chains of sweatshop conditions. Undoubtedly the climactic piece, high atop the fireplace in the living room, was a flesh-tone rendering of a hairless vagina. Voila!

"I admire your attention to detail. How long does it take to make one of these?"

"Very glad you say this. See curve?"

He stood by the hairless vagina and finger-traced the curve of its outer labia. He seemed to slip into a trance.

"It's well done, Jaspr."

"Yes!" He jabbed me with his elbow. "More vine?"

He took my glass before I could answer. The smooth jazz threatened to make me physically ill, but the panoramic view of perversion made me feel better.

"Can I smoke in here?"

"Ve go out. This vay."

He returned with my glass full and led us to a backyard and garden.

"You live here year-round?"

"Ya! Make house from... how ve say in anglish? From nozing."

"From nothing. From scratch."

"Ya, scratch." He gulped more wine. "I came, I vanted three-floor." He held up three fingers. "I make from nozing!"

"It's a beautiful place. I'm glad we'll be neighbors."

"You vith school?"

"I'm in law school, yes. I moved here to study."

"Many time, people come hee-yah."

The poor bastard had a parade of boring law students for neighbors. At least it was quiet for him to concentrate on those paintings. But I took heart in hearing this. It was a comforting reminder. I wouldn't be here forever.

Chapter 3

I was doomed to be alone, with cliques already forming like weeds, not unlike high-school. There were some students whom the rest of the 1L class ignored, like rejects from a fraternity pledge, and I was one of them. I'm not sure exactly how it happened, but after the second day of classes I was in a car headed to a fellow reject's house for a group study session. No one in this group, by appearances, resembled anyone I'd ever been friends with.

I was sandwiched in the backseat between two large, heavy-set women, and a munchkin-sized girl bounced on my lap. After two minutes in this predicament, it was clearly a full-blown hostage crisis. I was forced to befriend my captors.

"Can we play the name game?" I ventured.

The vibe in the car was decidedly unfriendly. I could feel every bump in the road, as this guy's Buick hadn't seen a tune-up since Eisenhower was in office. The munchkin girl shifted her little butt on my lap and my arm cradled her waist for traction, but the ancient Buick's hiccups inadvertently forced my pelvis into her backside.

Momentum continued downhill in a hurry as someone silently blasted one. I needed a window to roll down, though the driver had already apologized for the Buick's temperamental operations, including the back windows' tendency to be stuck. I reached over one of the heavy-set girls to attempt a manual roll down, but this was ill advised, as a nasty bump plopped my face straight into her ample cleavage. It was, if nothing else, a soft landing, and after a deep breath in that generous bosom, the storm passed and I righted myself in the middle slot once again.

"Yes, it's twice I have told you, but if you require a third time, I'll oblige. My name is Darby," the driver said, answering my inquiry.

This guy didn't need law school, he needed medication, but perhaps he deserved my understanding. After all, law school was like an intellectual boot camp, and we were all guilty of trying to sound smart.

"You're my first Darby! If you didn't catch it before, I'm Delton. In fact, we already sound like a law firm. At least, our first names do."

"I'm Ramona," the munchkin girl piped up. "Do you guys know that there will be a grading system on these tests and that they're designed to fail you? My older sister went to Duke Law and she said to watch out for tests with super-low score averages, and open-book tests too." She nibbled a handful of fingernails. "She said the system was like, if the top people barely passed, that was it. They passed and you failed, and the professors don't care at all. Oh my God."

Ramona's insight wasn't the burst of goodwill the group needed, so the energy in the car receded to its earlier subdued silence. I tried, valiantly enough, to smooth out the social edges, but now chose to focus on simply enduring the ride.

"Darby, are we there yet?" I whined.

He tugged at the part in his straight black hair.

"I would speculate that the duration of the trip, the remainder, shall approximate, shall we say, ten minutes," he said, making vaguely creepy eye contact with me in the rearview mirror.

"I'm Alicia," said the girl to my left whose bosom I violated.

"Wendy," said the girl to my right.

"Herc," said the guy in Unabomber glasses up front. I'd scarcely noticed him, but maybe that was precisely what murderous sociopaths counted on.

Darby finally pulled into the driveway of a large brick house. "We're home!" he announced.

We went inside with our book bags (Darby had an attaché case) and were ushered over to a long dining table. At a rocking chair in the living room sat a man under about sixteen knitted blankets, stroking a frazzled cat. The man looked infirm, wore trifocals, and was gray from head to toe. His shins stuck out, blotchy and purple, but the feet were thankfully tucked away in a pair of giant moose slippers.

"Hey grandpa!" Darby stepped forward to greet him with a hug and a clump of tissues, as the poor sot had a wet booger tumbling down his face. Darby blotted him and the geezer shifted in the rocker.

"So, Darby," he said, eyeing the group through the telescopes on his face, "this here is the fresh crop?" He retched up gook from his mouth, wiped it with a cloth he took from his robe, and vigorously cleared his throat. "I remember those first days, my goodness. You all are incredibly fortunate, yes you are." The cat on his lap didn't look like it was breathing.

"Grandpa was counsel to some major companies," Darby said.

I waited to hear how grandpa helped Lincoln free the slaves when a woman swept into the room with a plate of cookies and a bottle of soda.

"Nice to see y'all, I'm Darby's mother. I'm so glad he made new friends at school today."

"Hi mom!" Darby ran over and wrapped his arms around his mother's stomach.

We left grandpa to his hairballs and took seats around the table. Everybody took out their torts casebooks and the assignment. A collective groan sounded; even Darby's spirits visibly dimmed. The assignment was to read the next seven hundred pages and to brief every case. The idea was to extract the nugget found in each one, and from all the nuggets gathered over time, there was bound to be an alcoholic's moment of clarity where one suddenly started to 'think like a lawyer.' The tome of cases was foreboding; they were written in English, but the terms and meanings seemed more inclined toward men in wigs and enthusiasts of the dying Latin language. It might be best, after all, to sleep with Nate's dictionary under my pillow.

"Ok, it would appear that the petitioner in Zimbaud Construction is seeking damages . . ." Darby started.

"Wait, who's the petitioner in that?" Ramona said, her little legs curled up on a wicker chair, picking at a cookie. I noticed Darby sneaking a look at Ramona's thighs.

"The construction guy, right, Darby?" I added, motioning with my eyes, before she caught him.

"They're all construction guys," Ramona said.

"Why don't we focus on what the holding is," said the large-bosomed girl, Alicia, who was rubbing her neck as if it had gangrene. Her chubby face looked flushed.

"Good idea," said Wendy. She too gave a sidelong glance at Alicia, who was now visibly sweating.

"Are you okay, Alicia?" I said.

"There weren't any raisins—in those cookies—were there?" she said, voice shaking.

Oh shit.

"I'll see if my mother would be in a position to perhaps illuminate this line of questioning. Wait here," Darby said, rushing out of the room.

By now the poor girl was starting to hyperventilate.

"We need a brown bag!" I said, looking at Ramona.

"Why, have you hyperventilated before?" Ramona said.

"No, but don't they get brown bags for people on planes or wherever?"

"That's a barf bag," Ramona said.

"Alicia, do you want a barf bag to breathe into?" I said. But the girl was now clawing at her neck and gasping in heavy contractions.

"Maybe she's allergic to torts," Wendy offered.

"There were a few raisins in the dough!" Darby shouted, now back on the scene.

Alicia flopped face-first on the table.

"Holy shit. This chick has a raisin allergy, big time!" Ramona stood up, eyes wide.

"Maybe she needs a bag over her head," Herc contributed.

I leapt up, took Alicia in a bear hug and tumbled to the floor, landing underneath her sizeable weight.

"Herc," I wheezed, "pull her off me, goddammit!"

"What's the liability for wrongful death by homemade cookies?" Herc asked, tugging Alicia off my chest.

"Shuddup and flip her!" I yelled. "Call 911!"

Once we got her flat on the ground and face up, I lightly pumped her stomach like I'd seen on TV. Ramona tipped a little water into Alicia's motionless, open mouth. She grew eerily quiet, the only sound her shallow breaths. Paramedics stormed into the house, as apparently grandpa hit his 'fallen and can't get up' alarm to summon their speedy arrival.

"She's on the dining room floor!" Ramona said, flailing her arms and spinning in a circle.

The paramedics felt around Alicia's body and connected a long hose to give her oxygen.

"I'll make a copy of whatever we do today," I promised poor Alicia, as they carted her away on a stretcher.

"I think a near fatality excuses our unfinished briefs," Herc said.

Grandpa wheeled over to the front window.

"I wouldn't count on that, my boy," he said through his snot cloth. He stared off into the distance. "That is one thing I'll always remember."

"What might you be referring to, grandpa?" Darby said.

The group stood quietly by the window and watched the paramedics load our fallen study mate onto an ambulance gurney.

"The dang voodoo of it . . . law school. Little spooky, eh kiddies?"

Chapter 4

Back at the bungalow, I opened my casebooks to tackle the numerous course assignments, but quickly found myself in a sweaty panic; there were literally hundreds of pages to absorb. They didn't exactly ease you in. I read the opening two lines, lit a cigarette, and promptly face-planted on the desk.

The courses certainly sounded interesting—criminal law comes to mind—but the casebooks offered only endless reams of brittle legal minutiae. It was possible that a guy like Darby, who'd dreamt of law since suckling at grandpa's kneecaps, might find the material positively rhapsodic, but I'd wager even he was struggling. The professors' way of breaking our minds down was by Socratic Method. It was designed to strip the student of all dignity. Their cute bow ties and smug faces stank of self-importance. It reminded me of the goons from high school with their varsity letter jackets. I understood it was fine to have pride in one's appearance and position, but reflected that in my father's case, none of it was for show. His persona was extreme, but never embellished. He was for real.

The lecture hall for Real Property was packed with 1Ls anxiously scanning the room. We shared one long table in each row. A man in a dark brown bow tie entered and all activity ceased. He surveyed us from his lectern—the pulpit of raw power—and opened his casebook.

"Psst. Professor's a fag in that bow tie, huh?" The guy next to me had a ratty ponytail and smelled of sardines.

The bow tie eyed the name placards in front of each student.

"This class is gonna be cake," Rat-Tail spat. "Know how I know?"

"No, I don't, would you please shut the fuck–"

"You, Mister . . . Lowe," Bow Tie drawled.

Holy Christ.

"Do you see this paper, Mr. Lowe?"

"I do."

"Question number two, what am I doing now?" He gave it one long tear down the middle. "Don't answer that, Mr. Lowe. How about now?"

He ripped up both halves into little pieces and scattered them with a flourish, like a chef with spices, all over the floor.

"He's chumping you," Rat-Tail muttered.

"I'm waiting for your legal response to this query."

My heart almost stopped.

"You're, uh, ripping a paper into many pieces and scattering them on the floor?"

"Excellent, Mr. Lowe, except you are, other than in the strictest literal sense, frighteningly wrong."

Rat-Tail flashed me the thumbs up, then raised his hand.

"Mister . . . Girardi."

"You demonstrated how a real property interest is to be broken down into a bundle of rights."

"Not the worst response I'll hear. Now Mr. Lowe, the cases assigned addressed the notion that a real property interest, in this country, must be deconstructed as a bundle of rights, which we discuss at length in this course. Do you understand?"

"Yes, professor."

"Then come down here."

"I'm sorry?"

"Collect your things and step to the front of the room."

All eyes were on me as I walked the many rows down. Up close, Bow Tie had an enormous, misshapen moose-head, with thick glasses that obscured his eyes.

"Here, Mr. Lowe," he fished a quarter out of his slacks.

"What's this?"

"A quarter, Mr. Lowe."

"I see, but what for?"

"For you to call your mother and tell her there will not be a lawyer in the family."

The humiliation burned even after I retreated to the bowels of the law library, a cobwebbed, dank basement, where privacy was assured. How was I to make it alone in this academic wasteland? I needed allies, not counting the raisin-bunch gang. I feverishly contemplated this when, as if on cue, an answer came.

"What're you doin' in the basement?" An irritated voice snapped from the dark recesses.

"Well, I was trying to get away—I guess even that's difficult to do here," I said.

A guy emerged, laughing.

"I'm Finkle, Jerry Finkle."

Finkle was quite a specimen of humanity. He came up to about my chin, sported a tattoo on his forearm that read, 'heresy,' and had a lazy right eye. So it had come to this.

"Nice work in Property," he said.

"You admired that performance?" I took a little bow.

"See that bookcase?" He pointed to the far end of the basement. It was dim where we stood, but there was no light at all where he pointed.

"Yeah."

"Caught a hummer in there yesterday."

"Bullshit!"

"Okay," his lazy eye twitched, "you got me. It was a handy." He saw my incredulous look. "Wanna see the evidence, counselor?"

"You've made your case! But who? Most of these chicks seem pretty stiff."

"Give me fifty bucks and I'll let you in on it. Your life may change, my friend."

"You hustling me, Finkle?"

"Always. Okay, forget the fifty. You're in my torts class too, right?" he asked.

"The one with the bald professor and an obvious speed habit?"

"Yeah, Galler. Guy's off the wall."

"I still don't know what a tort even is, but now I know you can actually sue a Good Samaritan for screwing up a rescue. And that cute girl he grilled today? She was two people down from me," I said.

"That's just his way of flirting."

"What're you talking about?" I said.

"You hear of a young, hot professor named Becky Malina?"

"I didn't know there were any young, hot professors."

"Well, she was a 1L—like us—a few years ago. So Galler was married, like, to someone in her sixties or whatever. Becky Malina was a student in his class and he started banging her."

"No way," I said. How did he know all this? Finkle smoothed his Jheri-curl.

"Want the kicker? He knocks her up. They have a kid, he dumps his old lady, marries Malina, and a few years later, boom, she's a professor here. I think the horny toad is on the sauce, for real. Speaking of sauce," Finkle got this mad look in his droopy eye, "it's time for my own refreshment. You want?"

Two large desks were pushed together and he sat kitty-corner behind them. He unzipped a book bag and produced a plastic baggie with a yellowish powder. He crushed a lump of it with his student ID card and hastily chopped up a few lines. He looked up from his workmanship. "It's pharmaceutical, for focus."

"Yeah, I know what it's for," I said.

We blasted a few lines of Ritalin. For a moment, I forgot where I was. The tension in my system, thick and immoveable for days, completely vanished. We looked at each other and cracked up. Then he ran behind a bookshelf and wheeled out a book cart, the type you'd see in prison movies. He pushed it to one end of the basement, turned, and charged at me.

"You crazy bastard!" I screamed, leaping out of the way.

It wasn't easy to wrangle the cart from him, but soon I chased him with it. We wrestled on the floor like prepubescent boys. We pulled each other up, sweating and laughing.

The first week of classes dragged like a season of Dawson's Creek. By week two I was up to a pack a day, and discovered a constant vigil of strung-out, chain-smoking 1Ls in front of the library. I found myself between Finkle, Herc, Girardi, Ramona, and two people I hadn't met.

Kathy Benning and Lee Schmit, who knew each other, were riffing on strategies for negotiating year-one. Benning was thin with an eighties-style perm, long pink fingernails and a tan leather jacket. She batted eyelashes Finkle's way, which made perfect sense, as he wore the type of long shirt favored by rockers who shot junk, with a gold chain and high-top sneakers. If two people are equally suited to appear in a Whitesnake video, I say, it's a match!

"What about you, Lowe?" Schmit asked.

"Sorry?"

"Heard you saved someone's life. A big girl who ate raisins?"

Schmit looked a little older, mid-thirties, but dressed impeccably, like a waiter in a restaurant. There was still no reason not to bask in my heroism.

"We all helped, Ramona, and Herc over there–" I quickly added.

"Herc, my hero!" Ramona chimed. "You looked like you were waiting for her to croak right on the floor."

Herc didn't reply.

"Anyway, Delton, I don't know if your moves saved this chick's life, but we were all deer in headlights," Ramona said, punching my shoulder.

"Thanks, Ramona," I said, blowing out the last drag and flicking the butt to the ground. "Got another?"

The instant I made this request, Girardi's rat-tail materialized in my face. It is hard to quantify exactly what constitutes one's personal space, but whatever the most conservative determination, he surely breached it.

"You think you're gonna pass torts, property, crim law, with these casebooks, bub?"

"What are you talking about?" I asked.

"Taking dictation like lab mice?" he said, his intense B.O. forcing me to breathe through my mouth.

"What's the big deal? You're new like the rest of us."

"Yeah, but you see me answer their questions. I'll tell you right now, forget what they tell you to do."

His wisdom could be sheer madness, but I had no idea if it was or not, and that terrified me. School was going to be an assault from the bow ties, the loony 1Ls, and most of all, my own suffering mind.

The next day I ran into Jerry Finkle before torts.

"Would you hold this a second?" he said, as he held a taped box, crudely wrapped in lunch-bag paper.

"I didn't know you moonlit as a drug mule. The notion of a law school education now takes on real practicality."

He laughed. "No, I just wanted to see your reaction. Now give me my dick drugs back." He snatched the box. "I got a connection." We trolled up the aisle of the large lecture hall, and I spotted Herc in a corner at the back.

"Hey, there's a couple spots near Herc," I pointed out.

"The Unabomber? You don't have enough to worry about without being murdered?"

We settled into another space in the back row. Professor Galler, in a polka-dotted bow tie, silver mustache and black leather jacket, whooshed in like his kidneys were on fire. He had scarcely set his casebook down when he shot out the first flurry of questions. Finkle and I slumped down in our seats. The ability to be invisible was key, because if the bow tie couldn't see us, he couldn't call on us. Finkle and I were of like minds, essentially congenital twins with mental defects.

"In Construction, the company dropped a crane holding materials onto the street below. A pedestrian is injured from the falling debris. Is the company negligent? What's their duty? You," Galler lurched an arm at a man near the front, "Simmons, what's the duty? What's the defendant gonna say?"

It was hard to see the guy, but if I was having heart palpitations, then this poor fellow must be staving off paralysis. After three long seconds, Simmons coughed up a prayer. "The defendant will say they had no duty."

"Excuse me? None? You better read everything twice from now on, Simmons. Who's got it? Does the plaintiff have a negligence claim? What's the defendant gonna say in response to a negligence claim?"

In those first days, I could scarcely keep track of who the goddamn plaintiffs and defendants even were. Galler and his cracked-out style had me unhinged. The other professors were monsters too, especially moose-head, but at least the pace in that class was slower.

"Lowe, for the defendant to not be found liable, what's the defense?"

The son of a bitch was on top of me.

"Plaintiff's claim was alleged..."

"What?" He waved me off like he couldn't be bothered.

"Nice shooting, ace," Finkle whispered.

The worst part was that in future classes, when Finkle was called on, he actually didn't sound like an escaped mental patient. He started to get what the professor was teaching. This was patently against our pact of cluelessness. Even still, locked in an asylum with Galler, Moosehead, Herc, and Girardi, Finkle was the gold standard in sanity.

Chapter 5

It had been two weeks since I'd spoken with my mother or father. My answering machine was lit with their messages, but I had chosen not to respond. I wouldn't know how to answer any of their questions.

At the start of the third week I was presented with a most debilitating notice. An envelope in my locker contained a letter embossed with the school's letterhead. It could only mean one thing: I was to be summarily dismissed, as my attendance had been a grievous mistake. It was time to be sacrificed, like the poor and infirm from the flock. The letter asked me to report immediately to the Registrar's office.

Finkle read the letter, his high-top sneakers sticking out from under his barrack.

"You're toast for sure," he said. I watched him dip into the secret compartment of his bag, producing the familiar little pill, and smash it to crumbles with his student ID. He cut lines with a sharp corner. We each partook.

"How could I flunk out, Finkle? I haven't even taken a test yet!"

He laughed. "Maybe they pull aside an elite crew, like the Skulls at Yale? That'd be a sweet deal. Or no... they found out about the basement! You're busted! You're gonna wind up ratting me out, you bastard!"

"Finkle, the drugs have taken hold of your mind. I'll spare your career and take a vow of silence for a generous percentage of your future earnings."

"Well, that would be a good deal for me, since I'll be a waiter at Applebee's."

"By the way, before I get tossed out, I was curious what you thought of Benning? You know, the chick in the tan leather jacket... you checked her out."

"I check everybody out," he said, as he gave me an ear-to-ear grin like a carved pumpkin.

"Yeah, I'm aware of what a derelict you are, but she's got your look."

"They've all got my look."

This was getting nowhere. My panic returned to me, and Finkle's sex life wasn't going to resolve anything. In fact, I wanted nothing to do with it. He could find his own glam-rock chicks.

"Well, I'm off to the Registrar's. I'll report back. And I'm no rat!"

My head flooded with fearful thoughts about what my parents might say to my expulsion. On the main floor of the library, the Hebrew cabal advanced toward me. I was to be sacrificed, for crimes against the strength of the institution. The leader, Harry from orientation, had shorn his rangy beard and removed his tattered flannel in favor of a suit and buzz cut. They passed by, and as I hastened my pace, they didn't notice me. I took a breath, and privately wished goodwill to my brothers, but now was no time to risk a sighting. I would lead myself to slaughter.

The Registrar's office presented as a purely bureaucratic affair, with mental-ward walls and faceless cubicles.

A middle-aged, big-haired woman seemed to run the show. When she registered my presence, I raised the letter. This little gesture, a skill learned from waving cash at itinerant bartenders, finally came in handy. The woman hung up the phone and approached me.

"Hello, I'm Delton Lowe, 1L. I was instructed to report here?"

She glanced at the letter.

"Okay, let me see if Bertha is in. Wait here, please."

I slumped with my back to the counter and looked out the front window of the office. It was terribly dreary; students rushing to make their appointments with the library; the classes; the guillotine.

As the rush died down and the crowd swept out, one girl remained. She lingered by a poster board in the hall. I imagined myself in the woods at a halt, having spotted a lovely deer at close range, peacefully chewing on brush. She wore an outfit that showed off a curvaceous frame and flipped her long black hair. Was she posing for my admiring eyes? I had since pressed my face to the window, breathing heavily, and the glass began to fog, but as she turned to face me, a hand squeezed my shoulder.

"Mr. Lowe. Mr. Lowe!"

"I'm here," I said, a little disoriented. I regained myself, looking into the rotund face of Bertha.

"You are to report to your faculty advisor at once. His name is Professor Khaki. He's expecting you. Here is his office number. It looks like he should be there now. I suggest you drop by."

I took the info and quickly moved out to the hallway, but alas, this Bambi-esque vision had gone. Where had she come from? A 1L, perhaps? It stood to reason, as she appeared to take notes from an informational board. In other words, with the exceedingly limited prison yard hours at the school, I might not see her for some time. On the other hand, she probably set up camp in the library between classes. Regardless, a reason for living did not often present itself here, and for that brief moment, I was supremely grateful. Yet the rendezvous with Khaki awaited, and I feared this good feeling wouldn't last.

After blundering around hallways I'd never seen, in a section of the building I didn't know existed, I eventually came upon Professor Khaki's door. He invited me into a tectonic plate-shift of disaster, a broom closet stuffed with papers, books, folders, cabinets, tea cups, picture frames, lotions, lamps, clothes and cabinets. Somewhere in that maelstrom sat a small Indian man in a long coat behind a desk, except the desk was more like a collapsible card table, best suited for the local YMCA. Wisps of smoke swirled around the little man's head as he raised a teacup to his lips. Upon closer inspection, the smoke wasn't from hot tea at all, but from a lit stick of incense. I couldn't help but stare.

"Orange slice?"

He bore a turquoise tray with a Ganesh—the Indian elephant that symbolized prosperity—and slices of baby tangerine.

"Umm, I'm ok, thank you. I was sent here by the powers that be," I said, handing him the note with the pertinent information.

"Ah yes, they are always cutting down trees for such gibberish," he said, in a melded British and Indian accent. He crumpled the paper and tossed it atop an overflowing waste-basket. "Wouldn't you agree?"

"Honestly, Professor, so far, it's all gibberish to me," I said, weighing this unfolding scenario with the proper skepticism, but not without a certain curiosity. Who was this fellow?

"You may wonder," he said, sucking his lips around a tangerine slice, "why they sent you here."

"The thought had crossed my mind."

"In the early part of the semester, certain students whose performance on the collegiate level was, shall we say, hmm, on the borderline," his accent clipped the words, "are taken aside for additional instruction."

I absorbed this statement and immediately developed a fit of vertigo, the leaning stacks of books and incense conspiring to fizzle my circuits.

"This is tutoring I have to attend?" I squeaked.

Khaki stood up, all five feet of him, and examined the top of a stack of books. I feared he wouldn't reach what he was looking for, perhaps the Bhagavad Gita, which would have been lovely, but he didn't pull out a book at all. Instead, a bent bow tie was in his hand.

"Yes, do take it, you must prepare yourself to wear it one day, no?" He put the tie in my hand. I was too faint and sick to make any sense of this. "Tea, Mr. Lowe?"

"Please," I said.

"Of course."

He poured tea into a dollhouse-sized ceramic cup and passed it over. I gingerly took it and finished it in two sips, slightly restored.

"What are you talking about, professor?"

"I don't teach any class in the curriculum. I perform pro bono service for mentally infirm defendants at the school's criminal law clinic. There is no extra room for faculty there, so I maintain this office here. As part of my duties, I agreed to this extra-help nonsense. I care not for it. If you are an idiot, I cannot help you. If you are bright but in an adjustment period, you don't need my help. So, Mr. Lowe, you may simply carry on your miserable 1L life and need not concern yourself with this petty matter. I will fill out a time sheet for you. But, I shall leave you with one bit of instruction."

He reached out for my tiny cup and poured another thimble.

"Thank you, it's quite tasty," I said, feeling much better, mostly from being excused from tutoring.

"You're welcome. Now, you may have noticed I do not wear a bow tie, and that the one in your hand is in dire need of dry-cleaning. The reason I do not wear one is because the bow tie can be a noose around one's neck. Please remember, as you progress here, and perhaps graduate to practice law, that the law is far, far larger than a silly little bow tie."

He snatched it from my hand and dropped it to the floor. We nodded to each other and I crawled through the closet like an inmate to freedom. There was hope.

Chapter 6

My parents lived in a well-manicured suburb north of New York City. I arrived to find my father in the kitchen, wearing his Sunday pajamas.

"Hey, dad."

"Little Lowe."

We did a quick man-hug, more slap than embrace.

"Where's mom?"

"Getting food for you."

"Oh, okay."

He went back to reading his paper.

"Water?" He held out an empty glass.

I filled it up at our refrigerator door. The sun lit the kitchen through two oblong skylights, an addition made during a recent renovation.

"Dad, you ever miss the old apartment?"

He slurped the water down and lit a cigarette. He was almost certainly not contemplating the question. The newspaper on the table and news on the TV seemed to have him occupied.

After a long pause, he turned in my direction.

"No."

"Not even a little? You were there for like, fifteen years, even before I was born."

"The Bronx is my backyard," he said, smoke streaming out of his nostrils. "Let me know if you want to go in tomorrow."

"You know, I'm tied up with school. I have to get back. But maybe another time."

The truth was, I hated to go in to his work. The air pollution gave me a headache. The streets were covered in litter. The train near his office was so deafening, its force shook my mind with violence. The homeless men outside the shoddy Dunkin' Donuts on the corner always gave me the creeps.

"How about this for an idea, Dad? I'm up to my neck in shit tomorrow, even though there's no classes, but how about we do something now? It's the only day you're around, anyway."

He was out of water again. I thought he'd send me back to the spigot. I braced for his answer. For an instant, he stared into my eyes.

"You have work to do and your mother is coming home."

His pajamas did nothing to soften his presence. It was electric. Uncomfortable, I stood there, wondering if I should take a seat. I watched him watching the television.

"I have to get back tomorrow afternoon. You and I never really get the chance to do much."

"I gotta go in later today. Bobby & Monkey have an order from Fordham Road. Besides, when you're in the office full-time after school, you'll see me plenty."

"You'll be gone for dinner tonight?" I asked.

He nodded and stubbed out his smoke.

"Maybe later we can share a cigar?"

He said nothing. Then held out his water glass. I filled it.

"I'm going in later. You have schoolwork. That's the reality."

I hated reality.

Chapter 7

The first semester continued on, slow and painful, like a kidney stone, until exam preparation time was upon us. Finkle came over to my place with a special guest.

"Del, you know Amy," he said.

I'd met her briefly in torts class. She was the alleged handy-giver in the basement. Finkle had been quietly seeing her. He insisted she could be instrumental in passing our exams, as we were hopelessly inept at the little things, like taking notes and learning.

"What's up, Amy? Come in."

It was pouring out. Amy took off her raincoat and I noticed for the first time how nice her boobs looked in a form-fitting shirt. Her straight brown hair was wet and she pulled it out of a scrunchie.

"We can get some delivery. There's a pretty decent place down the road," I said.

They sat on the couch in my den, and I rolled a joint and packed a hookah with cherry tobacco. I placed the hookah on the old oak coffee table and passed around its tentacles. Finkle and I smoked the joint, and we ordered take-out.

"So, here's the plan," Finkle began, through a plume of white smoke, "tell him, Amy."

"It's all about outlines," she said. "I've been cozying up next to 3Ls who love to look at my ass."

"Baby, doesn't everybody?" Finkle said.

"Shut up, Finkle." She made a face. "So anyway, they're like, write your own, but the trick is getting your hands on other peoples'. Then they talked about how to make friends with your classmates," Amy continued. "I know you idiots actually need outlines, because you haven't bothered to make your own. Most people have been taking copious notes all along, maybe they made Saturday into outline day, I don't know, so they're not left holding their schlongs at test time. They use other people's outlines to supplement their own work."

It was a revelation. Why would anyone voluntarily come here to give advice?

"You just answered your own question. Wait, did you ask a question?" A stoned Finkle arched his lazy eye into a query. "Wait, what I meant was, you yourself said we don't need our own outlines. In fact, I would argue, to make your own would actually be a waste of time," Finkle said.

"Totally," I said.

"I thought you might feel that way, so the 3Ls gave me an important tip," Amy said. "For one thing, using their outlines from two years ago is a start, but not entirely reliable, as they're not current. I've tried to share mine in trade with another 1L, but the mother lode? That's easy. You camp out by the library photo copier and use your charms to poach people's work."

Finkle and I fell silent. Being the unfortunate recipients of barbs from bow-tied men all semester, this was the first morsel of real genius we'd heard. We could do this!

"That settles it. Del, you and I are gonna hang around upstairs in the library and woo the pants off these pricks. There's a whole black market to capitalize on," Finkle opined with new purpose. "Don't you just love this girl?" he said, kissing Amy. They started to make out on my couch. "Give us about twenty minutes, would ya?"

"Both of you, get out of my house."

The following morning, we loitered around the library copier. It was no trick to strike up little chats with 1Ls, as they felt the same way about the impending tests as we: mortal terror. The beauty was once we secured the first few outlines, we could sling them in trade. When the smoke settled, we had more outlines than notes of our own. We took our ill-gotten gains down to our basement hideout, excited to dump the booty, but somebody was down there! The interloper looked up and I recognized his large frame and plaid jacket from several classes.

"Hey, uh, Finkle, and don't tell me, Lowe?" His eyes darted between us.

"Yeah, hey man. Wait—if there's something important—like an actual reason for being down here, you gotta let us in on it," Finkle said.

"No, just taking a moment," the interloper said, voice cracking. "I was looking for a Shepard's book and couldn't find it. Okay, see ya."

He scampered past us and back up the stairs. Finkle bit down on his lip. I knew he felt territorial about our underground lair.

"Del, the Shepard's are all upstairs."

We made eye contact, and without a word, split up to investigate the area, peering into the ancient bookshelves.

Clumps of dirt made me sneeze and a long, intricate spider web blew back in my face.

"We don't even know what we're looking for!" I said, pulling spidery wisps off my lip and eyelashes. I didn't know if one was crawling on my skin or if it was already hatching eggs in my intestines.

"I got it!" Finkle appeared in my aisle with a book held over his head like a gold medal. "A Commentary on Criminal Law Codes! It's the one everybody needs for the final and couldn't find. This jackass ripped it off and came to our turf to stash it."

"Yeah, he wouldn't put it upstairs because that'd be too visible. The solution was to leave it where nobody would ever go," I said.

Finkle tossed the book onto a nearby table. He then dug out the book cart and rammed it full throttle against the radiator, making one hell of a racket.

"Jeezus, man! You want to get us pinched?"

"For which offense?" he said, shoving the stolen book into his bag.

"You're insane. Let's get out of here before I have a hay fever attack. We'll photocopy the pages we need, but we're not thieves—unsavory, but not criminals. We need to return it."

"I didn't know you were back from the leprosy slums, Mother Theresa," Finkle said, shaking his head, and he removed the book out of his bag.

It broke down like this: Finkle would speed to my bungalow around noon with bagels and schmear and coffee and cigarettes. The first day of finals prep he unloaded another huge satchel of outlines like it was loot from a bank job. We now had plenty of material to work with, though understanding it all was a different matter.

"You're a prince, Finkle," I said, pinching his cheek.

"Get the fuck off me."

"No, really, man, what are you doing in law school? A scoundrel like you, the way you bullshit and trade, you should be on Wall Street."

I unpacked a fresh carton of cigarettes and fired up the coffee maker. There was a knock at the door.

"Who the hell is that? Amy?"

"I didn't tell her to come today," he said.

Jaspr stuck his bald head through my living room window. He looked at our pile of outlines and stuffed ashtrays.

"Good, I vill need lawyer."

He grinned, glass of wine in hand. It must have been Saturday.

"Jaspr, we're trying to stay in school here, man. And in America we have fucking doors. What is it?"

"Vent to the Manhattan last night. Got girl, big titties." He extended his arms out for effect. "I punish good, need new condom." He swigged his wine, staring at me through the window. Finkle almost fell off his chair.

"You know what? I have no use for them."

I went to my bedroom and brought out my stash.

"Just don't let me hear your disgusting grunts while we're working."

"Is deal." He threw me a little wink and left.

"Can we get some shit done now with Mr. Furley gone, or is another kooky neighbor coming by?" Finkle said.

"No, I'm ready, really, I am. Wanna smoke a quick joint?"

We called it lockdown. Finkle left only to sleep, somewhere north of four a.m. every night. After a few days, we agreed that he could invite Amy to join us, at her own risk, of course. Why she'd want to place her lot in the hands of bottom feeders like us was beyond me, but I was happy to have her. Hell, I would've been happy to have Jaspr, if he could help. We scrambled to school for classes, but otherwise all contact with the world ceased. Amy arrived with Finkle at the start of week two.

"Ewww. Tell me I have the wrong house," Amy said.

She stepped into the living room, over little mounds of ash and cigarette butts. The place stank like a subway car from the trash, dirty clothes, and an unfortunate plumbing issue.

"Hey Del—uh-oh. Oh shit."

"Oh no. Don't even think about it."

Finkle made a dash, while my mouth was agape in horror.

"Dude, there's already a log in there!" But it was too late. Finkle detonated on top of my last offering.

"Oh my God." Amy was ready to have a stroke. She still had her coat on.

"Amy, mi casa es su casa," I said.

"Where's the reading material in here?" Finkle called.

"There is none!" I yelled back.

He opened the door a crack. "Not one goddamned magazine?"

"Shut the door! No magazines! Must you be entertained every second?"

I felt a draft and found Amy, who'd retreated across the room, opening every available door and window.

"They'll condemn this place," I said. "By the way," I blew a couple smoke rings, "I never got how the reading basket became this hospitality favor, like the masculine answer to the potpourri tray. You can't just enjoy your shit?"

"That's what I'm trying to do," Finkle called through the door.

"Shut the fuck up, Finkle! I'm not talking to you."

"But it's the little pleasures that keep me sane right now."

"Okay, tell you what, mister little pleasures. Next time, I'll have a variety for you. Perhaps the latest Architectural Digest?"

For the next ten days, we existed in a cycle of studying, eating, and more studying. The trouble was, I wasn't catching on; I wasn't 'thinking like a lawyer.' I couldn't make sense of it. Amy helped organize the material, yet I was close to a total meltdown.

"I got to get out of here. You guys—I don't know—stay. Tell you what, I'll get copies of the old tests at the library," I said.

Finkle crushed a beer can and threw it at me.

"More beer and Doritos, bitch."

"Yes, master." I did a deep, English-butler bow. "Anything for the madam?"

"Don't call me madam. Although..." Amy looked around the trashed bungalow, "with a piano and the right management, the place could potentially work as a house of ill-repute."

I stepped into the black cold. New York was a work camp, a frigid plain of dissatisfied souls that fed on pleasure of the flesh and professional success. I was killing myself so I could be one of them. The whole scenario felt so doomed. A few inches of old snow and slush muddied the roads, but behind the wheel, these elements didn't faze me.

I snuck a bowl out of the glove compartment and lit the green herb already there. An old eighties-rock tune came on the radio, something about breaking up with a chick, and I turned it up. Thank God for the heat—I could feel my hands again—and between the warmth and the weed kicking in, I started to smile in spite of myself, belting out the chorus. The car lost traction for a second and fishtailed toward the rail of the deserted highway, but I regained control as quickly as I'd lost it.

When the exit for the school came into view, I let the bowl cool and socked it away in the glove compartment. I lit a cigarette, slid into the lot and parked. It felt good to just sit in the glow. The plan was to run in, grab the tests, and run right out. Once out of the car I almost turned back, willing to chalk up the excursion to an aimless drive and a much-needed break, but I didn't want to return empty-handed. The heathens eating my food and clogging my pipes could use the tests.

The law library was still going strong as the school kept graveyard hours during finals. It was utterly quiet. I recognized 1Ls that dotted the tables, including the girl from outside the Registrar's office. I felt a rush in my chest. She was a French exchange student, I'd learned through moderate investigation, here to match her country's law degree. My mind was instantly filled with carnal images. But what had I to offer this beauty? She sat alone, her face in a casebook.

"You working on torts?" I said, after a throat clear.

"Yes?" she said impatiently, looking up.

"Well, you've been at this for hours, haven't you? I think I see a little crust around your eyes."

"Yes." She pointed to her casebook. "It's not making sense anymore." Her face softened.

"I'm Delton."

"Angelina."

"You know what you need, other than a spaceship to send us to a world without torts?"

"What?"

"A smoke break. Sometimes it's the simple pleasures. A friend of mine recently reminded me of that."

"I don't smoke, but I'll get some air with you."

We stepped outside. The air was so fucking cold. I took out a cigarette and tried to light it, but my hands were shaking.

"Is it ever this cold in Europe?" It was hard to be interesting. The smoke finally lit.

"In France it gets cold, but not like this. Y'know what? I will take one. I was trying to quit, but thank you very much."

The things I do for a girl, I thought, scraping my paralyzed finger over the metal lighter wheel until it almost bled. When it lit she took a drag, her lips slightly parting, and that was all I needed. I saw us walking the river Seine under the moonlight. I saw us in the basement of the law library. Either way, it didn't matter, I would be with her.

"So what are you going to do after finals, Angelina?"

"I'm going to France to visit my boyfriend." She took one more quick puff and threw the rest away. "It's freezing out here. See you."

She stepped back inside. Well, I hadn't come here to fall in love anyway. I waited until my pride froze over, then retreated inside. I went to the resource desk for the tests, but soon detected an unmistakable odor.

"You think that'll help you?" Good old Girardi, ex-fisherman and benevolent confidant, stood an inch away from my mouth.

"Hey man, there's a whole hallway here, could you step back a bit?"

I was haggard from weariness and stress, but Girardi looked like he just stepped off a tanker in Calcutta; his ponytail was greasy, his shirt was half-open, and of course, he wreaked.

"The old tests won't help you," he said, snorting into a sleeve.

"What does everyone other than you not know?"

"I could tell you how to get that Angelina chick," he said, through yellow teeth.

"You couldn't get within five-hundred yards of her."

"She's crazy about me. You had a little smoke with her? You don't know what we've had, bub."

"Sounds like one of your seagoing tales. She has a boyfriend, anyway."

"That's just a line. She was all over me. In fact, now it's starting to get in the way of my study method."

"You went out with her?"

"I went down on her."

This guy slayed me. "Listen, I have misery to get back to. It's been real, Girardi."

Didn't he realize I'm perfectly capable of flunking out on my own? I didn't need anyone's advice on how to do that. The woman at the desk handed me the tests. In the car I lit a fresh, pungent bowl of grass, but all I could smell was Girardi's bullshit.

Back at the ranch, I arrived in time to see Finkle's bare ass hovering over Amy's property casebook. He cried out like a tribesman in some distant jungle, "I'll do it!"

"No, you will not!" Amy shrieked.

He set his bare ass on Amy's casebook, then side-swaddled his ball sack onto her precious outlines. This work was her lifeline, her piggy blanket, her tether to any sanity left at all.

"I can't believe you did that!"

She screeched in psychic pain, mortally wounded, and covered her eyes to avoid the worst indignity of all—to witness Finkle's scrotum scrape off her work.

"I got the tests," I offered.

Finkle was hysterical, pants still around his knees, junk flopping about. He was a hairy guy, too. There was nothing aesthetically redeemable about any of this.

"Finkle, men coming home from war have seen more tolerable images. Pack it up!"

He finally covered himself, but the disturbing visual stuck in my mind like his nut sack to Amy's outlines.

"Oh, c'mon Amy, y'know I love you. Tell you what, you can rub your pussy anywhere on my books, all right?"

"That's as close as my pussy will get to anything of yours, ever again, Finkle!"

She tried a flurry of punches to his chest. He laughed, holding her elbows.

"Okay kids, break it up. Some of us have exams to flunk. Finkle, dinner is on you. Amy, get your stuff off the floor before he fetishizes your car keys. Can I get a truce here?"

I held out the menu for the pizza place. An hour later we were stuffed and enjoying after-dinner cupcakes and smokes.

Now that Finkle's one-act play was behind us, I was confronted with a grim reality; I was about to face the first round of finals and didn't have a clue.

A few days later Finkle came to the bungalow for the last study session. We sat around chain-smoking and just bitched a while. We spread out the old tests, written in recent years by the bow ties. We read the first question.

"It's negligence! The company breached their duty and caused the damage. Negligence! Holy shit, I think I got it," Finkle said, chewing a pen cap in his teeth. He moved on to the next problem.

"Wait a second. Hold your horses. What about the other person, the car that crashed—"

"No, it doesn't matter. There's still causation with the company. It was their duty. They breached it. Boom. Damages. All of that equals liability! They were negligent!"

Finkle was so exuberant I feared he'd pull his cock out for a tug. He inhaled a cigarette with an unnatural quiver caused by too much caffeine and too little sleep.

"You get it, bro?" he said.

"No, I don't fucking get it. Jaspr gets it more than I get it, all right? I've opened this law dictionary a thousand fucking times and definitely don't get how the concepts apply to the fact patterns. Okay?"

I leapt up and swatted at his greasy head. My stomach roiled from rising, acidic bile. I ran out of the bungalow into the cold light of day. A mess of crisp-brown leaves littered the road, and the bile shot from the back of my throat into my mouth. The burning calmed after what felt like several minutes; my forehead was wet, spittle was on my chin. It was eerily quiet out. Was anyone else alive, struggling for sanity? Back inside, Finkle was purposefully making notes. My insecurity was harder to bear, I'm ashamed to admit, now that he was getting it. I had no choice. I sat down to the table of fear.

"Okay, share your vision with me, Vishnu of torts," I said.

"The torts and criminal tests are different, but most similar of all the tests. But I realized that we need to plug in the concepts, y'know?" he said.

"No, I don't know."

"The bow ties always talk about issue spotting. That's really what briefing of cases has been all about. We're first learning what the legal issues are. Then, we're reading up on black letter law to understand what they mean. Then, we're reading these fact patterns for facts that relate to the issues. And finally, we'll argue the side asked for in the question, based on our interpretation of how the legal issue applies to the facts."

"Thank you, Oliver Wendell Holmes. But y'know what? What you just explained in thirty seconds has been more clear and helpful than the last few months of Socratic crap," I said.

Finkle stayed the night and we worked until we could forestall our fate no more. In the morning, we got into his car like convicted men, who have lost their last appeal.

"It's not too late to flee. Does Mexico have extradition?"

"Del, we'll be fine. If we pass everything, we can't fail."

We pulled into the school lot. I was greeted by EMPWR stepping from his silver Beamer, and to my surprise, he nodded at me, so I returned the gesture. Finkle and I headed into the melee of 1Ls gathered in front of the building, tossing lit cigarette butts and chattering away.

I made eye contact with Darby and Ramona, who were huddled in a corner, but they pretended not to see me. Darby was practically in a tailored suit. It was like he'd waited his whole life to take a law exam. It didn't seem, despite their apparent alliance, that he was privy to Ramona in any other capacity.

"Finkle, I don't feel that great."

I put a hand on my belly. Lots of bodies jostled together. Innumerable voices.

"Have a smoke and a piece of gum. It's an old trick for holding out in the sack and should settle you down," he said, handing me a stick.

"You smoke a cigarette when you bang? And chew gum? Do you juggle too?"

I felt a hand on my shoulder. It was Herc.

"Jeezus, Herc. Is that how you sneak up on your victims? I'm barely holding on here," I said.

He surveyed my pale complexion. His own face, as always, was inscrutable.

"A few make law review. A few flunk out. You ever been the best or worst at anything?"

"Good call, Herc!" I clasped him on the shoulder and almost went in for the hug, but he freaked if you got too close. I was curious to see Herc cross paths with Girardi.

"All right, they're going in," I heard Finkle say.

We took our seats for the first exam. Herc manned the back corner as usual, and Finkle and I separated. I don't know, sometimes you make weird decisions to quell anxiety.

After finishing, I glanced up to find that I was the last one there. I quickly left the room, whipped around the hall, came to the elevator, and stopped in my tracks. Angelina. She must have finished last too!

"Hey," I said. The light in the hall was a fluorescent bulb that buzzed in and out.

"Hey," she returned the volley.

I had nothing. I had never wanted to kill myself for two distinct reasons on the same day before.

"I'd ask you about the test, but I'd just as soon forget it. Are you going to—how are you going to unwind from it? I might take a bath," I said. A bath? Oh God, is it worse if I talk or don't talk at all? She peered at me sideways from under her long hair. She definitely pegged me for a total moron.

"I'm excited about Chinese food right now. I'll have that and hang out with my roommate a little and then get ready for real property," she said.

"That sounds chill."

The elevator opened with another person inside. It went down, silently, and then Angelina got out without a goodbye. This disappointment was quick-lived, however, as the crush of 1Ls gossiping about the test hit my ears. I did not want to hear what people thought were correct answers. Unfortunately, my classmates were not immune to such a psychologically harmful practice.

"Del! Over here!" Finkle yelled, an arm around Amy's waist.

The throng was several rows deep, yammering an amalgam of the following:

"There's no way that was res ipsa!"

"I told you he'd put in a contracts question."

"No way, that was a damages issue focused on tort liability."

"You egghead! Don't you know about tortious interference with a contract?! He designed it that way to throw you."

And so on.

"Amy, Finkle, hey," I said. "Let's get the hell out of here."

We started to walk away from the fray when I almost stepped over little Ramona.

"You ace that, Del?"

"With both hands tied behind my back." I winked.

"Is it too late to be a doctor?" she said.

"How about a vet?"

"How 'bout a pet detective?"

Her little dimples were spotted with freckles.

"Where's Darby?" I asked.

"I think the ecstasy of the first exam was more than he could bear. He ran to his car before I could catch up to him."

"Huh. Okay Ramona, catch you tomorrow. Round two."

She waved goodbye.

Finkle, Amy, and I got into his car.

"That test was rude," Amy said.

"Which part, or the whole thing?" I said.

"The question where it was sort of torts and contracts—when in the effin' hell did we talk about crossover issues like that? That's not in my outline," she said. Amy was visibly angry in a way I hadn't seen, even after Finkle's scrotum had violated her papers.

"It wasn't really the contracts, it was just him fucking with you." Finkle laughed, evidently finding humor in this. "There were lots of red herrings."

"What's a red herring?" I said.

"Fake issues to distract you."

He turned on the cassette player and cued a Metallica song.

"Would you turn that shit off?!" Amy yelled.

He raised the volume, his little hatchback shaking with reverb. The singer growled out lyrics having something to do with a sanitarium.

"You asshole!" Amy screamed.

Her anger broke into a smile. She settled her head on his shoulder, and he lowered the volume.

"Let's get a coffee, and then I'm going home. You guys are welcome to come over later, but if you find my head in the oven, do me a favor? Say I went out in a more memorable way, like autoerotic asphyxiation," I said.

"I like that because it's believable," Finkle said. "Anyway, I'll bring over Wendy's around seven? You want the burger or the spicy chicken combo?"

"I might stay home and try to have my period early," Amy volunteered.

"Uh, why would you do that, Amy? Wait, can you do that?" I said.

"She thinks better when she's riding the wave," Finkle explained.

"So what if I do," she said, laughing.

"Don't explain anything else to me, Finkle. I've got enough confusion in my life. Amy, you're out of your mind to actually find this man sexually attractive. You've filled in a lot of blanks for me about your psyche. Anyway, I don't know if I can handle four more of these tests. You know you're in trouble when Herc is a source of comfort."

"You'll be fine, just keep going, one test at a time," Amy dispensed her law review-bound wisdom.

"I guess so. Fuck it, get me the chicken combo, Finkle."

Chapter 8

After finals finished, there was a sense of profound relief, followed by a cavernous space of idle time. Finkle and Amy had long since vanished, and a couple days of lying around the bungalow convinced me it was time to venture out. Piles of smelly garbage bags covered the windows. A trail of ants roamed the carpet buried in crumbs, beer bottles and cigarette butts. I wanted to run for my life, but before I could leave, I needed gloves and boots and a sealed rayon suit to clean this crime scene, as well as find a willing plumber.

My folks lobbied for me to spend a couple weeks at home over holiday break. This seemed like a good idea, as the only prospects for meals at the bungalow were the takeout menus, which triggered flashbacks of acid reflux. The prospect of staying there alone was unbearable. I packed a travel bag and hit the road.

The world outside was icy and gray. New York City, especially in winter, looked positively ashen, from its grim beams and buildings and bridges, to the grimaces worn by the streets' shuffling masses. Fortunately, my parents' place was safely outside the city. I opened the door and immediately overheard my parents talking in the kitchen.

"I'm not sure you're telling me how it really is," mom said, her voice quivering.

"You don't know nothing," my father said, twirling a chewed toothpick in his mouth.

"Delton!" Mom leapt up and hugged me as I bounded into the kitchen.

"Little Lowe." The old man squeezed my shoulder hard until it buzzed.

"What's up, sweetie?" Mom said.

"Not much, other than finals. Thank God it's over!"

"How long are you staying?" my father said.

"Probably through the New Year." I didn't know if this was good news to him.

"Go wash up and I'll fix you something to eat," mom said.

The same stack of magazines and the painting of a lovely, sullen woman decorated the kitchenette. Upstairs the scent of pipe tobacco filled the hall. My parents' bedroom featured the usual overflowing ashtrays, an action flick on the large television, and the glow of flamingo lights that burned all day. The old man's reading glasses were next to an open crime novel on the bureau.

They had left my bedroom mostly intact, with its rock-band posters and photographs from trips. I looked carefree in those scenes, busy with friends in faraway places.

After a quick wash, hunger came on, so I scampered back downstairs, but at the foot of the landing, I heard a familiar discordant tone in their voices.

"It was the Assemblyman's function at Vachario's," my father said.

"Where else? I know you didn't make it home until after sunrise. I don't think it was your driver who dropped you off, either," mom said.

Silence. I imagine mom weighed whether to press further.

"And Kelly O'Brien was there too, I bet," she added.

"Kelly O'Brien? I can't believe you'd think I'd go for her."

The stress from their fighting made my skin feel hot and flaky. I splashed some water on my face, hoping the tension would die down before returning to the kitchen.

"Hi guys." I opened the fridge and took out orange juice. "Everything okay?"

The old man grunted. I teased a smoke from his pack, lit it, and poured a glass.

"Not really," mom said. She turned back toward my father. "What are you really saying, Larry. It couldn't be Kelly O'Brien because she is beneath you?"

"It couldn't be her—I still can't believe you'd think I'd go for her—because it was nobody." The old man looked at me. He took a deep inhale of his cigarette. "Don't you think if I wanted to cheat I could do better?"

"Not sure that's the point, dad."

It was all rather hard to bear. It's strange to be backstage for the drama of others, especially one's parents.

"What do you want me to think when you're out all night? That's the last time you come home in the morning. I mean it, *Larry*."

"I had business. That's the reality. The Assemblyman was honored, I put it all together, financing, and the right people." A flare flickered in his eyes. "I'm at the office by 7:00

every morning. I'm all over the city every day. Worst case, some nights I miss dinner at home."

"Delton." My mother turned to me, "Do you think it's right for your father to disappear all night?"

"I'm not sure I'm the right person to stick his nose in this . . ."

"You're in law school, so you can hear two sides of an argument," the old man said, fiddling with a matchbook before lighting up again.

"Dad, they don't make you a judge until the third year of school. Look, I think this is plain old lack of communication. Right?"

They were quiet. My mother leaned her shoulder against the kitchen door, and stared off into the dining room.

"How about a spring salad, dad."

"Honey! Spring salad? Sound good?" He went behind my mother and squeezed the back of her neck. She seemed to soften at his touch.

"What would sound good is to hear you truthfully say you were not with Kelly O'Brien, or any other woman." Her petite frame trembled, but her lips pursed and her eyes were wide.

"I wasn't with her or any other woman, Joanna. I was at the dinner, we drank and then went out, where I talk to people, make connections, set up business, do what has to be done. That's it. That's reality."

"Okay," she said.

"How about that spring salad?" he asked.

"There's no chicken in the fridge, dad."

"Crack open a tin of sardines. Be resourceful. Just hurry up. If you don't start it now, I'll miss the beginning of 60 Minutes."

Chapter 9

I managed to pass my tests, even civil procedure—a course as pleasant as a colonoscopy—thanks to Finkle's keen grasp of the material. It felt dreadful to be back at the bungalow, with fresh snowfall in the yard. The day blurred into evening, until Jaspr came into view, shoveling the walkway between our homes. I stepped outside to greet him.

"Hey Jaspr. Haven't seen you since before the holidays."

"Ya, hallo, Delton," he said, huffing from the workout, scraping an oversized shovel under mounds of hardening snow.

"You do good?" he said.

"You mean the tests?"

"Vat else? Health of cock?"

I managed a smile. "I did okay. I don't know, Jaspr. I'm not having a good time. There's sort of this expectation that I'm going to be a lawyer and work for my old man, and–I don't know."

This admission caught me off guard. It felt strange to hear these words spoken out loud.

"Vat?" He stopped to regard me.

"Nothing. I think I just feel a little trapped."

"Is good, this vat you do."

"Okay."

"Any trim?"

"Excuse me?"

"The sexy vomens? The girl I see in your house. Come, you talk and we have vine."

His place was as delinquent as I remembered. He had Sade's Sweetest Taboo playing on the stereo, and a large new painting hung on the wall. This one featured a pale, leather-clad woman in a garden, her mouth bright red, biting two apples at once.

"Interesting vision, Jaspr. I hadn't noticed this piece last time," I said.

He handed me a glass of red. "New von, ya. I know girl."

He looked both grownup and boyish, standing by his deviant work, sipping fine wine in his beautiful house.

"So you're the two apples, then? Metaphorically speaking."

"Ah, I get you! My package is like this!"

"Right. Anyway, the girl you've seen at my place? She studies with my friend Finkle and me. He's sleeping with her. As for me, I have nothing going on. Not since I stopped seeing a girl I dated briefly after college graduation."

"You give back meal ticket?"

"I didn't want to keep a girl around that wouldn't understand what I'm going through."

The Sade gave way to Sinatra. The wine began to warm my system. The conversation with Jaspr was bizarre as usual, but it couldn't be denied that the man had a point. I had no woman in my life. Jaspr slid a hand along the leather-clad body of his painting. Yep, he had a way.

"I vant you paint."

He guided me to a corner where he had an easel set up and a couple cans of paint with a brush.

"Jaspr, I can barely draw a stick figure—"

"Stop vith this bullsheet," he said, tying a paint-splattered apron around my waist. "Ve do slow, you make easy, this vay."

He popped open a can of paint and delicately swirled a brush inside, then fitting it in my hand, he gently moved my wrist onto the blank canvas. There was now a splotch of blue-violet.

"Do again. Relax shoulder." He added a half-used can of azure.

I let more paint fly.

"This color, too," he said, bringing me a can of orange and red mixed.

Before long, I was making actual sketches of various shapes. He asked me if I wanted more wine, but I didn't hear him. I was lost in what I was doing. The heaviness in my muscles slowly began to ebb away. Jaspr left me alone for some time, but returned to check on his new disciple. It didn't bother him to see a terrible mess on the canvas.

"You do it!" he said, patting me on the back.

"So there's this one chick at school," I said. "I can't figure out what to do. It's such a hard environment to operate in. I see her in the halls and that's about it. Besides, she has a boyfriend in Europe. I don't think I've even got a chance."

"Insanity!" Jaspr shouted."

"What're you talking about?"

"You be man," he said, shaking my shoulders. "You like her ass, her tits, she move good?"

"Yes, she move good."

"Then, be man!"

"I can barely get her alone."

"Make her friend."

"I don't follow."

"Make friend vith her friend," he said, handing me more wine.

"Get with her friends, like the Spice Girls' song, Jaspr?"

"Yah."

"My god, that's it! I think I know a guy in her study crew. Maybe I could swing a lunch out of it?" A smile lit up my face.

"Yes!" His arms shot out and suddenly his hands were gripping *my* package. "Then have meal again!"

I was in the main study area of the law library, for once, surrounded by motionless heads poring over their casebooks. I couldn't bring myself to focus on any of the assignments, feeling more incapable than at any other time in my life. Worse yet, an ugly insecurity had sprung up like weeds in my mind. For instance, if I sat next to Amy in class, the sheer orderliness of her notes made me want to squeeze her into a duffle bag and dump her at sea. The harder I tried to learn, the more disoriented and misplaced I felt. I was stalling out in what felt like the middle of rush-hour traffic. The whole 'learning to think like a lawyer' had gone horribly awry. My pocket law dictionary went with me everywhere, like a tourist, hopelessly lost in a foreign city.

"Delton. How are your studies progressing during this increasingly intensive period?"

"Hey Darby. How are you?"

"Splendid, thank you."

"How's Ramona?"

"She's tending to a matter of a personal nature."

"Is everything all right?" The blinking fluorescent light and Darby's maddening speech were a challenging combination.

"Yes, she's fine. Is that blood?" he asked.

"Where?"

"Well, you have a multiplicity of cuts around your face."

"I was a little careless shaving this morning, is all," I said. I didn't care that I'd left the house looking like the victim of a slashing. "Hey Darby, how's your legal writing paper going?"

"I've completed the body of work and am simply fact-checking the bluebook citations."

"Listen, I'm having a hard time finding these Shepard's cases. Maybe you might—if you have a few minutes—could you help me?"

"I have a few moments at the present time. It's really quite simple," he said.

"You're a lifesaver."

We walked through the labyrinth of students silently absorbing cases.

"I want to ask you a question of some delicacy, Delton." He averted his eyes, and tugged at the part in his hair.

"Anything."

"Well . . ."

"Go ahead. I'm pretty sure you're not going to ask me to brief your tort cases."

"It's Ramona, actually," he said. The little bugger looked pained. "I have, what one might call, an emotional—"

"You have feelings for her. That's great. And if I may, just talk to me, Darby, y'know, like you would an old friend."

"I don't have any old friends," he said.

Did anyone at this school ever have a friend? I felt a tinge of guilt that this revelation made me feel less alone.

"Let me help you. This is an area where I'm not a complete failure." It was basically true.

"She just wants to study with me," he said.

A sentence without seventeen commas. A good start.

"How do you know that?"

"Why would she feel anything more for me?"

I wanted to get his romantic aspirations off the ground, like a wounded little bird, but it was also an opportunity.

"It's funny you bring this up, because I wanted to ask you something. I've seen you with that girl Angelina. She wears pants with cows on them sometimes?"

"The cows had escaped my attention, but I'm aware of her presence."

"Darby."

"Yes, we trade notes, as she's in the other classroom section. Why?"

"I think we can help each other. I don't really know her, and I hesitate to suggest it, since you're already helping me with my paper . . ."

"Tell me."

"How about if we arrange a lunch to include you, Ramona, Angelina, and me?"

"I wager you will need a facial before such an undertaking," he said.

His dour expression broke open into pure light. He wrapped his little arms around me and snuggled his head into my chest.

"Thank you, Delton. Thank you."

"Relax, Darby, I'm not doing anything, but you're welcome. And quite honestly, I'm good at giving advice to others, but clueless when it comes to myself."

He pulled away and looked at me. "No, believe me, you are doing so much," he said, pulling down the Shepard's volumes I needed for the research paper.

This time, when Finkle came over for second-semester-finals prep, he looked despondent, as if a black sky hung above him. Without a glance, he roughly handed me the bagels and drinks, and slunk over to one side of the room to pout. He pulled out his laptop, and logged on to the Internet.

"Finkle?" No answer. "Finkle! You want me to toast your bagel, and use it as an ass warmer?"

Nothing. He stared into the screen. Every few seconds, *pop, pop*, he'd have a burst of typing.

"Who are you typing to?" I said.

From an angle, I could see the screen had a box with two names and lines of dialogue. Maybe he was scoring some fresh outlines. I peered over his shoulder and took a closer look.

"Whose junkinthetrunk?" I said.

"Can I help you?"

"Ok, so if you're not junkinthetrunk, then you must be pounder69. Are you in a fucking AOL chat room? You are! I don't even want to know you," I said, looking away. "Wait— think I could do it on my computer?"

"Get an account, I'll set you up," he said.

"Is that Amy on there? Is this some kind of new foreplay?"

"She—we kinda broke up."

He still hadn't looked at me. "She dumped you?"

"Not exactly."

"Holy shit, I'm sorry. I can't believe it. I mean, other than your terrorizing the girl with your disgusting personality, she seemed really into you. I liked you guys together," I said.

"I guess I did too," he muttered.

"Why didn't you tell me?"

"It just happened this morning."

"Wait, that's why she's not here now? Is she not coming for finals prep? Did you chase away our golden goose?"

He looked at me. "Fuck her and her goose," Finkle said, turning back to the computer.

"Do you even know where Amy is?" I said, feeling a sense of desperation. I felt like I'd broken up with her.

"I don't know, probably in the middle of a Debra Winger marathon, then off to get pounded by pipe-hitting crackheads."

"That's beautiful. It really shows how much you care," I said. I wasn't unsympathetic. It was a hell of a time to have one's heart broken, but feelings were a luxury we could not afford. "Walk it off, pounder69. Nothing like criminal law outlining to make everything all right," I said.

The phone rang in the bedroom. The creaky window was open and a light, early-spring breeze wafted in.

"Hey sonny boy!"

"Hey mom," I answered, smiling.

"How are you holding up?"

"I'm good. How are things with dad?"

"He's busy. The Russian and Polish buyers are in the city and they love to shop."

"Black bread and pierogis?"

Mom laughed. "I think they get plenty of that over there," she said. "They came with no luggage and left with suitcases full of clothes from your father."

"Need I ask how he managed that?" His garments were not high-end.

"Not by walking into Bloomingdales. But he has a guy with swag downtown, who gets it before the stores and boutiques."

"Sounds like good business. Anything else?"

"Nate is in the papers today. His recent trial, he won it."

"Mob client?"

"No, musician. A nice change of pace, I think. He's expanding his practice. Take a look, when you get a minute." She paused. "I wish your father would..." she trailed off.

"What, mom?"

"Nothing."

"No, tell me."

"It's fine. I just wish he would take more time with us, that's all."

"I know. I Love you."

"Love you, too. I'll check in on you soon. Give 'em hell."

I sat on the edge of my bed, lost in thought. I'd often wished I had a normal father. The kind that came home. The kind that was in my life. He was even harder on my mother. I let out a long sigh. Why was I so desperate to make him proud of me? And why was I drawn to his world, and yet at the same time, repulsed by it? Without any enlightening new insight, there was nothing to do but trudge back to the living room.

"Dude, I have to run to the store. Need anything? And what are we eating tonight?"

"Same as every night, shitty Italian takeout."

"It's great to look forward to something. All right, be right back."

Outside, the chilly air had surrendered to springtime warmth. The sun had faded, but the evening sky lay bare, no clouds, with stray violet streaks. I walked to the meager strip in the little ghost town. There were signs of the coming summer season. A couple kids played in a yard, while an adult washed a car on a front lawn.

The little general store had the papers, and sure enough, I saw the story on Uncle Nate's case. He was in a big photo next to his client outside the courthouse. I'd been vaguely aware of the case and its attention in the media. I felt a peculiar thrill, looking at the article and photos of Nate in a pinstripe suit, cigar in his mouth, commenting on his case. Criminal law in school was about as interesting as the writing on a cereal box, but Nate's work seemed different. Maybe one day I could be in the papers too. It was heady stuff, to see my own uncle as such a legal bigshot. It made outlandish success seem attainable. But a moral question arose in my mind: would I want to protect a wrongdoing client from punishment?

Chapter 10

"Little Lowe!" My father snapped through the phone.

"Yeah, dad."

"You'll be working at 2278 Strickland this summer. Norris's South Bronx office. Get there at 8:00 sharp, tomorrow morning."

"The Assemblyman? Dad, I don't think—"

"Do what he says and don't be late. Talk later." Click.

That's how my father operated. Fast, sudden, with no talking my way out of it. I sensed what I was in for; to essentially clean Norris' wastebaskets and keep his Scotch bottles unsealed. It was to be a wade into shallow city politics and the law practice embedded within it. I showed up at the appointed hour.

"Assemblyman Norris, it's a pleasure, sir. Thank you for having me."

"Having you? Are you a plump blonde with big tits and a juicy ass? Because that's the sort of thing she says to me when we're finished." He twirled a cigar in his lips. "You, on the other hand, I'm not giving my resources to so easily. What you do have, young man, is an opportunity. Got it? You can work hard and prove yourself. Then we'll go from there. Got it?"

Yeah, I got it.

"You're Larry's kid. Man, I love that guy."

Jack Norris leaned back in his swivel chair. He was young, tan, good-looking. His office, on the other hand, sat on a busted street corner in the Bronx. The building was ancient, its glass storefront was dirty, and the inside was all wood paneling. A couple metal, secretarial desks were shoved into corners, where old ladies pecked away on typewriters. The cigarette smoke was thick and suffocating. The place had the feel of a bygone era.

"My father has spoken highly of you. He feels you're a real rising star in the Democratic Party."

"Have a seat." He motioned to a stained chair in front of his desk. "Yeah, he helped shore up my base last election. In many ways, he's one of the visionaries of the district, hell, the whole city. He's the best."

It was astonishing to me that this man, who sat in the family kitchen in torn pajama tops, smoking and watching the news, wielded such wide-reaching influence.

"He puts things together in ways nobody thinks of," Norris added.

I had a terrible image of the old man, Norris, Kelly O'Brien, and an anonymous plump blonde all together in a wood-paneled nightmare.

"What can I help you with, Mr. Norris?"

"Fundraising. A number of things. I've got guys in the street and working the phones already, but you, you must be a smart kid. I'm gonna make sure you're put to use here."

"Fundraising, sir? Didn't you just get reelected a couple years ago?"

"First rule of politics, kid, you're always running," he said, blowing smoke in my direction. "Your war chest is constantly in need of replenishment. Just think of politicians as individual brands competing, and voters are always testing that brand," he said.

"Praising or blaming you," I said.

"Yes, something like that. They may know the man they're getting, but they need positive reminders, and reminders cost money. Got it? You're going to work on preparations for a big fundraiser I have coming up at the end of the summer. I need the phones hot with donor calls. You own a comfortable pair of dress shoes?"

"Sure, black ones."

"Good, because you'll work the street too, talk to business owners, hand out literature."

"I can do that."

"I also do legal work down the block in another office. You'll tackle both jobs. How does that sound?"

"Good, Mr. Norris. I'm ready, but is the legal work related to this office?"

"You have a curious little brain, don't you? The law practice is largely unrelated. They don't teach you that in school, but you'll learn," he said, stubbing out his cigarette. "First thing, here's twenty bucks, go grab me a pack of Camels and a Pepsi," he said, abruptly swiveling away and fixing his hair with a plastic comb and mirror set on the desk. I took the twenty and left for the A&P around the corner. I wondered if he acted this way at the fundraisers.

He stationed me in the office next door. It was basically a boiler room with two lawyers and two paralegals windmilling cases. It was perfectly legal, mind you, but felt like the low-end of the law business. Inside each file were the names and case information on injured clients. The practice was personal injury on a contingency basis. The name of each plaintiff and case caption were written on an erasable-ink chalkboard in the front of the office. Next to each case name was the main injury suffered, with a dollar amount next to it. The worse the injury, the higher the dollar amount.

Cummings v. Dawson, Case #. . . . broken tailbone-$25k. The object of the game was to figure out an injury's value as a dollar amount to reach for when negotiating with the defendant's insurance company. I waited for Norris to make me chase ambulances like a werewolf at night, where I'd stamp our fee on an injured person's forehead.

Did the client lose mental function? Was there actual trauma to the brain? This man fell out of a three-story window and you're telling me he'll walk again? That can't be! The graver the injury, the more the lawyers licked their chops.

I wasn't sent to court. I was left to man the phones and take statements from witnesses, but mostly I cut and pasted motions. Angelina visited my imagination in those dreary hours. We never did get around to doing the lunch. Darby conveniently dropped the ball, but I couldn't blame him. The fantasy of her was the only thing I missed about school. A hotshot mergers and acquisitions guy was probably making her promises in a high-rise office somewhere.

I went for smoke breaks and lazily watched the subway trains rattle into the nearby station, its parade of workers rushing off the platform into the neighborhood. They wore simple shirts, faded with use, and shoes I recognized from my father's inventory. The traffic kicked dirt up from the street where I stood. These gritty city blocks were, for now, where I belonged.

One afternoon, the usual pile of papers and phone calls waited back at my desk. I sat and stared into space for half an hour when another attorney in the office, Willy Rodgers, shoved a stack of pamphlets into my hand that said, in thin letters, *A Vote for Assemblyman Norris is a Vote for Community!*

"C'mon son, Jack wants you jumpin' into the political ring. Follow me."

Willy's office was the largest other than Norris's. It was, however, every bit as grimy and rundown, with its worn furniture and utter absence of luxury. There were two large filing cabinets stuffed full of blue paperbacks, the universal sign of filed documents in civil litigation matters. A black and white frame of John Wayne hung behind Willy, and on the desk sat two smaller frames of an older, attractive blonde riding horseback.

"Now these here pamphlets are worth a hell of a lot more than the paper they're printed on," he said, adjusting his Stetson hat and trailing a finger along his silver, walrus mustache. He was fond of rawhide jeans, and when not in court, he wore the denim with a huge belt buckle of a steer.

"What do you mean exactly, Willy?"

"You ever worked a street before?"

"I don't believe I have, no."

"You need to make them folks out there believe what you're sellin' is important, that they'd hand over their unborn babies for our support. This is their community, their future, and not to take a pamphlet and make time for you," he cleared his throat and crossed his legs, revealing a small pistol taped to his ankle, "is just plain crazy. Now by extension, what does it say when they do take one?"

"Probably that—"

"You ever hear of a rhetorical question, Lowe? They need to like you, before they buy in."

"Why do they need to like me just to take a pamphlet?" I screwed my eyes in earnest on old Willy. He pointed at the coffee machine, an offer I declined. It was always burned and the spoiled creamer could kill a steer.

"Because they'll wipe their white ass with it if they don't! Damn it, son, sharpen up. Now I like you, hell, the Assemblyman likes you, thinks you got the gift of gab and all, but you're askin' these folks, through your teeth, for only one damn thing. To give money. To contribute. And you're not gonna be none too subtle about it, neither."

I groaned inaudibly. All this political crap was as dull as drafting motions.

"How do I go about it? I take it you've done this before."

Willy pulled a pipe and a fold of tobacco out of a drawer and packed it. The window behind him looked out onto the street, but I couldn't see anything, its glass almost completely obscured with black streaks. Willy lit his pipe and thick curls of smoke floated along the wood paneling and evaporated against the window.

"Goddamn right I've done this before. Been through two election cycles with our man already. I'll be canvassing with you. The main thing is you make all them donors a promise, hear me?"

"What promise?"

"Every business owner has a gripe, from pedestrian troubles like not enough salt on the sidewalk, to graffiti, vandals, and thieves, to more, ehmm... intricate matters." He shifted in his squeaky chair.

"What matters?"

"Issues like city inspections, zoning rules, legal problems of that nature."

"How can Mr. Norris guarantee any of that?"

"He can't."

"I see. So how am I promising?"

"You're a lawyer—well, almost one—so figure out what to say. Say what needs to be said, leave out the rest."

"Leave the gun, take the cannoli."

"What the hell?"

"Nothing, forget it. You've been doing this for how many years in this city?" I said, my mouth contorted as if doused in vinegar.

"Long time. This is the greatest city in the world."

"That may be, so how come it smells like piss everywhere?"

Willy ignored the comment. "I'll spell it out for you. We—this office—everybody benefits. The Assemblyman gets his reelection, and we see more legal business for the firm. Keeps me smokin' this fine tobacco. You'll flank the westside of Betrayce Avenue, I'll take the east, and we'll work from there. To sum up: find the owner, give the pamphlet, have a sit-down, figure out what he needs, and give an assurance it'll be looked into. You've got to give this city, this district, a deep French kiss, son, you get my meaning?"

"Okay."

"You gettin' laid, kid?"

"Sorry?"

"I want you confident."

I was tempted to say not lately on account of your wife being out of town, but I kept my trap shut.

"Sure," I said, lying.

"Good. Oh, one other thing, very important. There's the big fundraiser in Manhattan coming up. Any significant local donor will attend as a special guest of the Assemblyman, and gets to glad-hand with all the bigwigs at the party. Wave that carrot around."

My first day of canvassing was muggy and overcast. It took about two blocks in my suit and tie before sweat was dripping down my back. I undid the shirt button at the neck and swathed my forehead with a hankie. The barrio streets were busy with foot traffic well before the lunch hour. Rodgers gave me a short list to kick it off, beginning with a radio and electronics store that was far enough distance from Norris's office to be a lengthy walk, but not so far that it justified a subway ride. I was out hoofing it to the fringe of his district; it was yeoman's work, pamphlets damp in my hand and my feet hardening over every step of concrete. I discovered for myself what Einstein said about the relativity of time: *When you sit with a nice girl for two hours you think it's only a minute, but when you sit on a hot stove for a minute you think it's two hours. That's relativity.*

Unfortunately, Einstein's intelligence was all too accurate, as with each block trodden I had an irrepressible desire to turn right around to head for the office, with its clangy, temperamental air conditioner that sputtered as much dust as cool air.

It felt as if I'd been on the street for forty years, like Moses had walked the desert, when in fact I had just stepped foot out of the office.

Leonard's Electronics sat on the corner of a block filled with bodegas and food markets, as well as a dentist's office and shoe repair store. Rodgers told me the idea was to work backwards from the periphery of the district, and to first target places that were either new to the neighborhood or hadn't yet donated to Norris. I couldn't figure out why I was tasked with turning around the deadbeats, but I imagine Rodgers was focused on keeping the prize gift horses in Norris's stable happy and attended to.

Before walking into Leonard's, I glanced at the plethora of gadgets and electronics in the store window. My heartbeat quickened. What did I know about convincing an electronics shop owner to part with his cash to support a politico he'd likely never met?

I retreated from the mouth of the store's entry and wound around the side of the building to collect myself. There weren't any shoppers up this way, so I took my jacket off, lit a cigarette, and paced along the block. My panic attack subsided and my senses returned. There was a little alleyway with overgrown shrubbery and trash behind a chain-link fence, and I saw what I thought was a loading dock behind Leonard's.

I took a drag from the smoke, rubbing my sweaty forehead with my thumb, and curled my other hand into the metal fence. Nobody else was around. Then a couple of Chicano guys in tank tops with tattooed sleeves came out of a warehouse door and started loading equipment onto a mid-size truck covered in artless graffiti. It looked like the old 'stereo equipment fell off the back of the truck' routine.

I chuckled to myself, imagining that these guys might be slinging product out of their shady truck by day's end, when a huge fucking canine snapped its jaws centimeters from my face. The whole fence shook as the animal jabbed at it wildly, my hand barely free before it was bitten off, and my ass now flat on the pavement.

The two Chicano guys stopped what they were doing and stared at me from behind dark shades. One of them jumped off the truck and whistled sharply, calling the name Guapo, which I think meant handsome, and was probably meant for the dog, because it relented its gnashing at the fence. I scrambled off the ground and tucked tail until I was safely around the corner in front of Leonard's. This first stop wasn't feeling like progress. Fuck it, I thought, ripping up a pamphlet—what Norris doesn't know can't hurt him.

A few blocks down, after a stop in a bodega for a cold drink and a trip to the pisser to assess any sartorial damage from the canine encounter, I approached target number two on my list: Eddie's Deli & Sandwiches. It seemed common to name an establishment after oneself in these parts. With the exception of dirt and smudges on the jacket and shirt, I was still presentable, and this time I didn't dawdle in front of the place. Upon entry, my olfactory nerves were hit with the aroma of sliced pastrami, hot dogs, and brisket.

"Hi, I'm looking for Eddie? I'm from Assemblyman Norris's office."

I directed this inquiry to the blue-haired woman filing her nails behind the register. She stuck a thumb toward the back of the store without looking up. The place was mostly empty, so I was rewarded with the attention of the one waiter in the dining area. He put a tray down and motioned for me to follow him. He disappeared momentarily, and then invited me into Eddie's office down a little hall.

Behind the kitchen was a door bearing the word 'office' on a sticky label curled with faded glue. It was half-open, and a voice told me to come inside. A man in a hairnet with long sideburns and a tussle of chin scruff pointed to a chair in front of his desk. A flip calendar of race cars hung open to the wrong month behind him. Eddie leaned back and slung his skinny legs on the cheap wooden desk, leaving a view of the bottom of his feet.

"You're with the politician's office? The one down the avenue?"

"Yes, that's right. Assemblyman Norris' office. I'm Delton Lowe." I offered my hand and he took it, not moving his legs. "So, I'm—"

"Woah, wait a sec, Junior." He dropped his legs off the desk and shook his head, clearing cobwebs. "You say your name's Lowe? As in Larry Lowe?"

"You mean the Larry Lowe off Mercer Ave. with Lowe's Shoe and Apparel?"

"Yeah, who else?" he said.

"I'm his son, actually."

"Sweet Jesus. Listen, Junior," he said, sitting straight up in his chair, "your old man, he didn't have to send you down here like this." He put his hand up. "What I mean is there's no problem. He doesn't need to worry about collecting from me. Listen to me, Darren—"

"Delton."

"Right, of course. Delton, listen to me. Larry will have last month's payment with this month's right on the first, all caught up." Eddie rubbed his hands shut, then open, palms up. "No need to call in the note, okay? There's no reason to send anybody down here. Do you understand?"

"Last month's...?"

He looked at me closely, and no doubt saw the confusion written all over my face.

"He didn't send you?"

"No, I'm really here with Mr. Norris' office to talk about his upcoming campaign and to solicit contributions." I put a pamphlet on his desk.

He let out a long exhale. "Oh man, I thought you came to give me my last warning." His whole body relaxed. He picked up the pamphlet. "As soon as I come even with your old man, I'll contribute to this, it'd be my pleasure." He tucked it into a drawer. "You know, I love Larry Lowe. I wouldn't even be in business if it weren't for him. Damn creditors were eating me alive. You tell him we had a nice talk, all right?"

I nodded.

"Listen, you wanna sandwich? Food? Anything you want, I'll make it."

After polishing off a pastrami on rye, a knish and a Coke back at the office, I went to the bathroom to pick out bits of meat wedged in my teeth. Eyeing my babyface in the mirror, I knew I was about as intimidating as a girl scout, and yet the mere mention of my father's name had struck Eddie with terror.

I hit the street again and walked my route for the rest of the afternoon. I spoke to three other local business owners, none of whom owed my father money, and even succeeded in signing two of them up for modest contributions.

I met my father, Nate, and a client of his, Rick Tischmann, for dinner. The restaurant was known for its authentic Italian food.

"So explain to me the no-menu thing?" I said.

"Tony goes to the vegetable and fish markets to find the freshest ingredients for that day's dishes," Uncle Nate said. My father lightly rapped his fingers on the table; he never did like to wait.

"Sounds good," I said. "By the way, has anyone noticed we're always eating at Italian restaurants?" I watched their blank expressions, then a man in a windbreaker lumbered over to Nate and kissed him on the cheek.

"He loves to eat, this one," the man said.

"It's an easy way to keep me happy, Gino. Gino, you know Larry Lowe and his kid. This is Rick Tischmann."

Gino shook his hand but pulled back sharply, and I recalled Tischmann having a clammy, wet-noodle shake.

"Good to meet you," Tischmann said, apparently not registering Gino's discomfort.

"Why don't you join us, Gino? We have penne coming out. It's the best in the city," Nate said.

"Nah, I gotta get back. But Nicky is around the corner and he wanted a word. I'll let him know," Gino said, pinching his nose and spinning his index finger in a flourish. "Nice seeing youse all," he said to the rest of us.

"Where's he connected?" my father asked after Gino was gone.

"Old Colombo outfit. I handled the underboss's RICO about ten years ago. Beat that one at trial. It was all over the papers."

"I don't read the papers," my father said, sliding back in his chair, a hint of amusement on his lips.

"You always were my favorite witness, Larry." Uncle Nate smiled back.

"What are you guys talking about?" I said.

"Just an old case, kid," Nate said.

"Gino mentioned Nicky. That's the Nicky who was at my graduation dinner, right? Is there a new case with him?"

"Attorney-client privilege. But yes, he was at the dinner."

"So, what line are you in, Tischmann?" my father said, eyeing the man and changing the subject.

"I run a private equity fund on Wall Street. I met Nate through our wives at a function."

"Which function?" my father asked.

"For Judge Dominguez, Larry. You were out of the country," Nate added.

"That was some favor the party boss did for Dominguez," my father said.

"What favor?" I piped up.

"Judge Sheila Dominguez is the youngest judge to sit on the bench in the county," my father explained.

"How'd she get placed?" I said.

"She's a young Latina," he said.

"So?"

"So, little Lowe," my father said, "the party boss made it happen."

"How'd it happen?"

"With her legs spread."

"Wow," was all I could think to say.

"Nate, we'll be in front of her?" Tischmann asked.

"No, whole different court," Nate answered.

"She was good to me," my father said.

"How so?" I asked.

"She cleared my traffic tickets."

I was pretty sure my father meant the Driving Under Influence case he had last year. He'd racked up a reputation behind the wheel amongst city law enforcement, with offenses ranging from driving on the sidewalk to taking some poor shmuck's open car door clean off its hinges, but he'd been arrested for drinking and driving and even that didn't appear to put him in too much trouble. He did, however, have to answer for it; his usual bounty of police union cards and stickers could not win his typical outright release. Nate had to represent him in court to keep him out of jail.

The platters of food came, and we fell into a contented feast. After a round of espresso with anisette, Tichmann took the check and excused himself.

"That guy's business is as slippery as his fingers," my father cracked. He didn't care much for the Wall Street boys club. I think he felt they were fake.

"How do you like Norris's office?" Nate said, pulling out a fat cigar. He handed it to my father and drew another from his breast pocket.

"It's good. I booked a few grand in donations this week in cold calls and street canvassing. I also help out with the firm's personal injury cases," I said, looking over at my father. He appeared distracted.

"They break their necks chasing ambulances?" Uncle Nate chuckled, as he lit the cigars.

"What do you think, dad?"

"You think Senator Rodd will show at Norris's fundraiser? I need to talk to him about that zoning ruling in District 13," he said to Nate, puffing on the cigar.

"Where's District 13?" I said.

"Senator Rodd should be there," Nate said.

My father turned to me. "Tell me about this street canvassing," he said.

"Okay, y'know—"

"No, I don't know. I never want to hear you hem and haw. That's for horses."

"One of the attorneys in the office, Willy Rodgers, gave me a crash course on how to solicit contributions."

The bartender tapped Nate on the shoulder, and whispered in his ear.

"I gotta run in a few minutes," Nate said.

"What's up?" my father said.

"Nicky needs me next-door."

"Hey Uncle Nate, is Tichmann a white-collar client?" I said.

"Of course, but he's a criminal defendant like any other."

"How's his case going?"

"Got moved to trial court. Should sum up next week."

"Sum up?" I repeated.

"Summation. Closing argument." He looked at me thoughtfully, switched his gaze to my father, then back to me, "You think you want to practice law?"

"Hey Nate," my father interjected. There was a forceful look in his eyes.

"Larry, is it a crime to ask a question?"

Before my father could answer, I said, "I'm not sure what I want." Even from my peripheral, I felt the disapproval from my father.

"Aha! This is good. Larry, sometimes we forget the kid has his own ideas. So, what interests you, Delton?" Nate leaned back and rubbed his chin.

"Not law."

Nate fell forward, cigar dangling. "Then what?"

"I can't say, except that cases and sales seem the same to me."

"It's all the same," my father muttered, then with voice raised, "It's all the same when you've got a roof over your head, bills paid, a car, food, and every other damn thing . . ." He put his cigar down, picked up his fedora, smoothed the crease in front, and got up from the table. "I gotta get back to the shop."

Nate answered by grabbing my wrist and pulling a ring right off my finger. Its carvings were symbols of earth, moon, and water.

"What the hell is this?" He looked cockeyed at the ring.

"It's an authentic Native American—"

He cut me off and held the ring up. "What's the difference between an amateur and a professional?" he said.

"You mean, like—"

"What is the difference between an amateur and a professional?" he repeated.

"A professional clips a napkin to his shirt when he eats?"

His face lightened with a tiny grin. He knew I was being a wise guy about his ever-present napkin.

"A professional gets paid, Delton. You take the money right off a client's finger." He twirled the ring around his palm. "Throw this piece of shit in the trash. What do you think you're doing in that school?"

"I'm not sure."

He tossed me back the ring. I slipped it on gently, respectful of its spirit.

Chapter 11

The fundraiser for Assemblyman Norris was held in a swanky supper club on the Upper East Side. A murmur sounded in the crowd as tuxedo-clad servers passed hors d'oeuvres, though the collective hunger was one of power and ascension.

I ferreted drinks and introduced Norris to the neighborhood donors that included jewelry, drycleaner, and furniture storeowners. Willy Rodgers was at the corner of the bar working on a double whiskey, with an eye on my progress. I finished my tasks, making it time to reward myself with a vodka cocktail, and I noticed a girl I couldn't quite place talking with Norris. She appeared to be reporting to him. She got up on the tip of her high heels to whisper in his ear. He nodded. She had his attention, and mine as well, looking quite fetching in a black cocktail dress, her thick brown hair tied up in a bun.

A shrill whistle halted the proceedings. The attendees looked to the source of the unpleasant interruption. At the top of the central staircase stood my father. His tan fedora matched his beige suit and the cigar he pulled from his mouth. A spotlight shone on him and lit up the gold ring on his pinky finger. A charged silence gathered around him.

"Ladies and gentlemen, I have the pleasure of welcoming you to this event. It is an important one, because we are here to offer our support to a dedicated public servant and a personal friend, Assemblyman Jack Norris. I'd like to call the Assemblyman up now to say a few words. Thank you."

Norris was caught off guard, in spite of the shrieking whistles, still talking into the cleavage of a young female supporter. He'd already had a few, and from the looks of the strong turnout, power had taken his brain to the clouds. The object of his affection, a fat-hipped blonde awash in mascara, had her hand on his thigh. The girl I'd noticed a moment ago rushed to his side and slid artfully between them. Norris snapped into it, or out of it, and finally made his way to the platform to a fresh round of applause. My father had a look on his face like Norris had spit at his feet; nonetheless, he recovered with a pat on the back and passed the microphone.

Norris gave a quick, if not garbled speech on the importance of leadership, flashed a few practiced smiles for the high-wattage cameras and promptly descended the staircase. The music resumed and there was renewed vigor among the crowd. I understood with my scant time in politics that no voter or donor wants hard (quite literally) evidence of a candidate's incompetence. Norris did manage to avoid that pitfall with a brief but coherent speech, and a line of well-heeled folks waited to shake his hand.

My father tottered off the stage, and to my trained eye, his gait exhibited the familiar signs of intoxication. He wasn't full-on, but the booze had already conspired to beget regrettable behavior. This was one of my mother's most wince-worthy difficulties in their relationship. She had elected to stay home tonight. My father spied me out of the corner of his eye and called me over.

"I want you to meet Jim Clemens. Jim, my son, Delton."

After we shook hands, my father said, "Remember this face, Jim," squeezing the back of my neck. "Jim is corporate counsel for the city. Did you learn what that is yet in law school?" I caught a strong whiff of cognac on his breath and tried not to show it.

"Not yet, dad."

"So how do you like law school, young man?" Clemens asked. He was polished, important-looking.

"Am I under oath?" I quipped. Clemens laughed. My father's grip tightened.

"Look, Devon."

"Delton."

"It gets easier, I swear," Clemens said, holding up his hand as if on a witness stand. "I didn't want to be in law school for the first year. In fact, I almost dropped out. But don't tell the mayor that." He chuckled. "Believe me, you'll find your way."

My father took his lobster claw off my neck and I peeled away, claiming work duty. The bar area was congested with people schmoozing, but I shimmied through for a drink. The girl who ensured Norris saved face stood next to me.

"I feel like I know you," she said.

"You do look familiar."

"No, wait," she said, "I do know you. You went to Albany, right?"

She had a pattern of adorable freckles on her cheeks.

"I did," I said, feeling off-balance by this sudden encounter.

"Yeah, like in '97. I graduated in '97. You too?"

"Totally."

After a long pause, our mouths opened at once.

"No way! I really just remembered you," she said.

"I knew you looked a little too familiar, but I couldn't compute why on Earth you'd be here, of all places," I said.

"Oh my God, you don't remember my name," she said.

Of course, I didn't.

"It's Carmen. And you're Delton, and you never called me, you jerk!" She swiped at my chest with her purse.

"As I remember it, we drunkenly kissed at a party, *you* left, then never returned *my* call. But who's counting?"

"Whatever."

"So, what are you doing here?" I said.

"I handle PR for Norris," she said. "What about you?"

"I'm his intern."

"I'm surprised you weren't like, aware of me," she said.

"It would seem wise to put us together," I agreed.

"Or unwise." Her eyes lowered ever so slightly.

"So how did you get into working with politicos?"

"I majored in communications and always wanted to do something impacting with it, and there's plenty of action in this particular arena."

"So you're the one person that actually watches C-SPAN."

She laughed. "I'm not sure about that, but I enjoy what they do. It's sexy."

"What about interns in political offices?"

"They're kind of cute, too."

"Listen," I said, taking the cue, "you want to go somewhere, like, after you're done with Norris?"

"You think I'm having a thing with the Assemblyman?" She feigned shock, cupping her hand to her mouth in a very Audrey Hepburn way.

"You know what I mean, done for the evening," I said, touching her hip.

"That would be nice. It has been a long time," she said.

"I'll look for you. Bring the Assemblyman, if you'd like."

"Now you're never going to find me." She disappeared into the mix.

"Delton Lowe," Norris said, out of nowhere.

"Assemblyman. I think things have gone quite smoothly." His tanned face was blotchy from alcohol.

"They certainly have, Lowe. Rodgers tells me you were a warrior out there canvassing, and you did well with the cases, too. I've passed that onto your father. Y'know, when you first walked into my office you were kind of a brat, but you got your act together. You're welcome back in my office, just not in my seat, you son of a bitch!"

He clasped my shoulder in a fratty, let's-do-a-keg-stand way. It was no wonder he won all these elections. He was a mainstream golden boy. What was my old man's benefit to the relationship? The connections were always veiled. I suppose the mechanism ran best that way.

"If I need a recommendation, your support would be greatly appreciated. I hope to be employable on a full-time basis someday," I said, but he was already gone, on the heels of the blonde from earlier.

I spotted my father off in a corner with two men, speaking with force, gesturing with his arms, fluid as a boxer. It seemed the whole world could not contain him. And yet, I had no idea if he was upset, or making a joke, or talking business, or perhaps none of these things. I only knew their attention was glued to my father. It was a common sight to see men rally around him. This time, however, I did not witness this familiar display as an outsider; I witnessed it as an outside employee.

As I turned to leave, Willy Rodgers' Stetson poked through the throng of people in the hall. He must keep to the shadows, I thought, Norris's secret weapon.

"How you feelin' there, young man?" He gave me a hug. "Havin' fun?"

He wasn't too far behind my father and Norris on booze. Sour-whiskey breath.

"Doing my job, Willy, just like you trained me. Everybody on my donor list is accounted for."

"Thatta boy. Not such a bad deal now, is it?"

"What's the report, cowboy?" It was my father's voice. How did he keep track of everyone? He was omnipresent.

"Hey, Larry Lowe, king of 'em all. You put this fundraiser together for our boy Norris, beautifully, as always," Willy said, throwing his arms around my father.

"It's what I do," my father said. "Now tell me about my boy."

Both men stood back and took stock of me.

"He's coming into the fold real nice, Larry, real nice," Willy said, and the two men shook hands. My father, beaming, rubbed my head.

"Hey Larry!" It was another partygoer coming to hijack my father's attention.

"You gonna stick around for a drink, Del? I gotta go to the can," Willy said.

I begged off on one for the road with Willy, found Carmen, and let her know I'd be waiting outside. I finished my drink in a gulp and left the hall, mildly buzzed and a little unsteady on my feet. The city streets were dimly lit by passing headlights. It started to drizzle, and the murky rain gathered into little puddles. The gloom of the city at night was reason enough to drink. A great majority of New Yorkers no doubt agreed with this, the city's bars packed most any night. A cab stopped at a light and on its hood an advertisement read, *Did you know there's a syphilis explosion?* A lovely public service announcement—and a moment later, Carmen emerged from the club. We walked about a block in the rain without an umbrella, and then ducked into a lounge. We ordered drinks at a candlelit table.

"So you don't remember blowing me off?" she said.

"If that's your opening salvo, this will be a long night."

"After that fundraiser, it's already long."

"We both remembered each other at the same time. That's kismet," I said.

"Don't be a corny shit," she said, slapping me on the arm.

"How'd you end up working for this guy?"

"I'm in PR. Nobody needs bull crap sweetened for consumption like politicians."

"Good point."

"Are you now his little bitch?"

"It's a special relationship, don't sully it. It's not our fault if you can't understand what we have," I said.

She laughed and tossed her wet hair. She'd worked it out of its ponytail and it fell freely on her shoulders. Lust pricked my heart, but before its usual chaser of bitter longing, I realized, *I had this girl.* This was going to be fun! My hand rested on her knee while I tilted my head into her neck and nibbled. She trembled, her hand moving up my leg. I came up for air and we looked closely at each other.

"You seem . . . older," she said.

"I am older. I've aged seventy years since college."

"From what?" she said.

"First year of law school."

"You might still be attractive, in an older man sort of way." She kissed me on the mouth.

"That was nice," I said. We sipped our drinks. A cackle of laughter came from the next table. A sixtyish man with a bad toupé had his arm around an attractive woman in her early thirties.

"Doesn't it seem like older people were all made that way? Like, God made one woman fifty-eight with gray hair and toenail warts, one guy sixty-four with hair all over his back . . . I just feel that I can't actually age. Isn't that a relief, Carmen? I was made as this beautiful specimen. What do you think?"

"What I think is you're drunk, so you won't call me. Or remember me."

"We only met once! Anyway, you're right, I don't remember much, except where I'm staying, so how about we go there? It's not far."

"Well, since it's the only thing you remember."

I settled the tab and we left the lounge, holding hands in the drizzle, then jumped in a cab. My college friend, James, was in Columbia for a couple months and left me the key to his Harlem apartment for whenever I needed to crash in the city. The cabbie prattled on in nondescript Arabic through the grimy partition; always an aphrodisiac, we started to kiss in a rhythm, going deeper, her hand inching toward my beltline. One good thing about New York cabbies is they get where they're going in a hurry. We pulled up to the building in Harlem, I jimmied the key through the chipped front lock, and we climbed the stairs of the three-floor walk-up.

Once in the apartment, breathing heavily, we undressed and fell together on the couch. Her hair was damp from the rain, skin fragrant, eyes soft and wide. She rolled on top of me, grinding, her breasts at my lips. It was over in moments. I peeled my back off the faux leather couch. The apartment was dark and still. I lay back down.

"I think I would have wanted that to happen in college," she said, running her hand gently across my chest.

"See, we should have slept together. You didn't want to."

She flipped over and whacked my face with a pillow. "Liar."

"Sometimes it comes naturally," I said.

"You are learning to be a lawyer. How is law school, really?"

"What sweet pillow talk," I said. "It sucks. I don't know, maybe it's me. I feel like I don't belong. And I'm practically flunking out."

"You're exaggerating."

"Maybe a little," I said, her hands on my chest, body curled in my arms. "I'm just glad that my work with Norris, y'know, that I didn't shit the bed on that one."

"What a lovely reference to make lying post-coital on some stranger's couch."

We laughed.

"Sorry, I can be thoughtless," I said. "But honestly, at school, in between panic attacks, the belief that I can succeed in the real world is my only bedrock."

"See, you do have lawyering skills," she said, sitting up, brown hair spilling over her breasts. Her sweat, or perhaps rain water, slid down and gathered around her belly button.

"Thoughtlessness and lying?"

"Yes, which is why you should be a trial lawyer. Norris might be a great weaver of bullshit, but he's not as smart as you."

"I've been too miserable to even consider something like that."

"Poor baby, is it really that bad?" She cooed.

"The worst. But it's not all bad. There is some amusement. I have a middle-aged, Eastern European neighbor that I'm pretty convinced I'd find on the sex offender registry, my closest buddy in school has a sinister lazy eye and still listens to Dokken, and the bow tie army of professors is determined to shame me in front of the entire student body at every opportunity."

"Shame is sexy," she said, biting down on my ear. I started to climb upward again. Her mouth closed on me and we were gone.

Chapter 12

"Ya, there is my law man!"

I pulled into the driveway with supplies on my first day back, and as I stepped from the car, Jaspr swept me up in a bear hug. He wore a black and pink jumpsuit, front zipper open. Not much had changed since I'd left the bungalow. At least not with Jaspr.

"Come vith me, leave all this sheet," he said, inviting me into his home.

"Listen Jaspr, if I'm interrupting anything . . ."

"Nonsense, vat you say! Vine?"

"I'm good, but actually, do you have any coffee?"

"Yes!" He snapped his fingers. "I have this."

He scampered off to the kitchen. It felt especially quiet without the usual smooth jazz playing. His computer was on, chair pushed back from the desk.

"I didn't mean to interrupt your work," I said, kicking off my shoes as I sunk into his burgundy-leather couch. I grabbed the cheetah-spotted throw blanket and crawled under its fuzzy coziness, blissfully drifting off.

"Delton." He stood over me with a mug of coffee.

I blinked awake. "Thank you, it smells delicious."

"Vant pill too? I get for you?"

"No, I'm good with the coffee. Is that what you've been up to all summer, popping pills and hitting the clubs?"

"I shake it," he said, rubbing his glistening bald head, "vith the hot vomans last night, bump, bump right heey-ah!" He pointed to where I sat and demonstrated with a vigorous thrusting motion.

"*Here*?" I threw the cheetah blanket into the air and leapt off the couch, hot coffee splashing everywhere.

"No vorry, I vear bag," he laughed, sensing my need to amputate all my contaminated limbs.

"Sorry about spilling the coffee, but hey, the good news is I'm awake now," I said, selecting a nearby chair in which to sit.

"I clean this," he said. He mopped up the mess with the blanket and tossed it in a purple laundry basket.

"There's a story I want to tell you. I know you of all people will appreciate it. There was this function—" He looked at me quizzically. "Like a party for a politician, to raise money for his campaign," I explained. "I was working for him."

"Ya."

"I saw this really attractive girl there, and it just so happens that I knew her in college."

"Ya." Jaspr's right hand trembled with excitement and pawed at his chest.

"Turns out she's working for the same guy."

"Ahhh." Jaspr nodded and now slid the hand through his open jumper.

"Let's just say I took a meal ticket," I said.

He lifted me off the floor in yet another bear hug. "Taste good!" he shouted.

He placed me again on the floor and a goofy smile lit up my face. His excitement was contagious. "Yeah! Was just a couple weeks ago. I'm excited to see her again in the city. I like her."

He scuttled back to the wine rack in a tizzy, throwing his arms over his head and forcefully grinding an invisible partner. He eventually returned with a glass that he pushed into my hands.

"Unfortunately, I also have some bad news. My mom may split from my father. Do you mind me bringing that up?"

"No," he called from around the corner, where he tossed the blanket in the washer. I wondered if the whole couch could be stuffed in. He came back and made for his stereo player.

"Oh no, dude, not the smooth jazz."

His Hi-Fi crackled and I heard the first drizzle of flute and sax.

"Vat smooth?"

"Anyway, I don't know what to do. I don't even think there's anything I can do, but it's confusing and sad."

"Ya, mother is good-looking vomans."

"You're an animal," I said, exasperated.

"Oh shits." He crossed his heart. I knew he was well meaning, just that he'd watch nuns shower if given the chance.

"It's all right."

"Ya, you make them proud, Delton," he said, patting my shoulder.

"I feel like I might be failing both of them."

As he pondered this, he fully unzipped his jumpsuit, revealing a tan, hairless chest. I imagined women must appreciate this, as opposed to the itinerant, curly black hairs that sprouted from my own. I wished he'd zip up.

"I am architect," he said, "but is takes much time. I make this my home. And I love design home for clients," he said, gesturing to his desk. "If house sturdy," he knelt into a crouch and slapped at his knees, "you sturdy." He stood back up and waited for my reaction. He was like my personal Mr. Miyagi.

"I think I get what you're saying. Sturdy."

"Like the voman's ass."

"I see. Do you ever go to fundraisers?"

"No need for this."

The smooth jazz had crippled me, but Jaspr's insight rallied my spirits. After all, I realized, he walked the talk; he had built a beautiful home of his own design and had his own business doing work he enjoyed. He was also in a good mood whenever I saw him, whereas my father and Uncle Nate were terminally cranky, impatient, and stressed out.

"Finkle, what the fuck!" The last piece of chocolate cake was crammed in his mouth, as he finished clipping his toenails on my kitchen floor.

"What?" Crumbs fell to the tile.

I lunged at the dangling, spongy cake and poked it out of his mouth.

"I bought that cake for the guys coming over, dumbass," I said.

"You're preparing dessert for Herc and Darby? You really are queer."

The four of us were in Real Estate Transactions. It was under the auspices of the moose-head bow tie from Property.

He had broken up his class into numerous little groups to attack tricky finance issues and their legal implications. The material was dense and complex, but at least this course dealt with actual business scenarios.

"Listen, I'm not preparing a baby shower, I just thought we'd not live like gorillas in the mist for one night," I fired back.

"And you think it was wise to let Herc know where you live?" he said.

"Would you really care if I turned up in a plastic bag?"

"That hurts, bro. Who else would let me violate their home?"

"I'm so glad this friendship is meaningful to you, Finkle."

"How long 'til they show?"

"Should be about an hour."

I sat at the little dinette and lit a cigarette. I stared at his back as he rummaged through my fridge again. Since his breakup, the vain bastard had put on enough weight to make love handles protrude from under his shirt. I was in a reflective mood, already burned-out from school work.

"What do you really want to get out of law school? I mean, what's it all about for you?" I said.

"Don't you have any milk? Or beer? I'd take milk or a beer right now."

"Forget it. I don't know why I asked. Would you please wipe up your putrid clippings?" I ran a couple paper towels under the sink and handed the bunched wad to him. "It's just . . . is there a point to any of this?" I said.

"What do you mean?" Finkle stared at me like I was nuts.

"Y'know, when you actually become a lawyer, dare I say. Is it to be a big shot, or have other people think you are?"

It was already cold out, as fall was giving way to winter. The swarm of smoke and dust in the bungalow made my eyes itch, so I stepped around Finkle's offerings, out of the kitchen to the front door. Outside, nightfall blotted out the last remnants of light. A gulp of fresh air cleared my lungs. Back inside, Finkle now sat on the kitchen floor, unusually pensive, smoking, cleanup job done.

"I thought about your question. You may have missed things like m-o-n-e-y and p-u-s-s-y. It might be fun to practice, too," he said, squinting through the smoke.

"No, not really, although I never understood what you loved so much about Civil Procedure. Besides, what about *helping* people?" I said.

"What the hell is that?" He giggled. "No, I just think once we're actually fighting cases with real clients and getting paid, it'll be cool. You think too much."

"I *think* you're an asshole. I also think you take too many dick drugs for your little AOL skanks."

"They're not skanks, they're just comfortable using the privacy of their computer alias."

"What about Amy? I haven't seen her this semester," I said.

"That's because she made law review and is busy fact-checking all those stupid articles. Ever poke your head in there? It's like a panic room, no air, no windows. But hey, she wants a job at a white-shoe firm, and because of that, I don't see her much, which is better for me anyways."

We heard stories about life at the white-shoe law firms, like associates having to cancel their vacations at the airport about to board a flight, and sleeping under their desks at night. The entire crop of aspiring 2L summer interns had come to school last week in the same soul-sucking gray suit, reading from the same script. Amy was now one of them.

"But you're still into her?" I persisted.

He scratched his goatee. "We're still hangin' out a little."

"Cool." I didn't expect more on the subject.

"You know what? Call off Darby and Herc. I'm not up for the real estate grind tonight," I said.

"You sure?" he said, spreading butter for a grilled cheese sandwich. He'd systematically gone through my meager supplies. I had let this house goblin in, and paid a terrible price.

"Make me one, too," I said. "In fact, I'm going to pack a nice, healthy bowl, if you'd care to join."

"I'm good. I'd take a belt of the Dewar's, but you're out of ice."

"I'm sure I am. I'm out of everything."

We called Herc and Darby and told them we'd meet tomorrow at school. There were moments when one just hit the wall. We sat in the kitchen for a long time. He took a glass of Scotch, neat, and I pulled rips from a glass bowl. I had him pour me a touch of the Scotch. We lit cigarettes and smoked quietly. The grilled cheese came off the stove and there was a pleasant short-order cafe smell in the air. We wheezed through a laughing fit, and after that I felt a lot lighter.

Finkle swiped the last of my sandwich off the plate and popped it in his mouth. "So what's the deal with you and Carmen? You haven't mentioned her in a while."

"I dig her. She doesn't seem to mind that I feature the winning combination of unavailability and anxiety. There must be something wrong with her."

"Well, as far as unavailability goes, we definitely don't make use of the weekends."

Finkle was referring to the problem of 'the weekend' in law school. We were always conflicted about whether to go to the city and blow off steam, or use the time to catch up on work. Invariably we felt guilty, whether out in the world or at home, as no work got done either way. The challenge to have guiltless relaxation was a formidable one. It also meant that I wasn't often able to visit the city.

"We're always behind. Maybe we should start our outlines earlier," I said.

"You smoke too much weed. Have another hit of the Scotch to return to your senses."

"I have an unbelievably stupid and simultaneously interesting idea. Why don't we bring the party to us?" I said.

"How? Have your boy Jaspr come by with his dominatrix?"

I'd given Finkle an account of Jaspr's paintings, and he had developed a creepy fascination with the man.

"No, *we* have a party," I said.

"You mean here?" Finkle got revved up fast. The ex-frat guy in him pre-ejaculated at the mere whisper of a party.

"Totally. We'll spread the word at school. We'll dispatch Amy, Darby, and Ramona as ambassadors."

"We'll get a couple kegs—"

"We don't need kegs. This isn't phi-epsa house. This'll be fifty law geeks around a punch bowl. In the kids' parlance, they're dorks," I said.

"A couple of those dorks happen to be cute chicks."

"You think Angelina would come?"

"Why not?"

"Think I should invite Carmen?"

"Probably not."

"Huh. This would be a chance to see her. Anyway, I don't think it's unreasonable to throw a harmless little party before everyone gets batshit crazy for finals," I said.

"Let's make it two weekends from now. Boom," Finkle said, grilled cheese stuck to his chin.

Jaspr caught wind of this idea and voted himself head party planner. He insisted my bungalow was too small to accommodate such a grand affair, so he took it upon himself to build a drastic attachment, and in less than two weeks he had it up and running. It was like an HVAC orgasm—essentially an outdoor heated beer tent, sealed and cozy, with furniture to boot. This way, he said, the revelers could party in the tent and not trash my place. The tent took up the entire driveway and curbage between our adjoining properties, but wasn't an eyesore. The guy had a gift.

In the same way Finkle and Amy had cornered the outline market, their outreach created a buzz. I was happy to see that in spite of her apparent detachment, they still made a great team. However, the tension between them was palpable, as I saw Amy roll her eyes at Finkle and tighten her ponytail in exasperation several times. She seemed like a good influence on him, but then again, who wouldn't be?

It wasn't easy to get him on board, but I assured Darby that since Ramona would be at the party, this would be an ideal time for him to bust a move. There was no avoiding Girardi, and he informed me that his attendance would be problematic, as all the women would only be interested in him.

I spoke with Carmen, but on Finkle's counsel didn't mention the party to her, opting to place my focus on Angelina. I then "bumped" into Angelina outside of evidence class a couple days before the big night.

"Hey, I didn't know you were in this class."

She was put-together in a power dress, and her silky black hair smelled faintly of berry. It was intimidating.

"I'm not. I'm going in for mergers and acquisitions."

"How is that?" I said, nearly choking on my tongue.

"It's incredible. Professor Mulvaney was on the Street for like fifteen years at Lehman, so he really knows his shit. It's exactly what I want to do."

"That sounds great, I mean, how many of us can say that about any of our classes?"

"I think a lot of people."

"I see. Well, anyway, I know you have to run, but not sure if you've heard, I'm having a party this Saturday night, not far from here. You should come, if you can leave mergers and acquisitions alone for the night."

"Maybe I will." A sliver of a smile appeared.

"Terrific. The address is in the students' mailbox. Hope to see you."

She wordlessly moved past me into the lecture hall, leaving me to enjoy the hint of berry in her wake.

Chapter 13

As belle of the ball, I wore a black bow tie, a' la Chippendales, in homage to our professors. Jaspr insisted on hiring a catering service that provided nosh to munch on, and even a little bar cart too. As per Finkle's fantasy, I'd agreed to a keg, so we made a day trip to a warehouse storage place. He ran up and down the aisles of kegs like a kid on the rides at Disney. Normally content to devour domestic swill, he became fixed on this costly Belgian import; seeing his enthusiasm, I couldn't help but splurge.

My crush-party dance mix was all set to go with a pair of giant, 90's style speakers set up in the corners. The tent itself was worthy of a home and garden spread; Jaspr's final touches included exquisite rugs, two sofas, multicolored throw pillows, and purple curtains. He even hung a couple of his more inspired paintings on racks, including the infamous Miami Vice three-way. I didn't have the heart to object to Crockett & Tubbs tag-teaming a suspect; after all, Jaspr had done so much to make this night special; the tent had the feel of a Turkish-themed, art installation party.

The guests arrived in droves. Finkle had it right, a local diversion gave our battle-fatigued classmates the opportunity to escape for a night. I sat at a table near a speaker, an eye on the entrance. The dark beer in my cup vibrated to the beat from New Order's Blue Monday. Purple and yellow lights flashed from the top of the tent, in sync with the arrival of Girardi, who not surprisingly, looked as if he'd just been pulled out of the Long Island Sound.

"Hey bub, brought you this," he said, handing me a sixer of Red Bull and a Costco-sized bag of nuts.

"You know how to party, Girardi."

"Are you kiddin'? You need somethin' to keep up with me," he said, guzzling a Red Bull. He pulled up a chair, flipped it around and straddled it.

"I'm gonna show *you* how it's done tonight," I said, gulping down the rest of my beer. But when I turned to face the entrance, my mouth went dry as a warthog. Angelina's long legs stretched out of the car with the EMPWR plates.

"Oh yeah, she wants me," Girardi said.

The meathead she came with hopped out in a muscle shirt so tight it would make Jaspr jealous, and simply left the car parked in front.

Rio by Duran Duran played, my buzz from the vodka tonic and joint I had smoked felt good, and I refused to be discouraged.

"C'mon Girardi, there's a party going on here! Let's go do shots!" I went over to the liquor cart, set us up with a round, and we knocked them back. I saw Darby nearby, staring at little Ramona.

She had her hair in curls like a grown-up Punky Brewster, flirting with a guy from real estate class who took her onto the dance floor. Darby locked mournful eyes with me and hopped over like a wounded rabbit.

"Delton, what do I do? I don't know what to do. I always see a linear path that when, once established, allows me steps to execute, but—"

"Darby, and I say this for your own good, stop talking. Relax."

The poor bugger was shaking. He wore a Teddy Ruxpin-inspired cardigan that clearly didn't afford him any advantage.

"Picture a circle. Nothing comes into that circle. It's empty and pure, with no fear."

"Stuff is coming into the circle!"

"Forget the circle," I said. "You're a tiger!" I squeezed his shoulders. "Let me hear you roar!"

"I eat with her, study with her, listen to her concerns about law. But now I can't even look at her without feeling like I'm composed of many broken pieces."

"Dude, I'm going to break into the dance she has going on, and you and me are going to take over. Then I'll run off, and presto, you'll be dancing with her. Okay?"

"No, not okay. Because then what?"

"*Then what*, what?"

"After I start dancing with her, what do I do?" Darby yanked at the part in his hair. Had I failed him so miserably?

"Listen, Darby, here's a better plan. We're going to get a drink, you and me and Ramona. We'll gently coax her off the dance floor and chat her up, then I'll disappear, and you'll ask her to dance. Then I want you to put your hands on her."

"Like her boobs?"

"Like her hips. Let's go."

Ramona was really moving to George Michael's Faith. She wore a rainbow shirt that sparkled, black leggings, and makeup that almost covered up her acne. She was a sweet girl. Then I felt a heavy hand on my shoulder.

"Delton Lowe, right?" It was the EMPWR guy. We'd never actually exchanged words.

"That's right. Wait, who are you?"

"John Dillsborough II."

"The next hotshot corporate lawyer?"

I'd had a couple drinks, it was my party, and I'd be rude if I wanted to. I signaled to Darby to wait a second.

"More like the lawyer who runs shit you never heard about."

His jaw angled upward and his nose wrinkled in distaste, as if suffering an encounter unworthy of him.

"So you want to be one of those goons that dismantles our economy for personal gain?"

He grunted and slugged the rest of his drink. I'd been a bit of a prick, perhaps, but couldn't stand a guy who thinks he's better than everybody. How could the lovely Angelina come to the party with him? I looked around, but couldn't spot her. John Dillsborough II gave me the slightest nod and walked off. So much for networking with classmates.

I'd lost sight of Darby. He had wandered off, predictably. Then I saw Herc enter the proceedings. He wore a tailored suit under a long overcoat and carried an umbrella, though it hadn't rained in days.

"Herc! You made it! Let's hope nobody leaves."

"I heard there was a meeting of the intellectual inconsiderates this evening."

"That would make the coolest indie rock name. Anyway, let me take your flasher coat and umbrella."

Herc surveyed the party from behind his Unabomber eyewear.

"Quite a turnout, Lowe. I'll hold on to my umbrella, thank you."

"See, some cute girls came too, huh?" I pointed out a few.

Herc scoffed.

"C'mon, there's a couple," I said. "What about those two Asian chicks in the corner there."

"If you say so."

"Herc, when was the last time you got laid?"

"I do okay by penal system standards." My mix produced an Oingo Boingo song, Dead Man's Party. That track always got me moving.

"So what kind of women *do* you like?" I queried.

"My turn-ons have changed. I used to chase so-called hot chicks." He looked at me intently through his plexi-glasses, as if he'd just confided a damaging secret. "Now, I look for females with nice bathrooms and clean kitchens."

"Cleaning ladies and nannies?"

"Finkle and that girl are fighting."

Sure enough, Herc pointed his umbrella at Finkle and Amy talking heatedly from across the tent.

I was quickly torn from that spectacle to another of a different flavor. My beautiful crush-jams mix scratched off and was interrupted with the dreadful, I'm Too Sexy, by Right Said Fred. A space opened in the center of the tent dance floor, and out sashayed Jaspr, bare-chested, naked from the waist up, thong-clad from waist down. He traipsed the floor, twisting his ripped abs, lights reflecting off his glistening, waxed head, declaring he vas too sexy for New York, Milan, and Japan.

With some impromptu choreography, Ramona popped in from stage left and bounced alongside Jaspr's gyrating, thonged manhood. He twirled her around like he was Swayze, finally hoisting her above his shoulders as she extended into an airplane, before he let her down into his arms.

The song and performance mercifully ended, and the murmurs of partygoers resumed. Finkle and Amy's fight was now loud enough for the whole tent to hear.

"You bastard!" Amy yelled.

"But I didn't do anything!" Finkle pleaded, arms outstretched.

"Oh really? What do you call getting me pregnant?!"

Silence.

I thought this was a good time to cue up my mix again, leading with Joy Division's Love Will Tear Us Apart, along with the announcement that the catwalk portion of the evening was over (along with Finkle's life).

It was then time for me to take a break and get stoned again. I snuck out of the tent and crept into my dark, empty bungalow. The bag of weed, rolling papers, and lighter were on the coffee table in the living room. As I collected the items, I heard a rustle. Somebody was in my house!

Like a cat burglar, I tiptoed through the living room toward the source of the sound. My bedroom. Fast, breathy grunts, cut with high octave moans, reverberated through the closed door. I kicked it down like a cop in a drug bust. First visual: ratty ponytail attached to a leathery face licking a na-ked bosom, on my bed! Girardi lay there, his sunburned arms pressing down onto supple, female flesh, her long, black hair splayed across my pillow, and a pretty face—Angelina's. As they looked up at me wide-eyed in the faint bedroom light, a heavy silence hanging between us, I thought of only one thing to say.

"You guys wanna smoke a joint?"

Chapter 14

I had not invited Carmen to my party, and so the gods administered harsh, but just punishment. After bearing witness to Girardi's defilement of Angelina in my own bedchamber, hungover the next morning, an epiphany over Red Bull and eggs came to me. This insight, in sum and substance, revealed that my interest in Angelina was akin to chasing a rainbow. If Ms. Mergers and Acquisitions was close to EMPWR and enamored with Girardi, I'd be nuts to continue this one-sided courtship. At least she'd been in my bed, I ruefully thought.

Why not invite Carmen for the following weekend? She certainly didn't need to know I'd blown her off. Perhaps telling her to pack a bag might be a tad forward, so my solution was to present the invitation as a late dinner with friends, and naturally, she was welcome to stay.

Darby and Ramona both agreed to come for dinner—as did Jaspr, who had no invitation, but insisted—and Finkle was certainly eager for any excuse not to study. His only condition was that Amy, the mother of his unborn child, not attend. I admonished the invitees to avoid any mention of the previous weekend. That aside, it was a finalized plan and Carmen agreed to it, provided I would scoop her up at the train station.

No one could ever accuse me of great culinary talent, but I wanted to prepare my masterpiece: penne with marinara, sausage, steamed broccoli, and peas. On Saturday night, the kitchen was warm with the smell of fried onions, garlic, and a lit joint on the countertop. Miles Davis's Birth of the Cool played, and for the next two hours I stirred sauce, cut vegetables, and flavored meat.

It was almost time for Carmen's train to arrive. We had spent the night after the fundraiser together, and spoken on the phone frequently thereafter, but my thoughts drifted to the impression I'd make tonight, and if she would still find me attractive. This stage of a relationship was perilous; a woman turned off for any reason skips town faster than a drifter wanted for questioning.

The traffic moved easily down the long roadway to the train station. It was easy to find a parking spot on a Saturday evening. It occurred to me as I cut the engine, the train set to arrive in minutes, that I reeked of garlic and onion. I lunged for the glove box, rifling through the compartment for a mint. No dice.

The train hadn't yet arrived. It was damn cold out on the platform, and I'd foolishly left my gloves and hat at home. The edges of my ears tingled and I felt my nose starting to run. There was no one else in sight. I leaned over into the blackness of the track, neck craned toward the distant bend. Darkness.

Then a glimmer of light shone. The silhouette of a train appeared. Carmen was coming, down the stretch, rails shaking, lights flashing, and finally, grinding to a howling halt. She was here.

A few stragglers got off, kids and the elderly, mostly, with Carmen zig-zagging past, our eyes locking as she made her way around them. She kissed me on the lips and transferred her tote bag to my hand in a smooth, almost practiced movement. We held hands all the way to the car.

"So this is it. The final frontier," she said, once settled in the car. "Tell me, who's about to charm my pants off?"

"Taken literally, I'd answer myself, but I think you probably meant that as an expression."

"I did, Casanova."

"You'll meet Jerry Finkle, my best friend in law school, a guy named Darby, our friend Ramona, and my neighbor, Jaspr. Just so you know, they're all a smidge on the eccentric side. Ever see Girl, Interrupted?"

The car felt cozy and I breathed a little easier, less self-conscious as I started to relax.

"I specialize in eccentrics, and love that movie, by the way," Carmen said, gazing out the window at the beach town's assorted tackle shops and shabby dining spots.

"How's work lately?" I said.

"Oh, don't get me started. This state senator, he's such a big shot. Four terms running in Queens and everybody sucks up to him. He actually thinks I'm another one of his handlers. I'm supposed to fluff his hairpiece before cameras roll, and that's not even the worst of it! He's like sixty-something and blabbers with whiskey breath all over his dentures, begging me to introduce him to my girlfriends. Disgusting."

"Jesus, why didn't you go into entertainment PR or something? I can't believe you found an industry even sleazier."

"Don't be mean. I'm good at what I do, Delton."

"I know you are. Anyway, this is my one-horse town," I said, hopeful I didn't spoil the mood. "It's real small, but I find it charming."

I piloted the Volvo into its tight spot next to Jaspr's orange Spyder. We got out and I reached for her bag.

"Oh my God, is that the beach right there?" She jumped up, excitedly pointing at the boardwalk down the block. She smiled wide and I noticed one tooth was chipped and stuck out a smidgeon. It was cute.

"Yeah, totally. You want to come inside? It's nice and warm . . ."

"Put my bag down, c'mon!"

We ran arm-in-arm, through the opposing wind, and stopped short at the foot of the sand. The long, desolate beach stretched before us. We took a few steps toward the water. Cloud cover masked the moonlight. It was easier to hear than see the waves. Carmen led me by hand closer to the shore. Her panting body rested against mine, and I slid an arm around her waist, bringing her closer, and we kissed.

We came home to a toasty bungalow, as I'd smartly left the heat on, and it wafted the smell of fresh pasta and sausage. Carmen tried to peek at the fruits of my culinary labors, but I scooped her butt with both hands and shooed her out of the kitchen. I put Miles back on, his Blue in Green tune, and lit rosemary incense next to the stereo. I offered her the last remnant of the joint in the ashtray. She put it to her lips and sipped Chardonnay, seated atop a pile of pillows like Queen Nefertiti.

"Roll another one," she said. "For us to share."

"Your wish is my command." I broke out some weed and arranged it on the coffee table. She poured more Chardonnay and watched my clumsy attempt to seal the rolling paper with buds sticking out of both sides.

"Snoop Dog you are not." She laughed.

"Hey, you're not exactly helping. I'm under a lot of pressure here!" We cracked up, and I passed her the shittiest joint ever rolled. She cheerfully took a hit and sipped wine, my arm draped across her shoulders.

I wondered why I hadn't had her over to the bungalow sooner. Her presence really lit up the place.

Darby and Ramona soon arrived, and as I hung their coats, I whispered another reminder to keep last week's party quiet. Finkle wasn't too far behind, and just as I offered everybody drinks, Jaspr's head bobbed past the living room window. I learned to leave my windows closed with him roaming the grounds. Finkle's droopy eye twitched with pleasure as it followed the length of Carmen's body, and Jaspr threw her a wink, the bastard. The guests gravitated to the dining room table.

"So, Carmen, you live in the city?" Finkle asked.

"Yes," she said.

"Cool. What do you do for work?"

"I help politicians craft their image, marketing, and PR, basically. Del, let me give you a hand," she said, cutting short Finkle's interrogation. We set the dishes down and took seats, in time to soak in Jaspr's political commentary.

"He should get blowjob. This voman, Levinsky, is patron." His jowls sagged a bit in the light.

"I think you mean patriot," I said.

"Ya, Levinsky is patriot. And to punish Clin-ton, this is lucrative."

"Ludicrous," I corrected.

"I see it similarly," Finkle chimed in. "A man's blowies are his business. Who cares if the President likes chubby chicks? I'm certainly not going to sit here in judgment."

"You're an idiot," Ramona said, flinging a pea at his head, but Finkle was too agile for her and ducked.

"What about Hillary?" Carmen said. "Maybe we're missing the bigger issue here?"

"Actually, Hillary is the problem. You think after Big Willy deals with Kosovo all day, she's recharging his batteries? *Pfft.*" Finkle scoffed.

"She has must'ache." Jaspr shivered.

"Animals," Ramona said. "What about you, Darby?" she said, exasperated.

"It strikes me as terribly inappropriate that the President lied under oath," Darby said.

"Okay, fair enough," I weighed in, "I think Bill's parsing of the word 'is' under oath was pretty insulting to the country, or anyone who speaks English. But is an impeachment really worth the country's time?"

"I believe it is," Darby said, chewing a fat sausage. "Not to mention," he continued, "Lewinsky is about twenty-one. The most powerful man in the land would intimidate anyone, and especially when adding that he's thirty years her senior. It's deplorable behavior and an exercise of terribly poor judgment, especially for a sitting President."

"He'll need some serious legacy building to restore his image, that's for sure," Carmen agreed.

"Want more sauce with that?" Finkle said, pointing to the battered sausage on Darby's fork.

"Yes, Jerry, thank you." Finkle passed him the sauce.

"What do you want, Darby, Bush back in office, or one of his Bush babies?" Finkle said. "How about another Bush in office and another war in Iraq? How does that strike you, you lousy Republican."

"Hot!" Darby yelped, spitting bits of chewed sausage out onto the tablecloth.

Finkle smiled.

"Okay guys, this isn't The Mclaughlin Report. I say no more talk of politics before somebody loses a tongue," I ordered, looking sidewise at Finkle. "Besides, what idiot would ever send us back to Iraq?"

"Agreed. And if we can all agree on anything, it's that going down on someone is a beautiful thing. Amen," Finkle said.

"A poet and a peacemaker," I said, clinking his wine glass.

Ramona stuck out her tongue at us. "Whatever." She shoved veggies under the barely touched pasta on her plate, like a child.

A blanket of silence fell over the table. Darby broke the tension.

"I must say, Jaspr, your moves were rather impressive last weekend."

"Yeah, you and me, Jaspr! Soul Train here we come!" Ramona put her little hand up and slapped Jaspr five.

"What moves, Jaspr?" Carmen said, giggling.

I stared at Jaspr from behind Carmen, eyes bulging.

"Ya, is nozing." He put his head down.

"Right," Ramona said slowly, remembering my admonishment. "Yeah, we went to this club to dance. See, I started dancing in the third grade. My dad made me take ballet, tap, hip-hop—"

"Your father made an eight-year-old take hip-hop dance? Wait, did they even have that back then?" Carmen said.

"Oh absolutely, it was cutting-edge, like the Sugar Hill Gang, but my dad's favorite was Michael Jackson, and Michael's father was his role model. He pushed me to become, like, the queen of pop, and made me practice routines and drills constantly, and I never saw my friends. But after one performance I did in Nashville, I was like, fuck you, dad, and I ran away. It took years of therapy before I could hear a song and want to dance again."

"That's quite a story, Ramona. It sounds like Jaspr's got the right stuff then," Carmen said.

"Ya, this is right stuff," Jaspr said, pointing at himself with both thumbs.

"Maybe you guys can give me a taste of what I've been missing," Carmen suggested.

"Uh-huh," Ramona said under her breath, getting up from the table with her plate.

"I've got it, Ramona. Sit, sit," I said, silently conveying my approval of her bogus story.

"How'd you guys meet?" Ramona asked Carmen. Finkle and Jaspr had gone into the kitchen.

"We technically met in college, but really we ran into each other at a fundraiser in the city," Carmen said.

"She stalked me for two years," I said, kissing her cheek.

"So, you guys ran into each other at this fundraiser thing? No way," Ramona said, biting a nail.

"That is quite a serendipitous encounter," Darby added.

I poured more wine for everyone.

"No more for me, thank you," Darby said. I filled his glass anyway. "I believe you have a coffee grinder in the kitchen, Delton. I'll help you with that endeavor, if you like," he said, tugging at the part in his hair.

"Of course, great idea. That's Darby—always with the great ideas," I said, catching a queer look from Carmen.

In the kitchen, Finkle and Jaspr were lost in conversation. ". . . you have to show it to me," Finkle said, eagerly.

"Ya, is key," Jaspr said.

"What are you degenerates talking about? Move over, please, I need to get the coffee going," I said.

"Jaspr says he has this 'swing set' at home," Finkle said.

"Ya, like playground. The vomans bounce on it," Jaspr said.

"You mean like a sex trapeze?" I said, laughing.

"Ya, sving like in jungle," he said, beating his chest.

"We're gonna go check it out!" Finkle said, spittle on his lip.

Darby and I ground coffee and put sliced chocolate cake and a bottle of Scotch on the table. After a round of coffee the group was reenergized. Jaspr and Finkle finally came back, and I poured Scotch for everybody.

Carmen slipped her hand in mine. She looked at me with shining eyes.

Then she said, "Hey, c'mon Del, put some bumpin' music on so I can see this dance team in action!" I was somewhat drunk by this point, so without hesitation I put on Human League's Don't You Want Me, Baby.

"Dance Party USA!" I yelled.

Carmen and I moved the coffee table in the living room out of the way, and I gave her my opening move, a twirl and spin combination that resulted in my arm stuck in her hair, but she spun around and we faced each other.

". . . And we'll both be sorry, don't you want me, baby! Don't you want me ohhh, oh, ohhh!" We shouted, tipsy, lunging, spinning, holding each other. Meanwhile, Jaspr had taken off his windbreaker, arms rippling in a spandex shirt from Club Monaco, and he tossed little Ramona clear over his head. He caught and guided her down slowly, placing her arms around his neck, her legs around his hips, and locked her into a tight grind. They moved smoothly, leaving little doubt Carmen would question Ramona's doctored pedigree.

Old Darby was stranded at the table, stooped forward in his chair, pale and unblinking. I asked Carmen to run interference on Jaspr, craning my neck toward Darby in an attempted signal. Carmen played along (perhaps too easily) and cut in on the duo, but not before I cupped the air near Jaspr's junk and made an exaggerated squeezing motion, for his understanding.

Ramona and I were doing a little can-can thing when I waved at Darby to come over, but he wouldn't budge from the table. Finkle dumped the poor guy out of his chair and shoved him forward, toward the floor. I rescued my girl from Jaspr's swarthy embrace and steered Darby into Ramona. He just stood there breathing on her, but with her encouragement he managed to actually get his hands on her hips (not boobs). She looped her little arms around his neck and they swayed, timidly, off-time, to their own beat. I couldn't have been prouder of him.

The group left a little while later, exhausted and happy.

"We could still catch the last train," I offered, insincere as hell.

"Shut up."

"Yep, copy that."

I shut off the lights.

"What about the hurricane in the kitchen?" Carmen said, stripping off her evening wear.

"The good news is, it'll still be there in the morning," I said, playing with a Zippo—snapping it open and shut, cklickclackclickclack.

"Would you mind stopping that? I have a terrible headache coming on."

"Did baby get drunk under the table by a bunch of law students?"

"No, not exactly. Well, your friend Finkle can put it away. He is definitely a man of large appetites."

"What the hell is that supposed to mean?"

"Nothing, jeezus. Only that he reminds me of a lot of men. He has urges—and he satisfies them. I'm not saying anything sexual—although I'd bet that would be the case, too—I'm just referring to how he eats and drinks and inhales everything he comes into contact with. It's only an observation."

"Thank you, Carl Jung. While we're discussing observations, what about Jaspr?"

"Well, he can dance. I haven't seen a white guy move his ass like that since Europe."

"Is that what you like, European guys?"

"No, of course not. Will you stop? I thought it was sweet of you to help Darby out with Ramona. He's adorable. Now let's clean up the kitchen."

"Carmen, to hell with the kitchen. I think going to bed is a much better idea."

"I can't fall asleep right now."

"Who said anything about sleep?"

Carmen put her hands over her eyes and rested her head on my shoulder, suddenly sobbing.

"Was it something I said?" I had no idea if I hurt her feelings.

After what felt like a long time, her chest spasms relaxed and the noises quieted. She sat upright, wiping her face with her hands.

"Wait here, I'll get tissues," I said. "Would you like some water, too?"

"Sure."

I returned with the collected items.

"Don't worry, this bungalow is designed for emotional purging," I said. She smiled a little. "We can talk about it if you want."

She turned away. I could almost hear the levers in her mind moving, weighing whether to discuss the matter with me.

"Well, remember the stupid Bill Clinton blowjob talk?"

"What about it?"

"I don't know. I'm sorry I had this little breakdown. I'm a little embarrassed. It doesn't really make sense."

Her legs crossed stiffly and eyes darted from mine. I wondered whether to push.

"It doesn't matter if it makes sense, and please don't feel embarrassed. I want you to be comfortable and know it's okay to talk to me, if you like," I said, rubbing her back.

"Something about that Clinton creep set me off, and I didn't know why until now." She blew a honker into the tissues. "And I deal with politicos for a living, half my job is to clean up their mess. You'd think I'd be immune to it by now."

She uncrossed her legs and lit a cigarette with the Zippo.

"The thing is, he wasn't just President, like Darby said, he was so much older. She may have been brilliant enough to intern at the White House, but she was still just a kid."

"Are you suggesting she was taken advantage of?" I said.

"No. But then, I don't know."

"Did you ever have a bad experience?" I touched her shoulder, but she recoiled.

"It was just a thing that happened once."

Without another word, she got up from the couch. I heard the bathroom door close behind her, the sink run and stop, and the door open again, footsteps, then silence. I sat still for a moment. It was sad to see her hurt. I got up and went to my bedroom. She was already asleep.

Chapter 15

Monday morning, I found Finkle in the basement before evidence class, staring into the black distance.

"It's official. Amy's getting an abortion. Not that she asked me what I thought about it. I guess having me as the father wasn't an option."

"You would want this baby?"

Finkle chortled. "Fuck no. But the fact that she didn't even stop for one second to ask me."

I sighed. "That's hurtful," I agreed. "It might've been nice if it was at least a choice. But remember, this isn't about you, it's about Amy not wanting to derail her life plans."

"Yeah, I know. Thanks, man."

"Of course. We have to take part in the shitty side of the human experience, whether we like it or not." I paused to let the awkwardness pass, but in the silence, it only seemed to grow. "Did you have fun the other night?" I asked.

"Yeah, it was cool. Your neighbor is a trip. And the swing he has? Now that's a guy I can learn from."

"What'd you think of Carmen?"

"She's cute, plus she can take a joke."

"Yeah."

"What's the matter?" Finkle said, eyebrow raised.

"Nothing. I had a super time with her. It's just, well . . ."

"What?"

"It's kind of private, I don't know."

"Spill it."

"Fine. Remember the Clinton blowjob chit-chat?" I said.

"Yeah. So?"

"So that was hilarious, but she wound up telling me about an episode in her past where she was assaulted, y'know, sexually."

"Oh shit, that's heavy," Finkle said. "How about a bump? Might make you feel better."

"No, but that's thoughtful of you. Anyway, it wasn't really a problem as far as we were concerned. The next day we had a pleasant breakfast, cleaned up the kitchen, fooled around a little, and I took her to the train. I just felt awful about whatever it was that happened to her."

"And you're a little wigged out by it."

"Maybe, a little. You ever deal with a girl that had an experience like that?"

"You kidding? All the time. These days, I'm surprised if a girl hasn't had that happen. The thing is, there's no formula for dealing with it. It's common for girls to suppress it, but a lot of them act out."

"Act out?"

"Y'know, drugs, weird sex stuff or whatever else to escape the pain, guilt, or anger they feel. It's a bit of a wild card, because a girl like that, and I don't mean to sound like a dick, is a trauma case. The good news is that like everything else, there's an upside." He started to pack his books. "We've got evidence in ten minutes, let's get over there," he said.

We had Galler, again, this time for evidence. He was the same hopped-up terror from torts. My head was spinning after Finkle's diagnosis. And what exactly was this upside? The last thing on my mind was evidence, but I had to get dialed-in for class. I actually wanted to read the case assignments; evidence had a cinematic feel, slippery and elusive in its content. I was intrigued.

The class was held in the auditorium used for orientation, and with only faint light from the stage, a dim pall was cast over the students. Galler liked to roam the space, prowl the aisles, and pretend he was on trial. He was short and slight, gray and wrinkled, but his Socratic attacks were as sharp as a ninja's star.

"All right, folks, today we talk about hearsay. Here's the main clincher: your client doesn't care what you think hearsay means. He needs you to understand hearsay, to understand evidence, to use it, object to it, get it in, or keep it out."

He faced the class, motionless, bloodless, fingertips at his bow tie. His arm lashed at his first victim.

"Mahler, what's the hearsay testimony in Ramirez v. Randolph?"

Mahler's answer was hard to hear. We were, for the moment, shielded by many rows in front of us.

"I've dealt a lot with abused chicks," Finkle mumbled in my ear.

Did he actually have a hand down his pants? "Dude, not now."

"This one girl, all she wanted to do was this weird role play where she dressed up as a unicorn, with glitter and a horn on her head, and I was a brave knight in tights who had come to mount her." A little spittle slid out from his mouth.

"You're disgusting," I said, an eye on Galler, still near the front, miles away.

"If you play this right, you might've hit the Powerball of poontang, my friend."

"What the hell are you talking about? I'm trying to get to know this girl."

"Sure, you are," he said, grinning.

"Wait, what Powerball?" I said, submitting to the dreamy image of a naked Carmen, glitter on her unicorn horn—

"The defense will object to the introduction of the statement on what grounds? *Lowe! How're you getting it in?*"

My sphincter immediately compacted into a tiny, squeaky fart, my forehead got thick with sweat. What the hell was the question?

"Sorry, would you repeat that?" I beseeched the grand wizard of humiliation. He leaned over me.

"Lowe, what class is this?"

Law & perversion. "Evidence."

He pulled a hanky out of his sport coat and dabbed at his reddened honker. He stood so near, I could see two grey neck hairs sticking out from his bow tie, and track the orchestral movement of his post-nasal drip.

"Now that we've settled that, if Jones looks to get in James's statement at the scene, and it's objected to as hearsay, can Jones still get James's statement into evidence?"

If a train leaves the station at 100mph for Chicago, and a second train leaves at 75 for Milwaukee . . . "It's a prior inconsistent statement—"

"We're not talking impeachment, we're talking hearsay."

"There'll be an exception to hearsay," I said.

"What exception?"

"Well, since the statement was made at or near the scene, it'd be a present sense impression, which gets around the hearsay problem, as it lets in the testimony for the truth of the matter asserted."

"That might've been so with a completely different set of facts. Here, Jones wants it admitted for the fact that it was said, not for the truth of the matter asserted! Read your facts! Your client just lost a million bucks. Ladies and gentlemen, if you ever want to be hired to work as a lawyer, don't do what Lowe just did."

I felt a tap on the shoulder and heard Finkle's creepy mumble in my ear, "I'm tellin' you man, be a knight in tights."

"I miss you," Carmen said.

"I miss you too." And I certainly did since her visit. We had worked up to four or five late night phone calls a week, even during the semester finals and the holiday break while she was away on the West Coast. I was aware of the argument against frequent contact; Finkle pointed out she could develop feelings for me too quickly. My response was that such a scenario was unlikely, given my study quarantine. Besides, these were phone calls. It had been a while since we'd seen each other. But more importantly, I was enjoying getting to know her.

"Are you alone?" I ventured.

"I get scared when you ask me that," she said, lowering her voice an octave.

"I was just imagining your neck between my teeth."

"Is this your tweenie-vampire fetish?"

"I want you to be my first kill. We'll go out for ice cream. I'm in an unseasonably warm trench coat. You're wearing goth eyeliner and a miniskirt. Shall I continue?"

"I don't think you should. The blood-sucker thing doesn't get me going down there."

"Maybe you're just scared. I'd think that'd be natural, chased down by a sexually provocative man with very pale skin and a deep hunger for your essence?"

She giggled. I pictured her in bed, only wearing panties, stuffed animals and soft pillows surrounding her. I clutched the phone, which had grown clammy.

"Listen, I really need to take a day off from studying, and we haven't seen each other in way too long. Do you want to get a bite and a drink in the city this Friday evening?" I asked.

She agreed.

Waking up on Friday morning, the appointed day for my date with Carmen, I could not bring myself to get out of bed. In spite of my excitement, the assignment for today's criminal procedure weighed on my mind. It was another gem from Galler, a sphynx-like mix of concepts that had me up half the night flipping through notes and cases. And yet, in spite of his being a prick, Galler's classes were eye-opening in matters of trial theory. The good news was, over the course of the semester, I slowly began to connect the dots between torts, evidence, and criminal procedure, in as much as they all dealt with aspects of the courtroom.

I showered and regarded my bony chest and its nest of black hair in the mirror. It was a good idea to fire up the man-scaper razor and do a bit of pruning. At the last moment, I was inspired to switch the focus to the family jewels; Carmen would appreciate an aesthetically pleasing garden.

Unfortunately, my effort down there was a tad enthusiastic, as I'd gone too close and now lubricant was needed to address the irritation. After rubbing a generous amount into the afflicted area, I plowed upward to raze the chest. I was more ginger with the blade this time, and one pectoral quickly looked clean and smooth. That is exactly when the manscaper's battery died. There was no plug, and after rummaging through the bathroom drawer, I could find no spare. The finished product of this beautification project was an inflamed scrotum and a half-hairy chest.

There was nothing to do but soldier on and brush my teeth. Then I dressed hurriedly, and in the kitchen, neglected the cardinal rule of no orange juice after toothpaste, spitting up the sour mix onto my button-down shirt. While applying water to the stain, I lit a cigarette and began packing up my books. A thin light slid through the blinds. A fuller, more alive world beckoned.

I managed to not get called on in Galler's class. It felt so much better to simply listen and learn, without the panic of being picked on. My attention happily shifted to seeing Carmen.

In the city, I finally found the right block after muddling around the Meatpacking District. The hip crowd had recently turned up there in droves, and stylish women now walked its cobblestoned streets. Trance music leaked out of bars and cafes. This area used to be a wasteland; I'd not seen the glow-ing lights, nor lively activity here before.

"Reservation?" The hostess's sequin dress bore ample cleavage.

"Just meeting someone at the bar."

"Don't have too much fun," sequin winked at me with long, dark eyelashes.

"Without you? Hardly possible."

"Hey Delton!" Carmen waved at me from the bar, which was chatty with an early Friday-night energy. She wore a bright orange sash over a skirt that showed off stockinged legs. Her cocktail was at its dregs.

"Looks like you got here early. Couldn't wait to see me?"

"Maybe I couldn't," she said.

"I'll order you a fresh drink," I said, summoning the tat-tooed bartender.

"So, how's life by the sea?" Carmen said, tilting her head to reveal a fair and exquisite neck.

"Since we spoke two nights ago? Lonesome."

"Without me," she said, thin red cocktail straw in her shiny lips.

"How's helping politicos sound like they care about their constituents?"

"Eww. That's harsh. I help them present their message. I'm not in charge of whether they mean it or not," she said, bottom lip curled.

"You should teach at law school. I think I could learn from you."

"You just figured that out?" She gave me a kiss, leaving a cherry-balm residue. We'd been on the phone regularly, and yet, the floral perfume scent and skin tone, even the sound of her voice, were not entirely familiar. It all required a certain reorientation.

"How's Norris?" I asked.

"He'll win, thanks to my PR campaign."

"Think highly your efforts?"

"He's dumb as a stump and stays in office. Why do you think that is?"

"The large cougar demographic? His artificially tan face?"

"Maybe, but I am good. I have many clients. Lawyers included," she said.

"Lawyers?"

"Sure, you think your Uncle Nate gets by on his good looks?"

I hadn't expected this connection at all.

"Actually, I did. He's defended racket guys, politicians, and movie stars. Why does he need PR? I'm pretty sure the mafia doesn't pick its counsel based on an article in Vanity Fair."

"You'd be surprised. Hey, speaking of which, I wanted to tell you. There's a corporate-sponsored trial workshop at the start of the New Year. You should cut your teeth there. You'll meet a lot of lawyers and judges. I can send you the details, though it might just be for attorneys. But I imagine law schools spread the word to their students."

"I didn't hear boo about it."

"That's because most of your classmates will never see the inside of a courtroom, unless it's on Ally McBeal. They're going into finance, with big firms. But you're not concerned about money and prestige, right?" She cocked an eye at me.

"I don't see how a big firm serves mankind. I'm not anti-money or success. I just don't want to be another puppet shilling for large companies. Does that answer your question?"

"It's a little black and white, no?"

"I guess, but if Bob Dylan said 'you gotta serve somebody,' I feel I should get to say who."

"Fair enough. A Dylan reference is a knockout in my book," she said.

"I rest my case. And by the way, trial lawyers are hot. You know, the way an older man with a receding hairline takes command of a courtroom. This is like dirty talk to you."

"I just think it would suit you," she said, crossing her stockinged legs. I could hear that nylon scrape in my brain. "Of course, it would be pretty lean until you were established, unless you worked for somebody like Nate."

"Probably. Let's finish these drinks and get out of here," I said.

We took a cab to her place. She lived in a doorman building on the Upper West Side. In the kitchen, I chopped up a lime and mixed Ketel One vodka and club soda into two glasses. She put on music in the living room.

"Hey Carm, it's great to see your place, and I love Leonard Cohen, but isn't his stuff a wee bit depressing? Got anything a little more, I don't know, optimistic?"

"Optimistic? You're the one that said everybody has to serve somebody."

I brought the drinks out.

"You do have an impressive record collection," I said, handing her the glass.

The girl was a rarity; a predilection for good vinyl, folk, blues, jazz, '80s new wave, Stones. Impressionist prints on the walls. Jaspr would totally falsely imprison this chick. We sipped our drinks to Roberta Flack's Killing Me Softly.

She curled up in my arms and I pressed my lips into hers, clothes came off, and it wasn't long before my free hand fumbled for protection. She undid the clasp of my belt, tugging at my jeans until my feet wriggled out of them. Her tongue ran down the length of my half-hairy chest. My head rested, light faded, and only her warmth remained.

"Del, wait." She stopped what she was doing.

"What?" I mumbled, clenching a fistful of her hair.

"It's just, I might—" She looked me in the eyes. "Nothing."

She climbed on top of me and stretched upright. After we finished she slid off, turned on her side, and leaned into my chest. We lay in a contented silence, passing a cigarette between us.

"Baby, put another record on," she implored, her hair spilling over my shoulder.

I sighed. "What do you want to hear?"

"More soul. How about Al Green?"

Her big eyes fluttered at me and she made a little purring sound. These were the feminine moves a girl introduced once she got comfortable, and I loved them.

"Al Green it is." I extracted from her twisted legs and stood up, buck naked.

"Get a load of that ass!" she whistled as I went to the rack with records. I extended my arms and twirled around, giving her a show, slapping at my backside. She directed me to Al

Green and I took it out of the sleeve and heard the first notes of Let's Stay Together crunch under the needle. Al's voice and those horns sounded so warm, as natural as love itself. I shimmied to its beat and her chest rubbed against me and we kissed. I wanted her again. Fortunately, there was another condom in my pocket and I tore the wrapper off while on top of her.

"Del," she whispered in my ear. "I'm really happy."

"Me too," I breathed back.

"Like falling for you, in love with you, happy."

I thought I heard the record skip. Al's garden of sunshine was gone. My cock, hard as a WWII canon, wilted like a parched plant in the sun.

"Del? What is it?" Carmen said, examining my shriveled member.

"Nothing. It's just—" I pulled away and rolled over into the couch, hands searching the floor for my assorted clothes. In no time at all I'd tucked myself into underwear, pulled up my pants and had my shirt on, though socks were a challenge. The delightful pre-coital moans had morphed into an awful silence.

"So you're leaving with the condom wrapper still on the floor? Classy, Delton." She wiped hair from her eyes, which had started to tear. I knew my reaction was terribly immature, but I was given a fright, like when a serial killer in a hockey mask catches you having sex. I picked up the wrapper and stuffed it into my pocket.

"How do you even know something like that?" I said.

She sniffled into a blanket she'd pulled under her chin. The last touch of sunset was gone and twilight shadowed darkly through the window.

"I just, do."

She motioned for tissues on the cabinet. Why did it always lead to tears and tissues?

"There's a pack of Virginia Slims in the drawer next to the sink. Grab me one, and make me another drink."

I went to the kitchen for the pack and vodka.

"Virginia Slims? Who lives here, Chris Evert Lloyd?"

She laughed. "Shut up."

"Forget Chris Evert. I'm starting to feel like Mr. Belvedere."

I fixed us both drinks and returned to the living room. "Where was this taken?" I said, holding a framed photo of Carmen backed by a jungle.

"Costa Rica. I went with my sister after she finished graduate school. We had a total blast."

"Yeah? I've never been. Heard there's lots of monkeys," I said, sipping my drink and motioning for Carmen to do the same. She did.

"My favorite was getting up close to this incredible volcano—as near as we could to this beautiful orange lava running out of it. Then the volcano stopped popping, and everything went very still."

"That sounds amazing. Do you have photos of that?"

"Totally. I'll get them."

We looked at her photos and talked about other places we'd traveled. Most importantly, I told her how sorry I was, that I acted like a total jerk and didn't mean it. She rested her head on my chest, I put my arm around her waist, and we fell into a deep sleep.

Chapter 16

It was hard to comprehend that two years of law school were over. The celebration dinner at Carmine's felt like yesterday. Carmen was in Chicago for most of the summer, working on a campaign for a state senator. Finkle had a gig with a local lawyer, a solo practitioner civil litigator who needed office support.

My father planted me in the bowels of bankruptcy court to work for a judge and his staff of attorneys. He felt it would connect me with players in city government, and offer more legal insight in a business context. I figured I would find out if he was right soon enough.

Judge Williams had bushy eyebrows and little eyes like marbles stuck in their sockets. His default expression was a scowl. One reason for his sour disposition was an ongoing battle with irritated bowel syndrome, and it was common knowledge that his mood, and therefore his decisions on the bench, could be traced to the state of said condition on any given day.

Several attorneys assisted the judge, and their excitement level for the post would be an absolute flat-line, were it visible on a heart monitor. They were rounding middle-age and passed their work for the judge's review like drones in a Dickensian factory, clocking out every day before five. Judge Williams, however, was a player in the city's power circles, always in attendance at the various political fundraisers, including Norris's.

I didn't spend any time with Williams, other than in the gathering of attorneys in his chambers for weekly case reviews. They still sat me at the table despite my lack of any meaningful contribution. Williams seemed to resent my insertion into his little kingdom—no doubt something of a tax for his secured seat on the bench. The fact that I routinely dozed off at these meetings, even snoring on occasion, certainly did little to inspire Williams's affection. He almost never spoke to me.

I spent my free time with an African-American woman who worked as secretary to the attorneys. She couldn't teach me much in particular, but she was hip to the game.

"You don't like it here much, do you, hon?" she said.

I'd been with the department almost two weeks. I was nibbling a sandwich at my desk, which was practically in the hallway.

"You won't be comfortable eating out here, all alone. Why don't you come and sit with me?"

She was carrying a takeout order and a purse larger than most studio apartments. I gathered my half-eaten food and followed her back to her desk. It was the only one in the office filled with tall, thick plants and assorted picture frames.

"Here, pop a squat," she said, pulling a chair from a neighboring desk. "Would you like some water?"

"I'm okay, thanks."

"My name's Roberta, but call me Bilkees. I'm sorry we haven't met until now."

Her hair was permed and fluffy. Bilkees was by no means unattractive, but I didn't consider her in that light.

"I'm Delton. How'd you get that name?"

"What, Roberta?" she asked, teasing. "My friends call me Bilkees, and I have a feeling we'll be friends. I've seen you around, doesn't look like you'll be here for long, though. Am I right?"

A rusty fan twirled from the ceiling. It was hot in the government office. I loosened my tie and tried to relax.

"Yes, you're probably right. This is a summer internship and then I go back to law school."

"Like a summer romance, except not," she mused.

"Yeah totally," I said, not really getting it.

We sat munching. Her sharp, cat-like eyes peered at me over her sandwich.

"But you need to be here, don't you? You didn't dream of bankruptcy court as a child."

"No, I didn't. You got me there. But then again, I don't think I dreamt about law at all." I thought about growing up around Uncle Nate and his clients. "Well, maybe a little. What about you, Bilkees, what did you dream about?"

"I was quite the little songbird as a child, always hummin' a tune if I wasn't already singin' it. I loved to play with bands, then I started performin' in the city."

Her dimples rose at the remembrance.

"That sounds amazing. I wish I could have seen you. So what happened?"

She motioned with her eyes to the picture frames on her desk. They were shots of her and a young girl in her early teens.

"You really want to hear?"

"If you don't mind sharing." I thought maybe I shouldn't have asked, but she didn't seem to take offense.

"Well, it wasn't some kind of Ike and Tina thing," she started, laughing softly. "Ray was a good man. Tall, broad-shouldered, handsome as all get out, I mean, he was then. But the best thing about Ray were his brown eyes when he looked into mine. He was a man who hadn't lost that innocence. And he could choreograph numbers with a troupe—that kind of energy, but he could slow it down and really groove on it, too."

"Did you guys perform together?"

"Eventually, but that's its own story. To cut to the quick, we rehearsed for Showtime at the Apollo. Our biggest night. And in the dressing room right before me and the dancers go on, I find out he'd knocked up some girl."

"How'd that happen?"

"Dumb young thing came up in the room and made a racket, screaming about childcare."

"Did Ray deny it?"

"Hell no! I mean, he tried for a minute—but he couldn't look me in the eye. So I went out and tanked on our big night, at the Apollo Theater, of all places! I'd dreamt of knockin' 'em dead on that stage since I was a little girl."

"That's terrible, Bilkees."

She reached into her mammoth purse and took out Chap-Stick. Her eyes dimmed.

"That wasn't the worst of it."

"You're kidding."

"I found out I was pregnant, not long after that night. So now this man has himself two babies from two women."

"This might seem a little personal, seeing as how me met a half-hour ago, but I take it you had the baby?"

"See that beautiful girl in the picture? There's your answer."

People started to come back from the lunch hour and the sound of phones and other conversations seeped into my awareness.

"She is beautiful," I said, picking up the frame with Bilkees' daughter. "Is Ray still around?"

"Ray? Hell no. He couldn't handle all that drama. Not the most uncommon story you hear, right?"

"I guess not. I'm really sorry."

"So now you know why I don't perform no more."

"You needed to support your daughter?" I ventured.

"I been here since she was born. Right at this desk. Twelve years."

She was in a maze with no exit. "You seem okay with it. You have a brighter attitude than most."

"I may need to be here, but I don't see it that way. There's a plan a whole lot bigger than me, and my love for my daughter is a major part of that. There's a plan for you too, Delton."

She wrapped up her food and put the ChapStick back in her purse.

"So, what do you think?" she said.

"I think you know why the caged bird sings."

She laughed.

"You're a good boy. But remember, you gotta find your own freedom, baby."

We smiled at each other. I thanked her for the hospitality and went back to my desk, watching dust accumulate for six more weeks in my section of the maze.

Chapter 17

"**F**inkle, calm down!"

He was freaking out, throwing casebooks at the wall and stomping the ground like a child off his meds. It was no surprise—two plus years in a basement dungeon will do that to you—but we weren't free men yet.

"We have state and local government in fifteen minutes," I said. "Don't you think it's time we get our shit together on this huge paper for moosehead?"

He quit his tantrum. "I've already looked into it."

"Great. Then let's just go with whatever sleazy idea you came up with."

"I already mentioned it to you. The legal issues surrounding the closure of strip clubs around Times Square. It's very topical." He smiled.

"Tell me again, what's the controversy?" I said.

"The city is trying to clean up Times Square by shuttering these houses of free expression. The courts are set to hear oral argument on pole dancing as a First Amendment issue."

"I'm sure it'll be a ruling of sterling legal significance."

Finkle ripped a loud fart. We stared at each other.

"What if we don't pass this paper?" I said.

"You worry too much. Soon, no more bow ties. No more bungalow—"

"No more outlines," I added.

"No more sacrificing our lives to law school. All becomes possible. Look, even Darby's getting laid these days." Finkle outstretched his arms wide toward the ceiling, humbled by this miracle.

"No way."

"I have a reliable source. Now, if that isn't proof that all things will work out in the end, I don't know what is."

I stood up on my chair, clapping. "Alright, we're doing the strip club paper!" I announced before stepping down. "But we need to do a field trip to one of the clubs involved in the lawsuit. Consider it research," I said.

"I'm way ahead of you. I've got a hookup."

"What hookup?"

"This chick from AOL. We shot pool once. I played with her titties in the parking lot, but she wouldn't let me kiss her."

"How unfortunate. And?" I said.

"We're still chat friends. She actually works at The Palace, in Times Square, a strip club connected to the suit. I set it up for us to go backstage and interview her, as a dancer, to discuss the artistry of her work. Bring a camera and we'll snap a couple shots and add them as exhibits to the memorandum."

"Will there be complimentary dances?"

We gathered our things and headed upstairs for class. As usual, the law library was packed with students quietly studying.

"Are you kidding? We'll totally get dances," Finkle gushed at full volume. Somebody shushed us from a corner. Finkle continued his train of thought. "The last time I hit the club, Nicky Beemer—y'know, the porn star? She gave me a dance and stuck both her nipples in my mouth."

This killed me. "How'd that happen?" Outside students choked down cigarettes and compared class notes.

"Like this." Finkle made loud sucking and smacking noises with his lips, his hands squeezing imaginary boobs.

"Eww. Gross." A group of female undergraduate students witnessed this demonstration of low-class law students. We were a shining beacon to all.

"I'm already a little hot."

"How hot?" I said.

"My panties are slid past my butt and I want you to touch my wetness."

Carmen's voice sounded extra throaty on the phone. I loved these late-night calls.

"Mmm. You're making me touch myself. But the good news is I have a hand free to touch you too."

"Where?" She purred.

After we finished our little dalliance we clicked off and I jumped in the shower. I toweled myself off in the living room and saw two missed calls from my mom. I started to pick up the phone to call her back but it rang.

"Del."

"Hey Mom, what's going on?" Background noise garbled the call.

"Del, it's your father, he's had a heart attack."

"What? Where are you? Where's dad?"

"Lennox Hill hospital."

It was two in the morning. "I'm coming in."

"No, not now. He's passed out from the pain meds. They say he's stable, they're just keeping him for observation."

"I don't care, I'm coming."

"Come tomorrow when you're through with classes. He'll be conscious then, probably, and we'll know more."

"I don't want to leave you alone."

"I'll be all right. Love you."

"Love you too, mom."

I smoked a cigarette on the couch, struck dumb. Then paced the bungalow. The thought 'this can't be' pelted my mind over and over in an unrelenting downpour. One window in the living room wouldn't open. I flexed with all my might, sweat spilling off my forehead, but it wouldn't budge. That was the reality. Then I remembered the baseball bat in the closet near the kitchen. I grabbed it and whacked at the lock on the window, then another, then took full swings that stung my hands. Nothing. I took a step back, rushed the window with the bat, and this time smashed the glass. Shards flew out in all directions. I collapsed to the floor in a fit of tears.

When I awoke—asleep on the floor with glass everywhere – it was early light. I got up, panicked and horse-tired—and stuck a fistful of coffee grinds into the machine. I slurped down a cup, put the rest in a thermos, threw on a dirty shirt from the hamper, and sprinted to the car, peeling out of the driveway but hitting the curb, spilling hot coffee on my lap. On the highway, I opened it up to ninety-five, weaving in and out of lanes into the city. A knot of morning traffic greeted me in Midtown, but I channeled my inner cabbie and cut down side streets, dodging most of it.

In the hospital diffused wails of terror and a wave of disinfectant assailed my senses. Why would anyone come here to get well? To enter this madhouse was to seek ailment itself. A cranky woman at the nurse's station directed me to where my father had been admitted.

My mother sat at the bedside, staring at my father, a look I had never seen on her face. The swiveling television had one channel. Sally Jessy Raphael's guests squawked at each other over a cheating boyfriend. The window gave the view of a brick wall, and the patient on the other end of the sheet coughed in heavy fits. My father wriggled around in the bed, eyes lucid, searching. They did not meet my own.

"Dad, how are you feeling?"

"Mmm." It was the drugged version of his typical response.

"Mom, what do the doctors say?"

Her cheeks were pale and sallow. She was terrified but resolute, her hand resting on my father's IV'd arm. It moved me to see my dainty mother hold his wild spirit.

"They're running tests. Once they understand more, they'll discuss options with us."

"Is he able to go home soon?"

"We don't know. Get that pitcher over there. Your father wants a cup of water."

I poured a cup and he took it feebly, sipping, my mother dabbing at his lip. A nurse bounded in and came to the bedside.

"How's the patient this morning?"

She seemed sweet, an older lady with a face full of blemishes. The old man looked up at her.

"Phone," he said.

The nurse chuckled. "Mr. Lowe, I'm going to take your vitals now. What's your pain on the 0-10 scale, 10 being the worst?"

No answer.

"Okay, let me get the drip going again, shall we? We'll fix you up."

The nurse took his blood pressure and checked his vitals. But when she tried to stick the IV in his vein with fresh pain meds, he balked, twisting his arm away.

"Mr. Lowe, I'm supposed to give you this medication. Doctor's orders."

He turned his head in defiance. She made a sound, surely perfected over years on the job, somewhere between a grunt and a sigh and left the room.

"Gimme phone," he directed, in the general vicinity of my mother. She stared back at him unmoving, long accustomed to the ferocity of his nature.

"You'll come home and make all the calls you want," she said.

"Gotta talk to Monkey. Queens job tomorrow . . ."

"I heard you, but you're here now, and that's the reality," she said, pinching his cheek.

"She stole my line," he said. "Delton, I need you to—"

"Go get your father's book from the car," my mother said, interceding.

Back in the lobby, I was actually relieved to find that my father looked better than a lot of other patients. One guy was almost upside down in the bed, bandaged around the head and legs, and he was the envy of the floor. The patients in gowns shuffling the halls had vacant eyes that seemed stricken with illness.

When I stepped outside, I smoked a cigarette on the busy sidewalk. Ambulances came into the ER, their sirens shrieking. People were everywhere, but my attention was drawn to a New York City bus stopped at a light in front of me. A teenage boy looked through a window and caught my eye. I held his gaze and he smiled, but the bus crept forward and a sharp glare beamed off his window. I couldn't see him anymore.

I found the car, with its familiar scent of cigar smoke and after shave, and snatched my father's true crime book from the backseat. I returned and when passing the nurse's counter, I heard laughter coming from my father's room. Nate sat on the windowsill. He was fresh from court in a pinstripe suit, a hankie the color of peacock feathers peeking out of the jacket pocket.

"Delton! Come here, my boy." He slid off the ledge and wrapped me in his arms. "I heard you're taking a trial class. Your mother said you like it."

"It's the only actual trial advocacy class offered. Yes, I like it. Trials feel more real."

"After two-hundred jury trials, I'd have to agree."

"Thanks."

"You're thanking me for agreeing with you?"

"Well, for your support . . ."

"It wouldn't be supportive to disagree? Am I worth thanking only if I agree with you?"

"Nobody busts chops like my Uncle Nate," I said.

Taking stock of him, his suit and self-assuredness, I wondered if I wanted his career, his life. He defended people whose freedom hung in the balance. Wasn't that a worthwhile career?

"What do you think, Larry?" Nate said, knowing full well what my father thought.

The old man blinked a couple times. "Family business. I don't wanna worry about him."

"You never had to worry about me, baby," Nate said, folding his arms.

"As I recall, Nate, you had a close call once before," my mother said.

"Delton, call Monkey . . ."

"Dad, I really don't know how to handle issues with your men."

"Just—listen to me . . ."

He clutched at his chest. Thick purple veins bulged on his neck.

"Hit the call button!" I yelled to my mother.

He thrashed about, yanking the drip out of his arm. It was like watching the Incredible Hulk transform.

"Dad, just try to—I'll get help!" I darted into the hall and grabbed a nurse, who immediately summoned an orderly. They rushed in and the orderly forcefully subdued him while the nurse fixed his drip and injected the fresh pain meds. After a long moment, my father's tension relented and he eased back on the bed.

"What the hell was that?" Nate snapped at the nurse.

"Probably just cramping, because he refused the meds. He should settle down now," she soothed.

The old man's eyes closed. My poor mother was trembling. I put my arm around her. I simply could not digest the reality that this was my father in the hospital bed. It was not possible for him to be in any danger to his health.

"I have something for him," Nate said, pulling a Saran-Wrapped plate out of a bag. It was a platter of pastrami, corned beef, and knishes from 2nd Ave Deli.

"Are you serious?" my mother said, looking at Nate sideways.

"I'm not sure corned beef is the best thing for a heart attack," I added.

"Nobody knows what the best thing is. Besides, the food here is shit, and he'll be hungry soon," Nate said.

"Take it away, Nate," my mother said.

"Brent always liked it when I brought food," Nate said, turning away and dabbing at his eyes with his colorful hankie. "They didn't know what he needed." He gestured toward a random doctor in the hallway.

"What happened to your son was a freak accident on a playground, not in a hospital room," my mother said, rising up from her chair. "And you know that."

"Can I just leave the sandwiches, Joanna? It's Larry's favorite," Nate whined, like a little boy.

"You were at 2nd Ave Deli and didn't get any chicken soup?" I complained.

"Okay, I have to run. I have an arraignment in federal court," Nate said, straightening his tie and smoothing his hair.

"A big sweep, Uncle Nate?"

"Not this time." He glanced back at my father. "I'll visit the house when they let him out," he said, kissing my mother. He left the room and took his fatty meat platter with him.

"Do you have to go back to school today?" my mother said.

"No, just need to study, but I can stay."

"You study," the old man said, quietly. His eyes opened a little larger. "Come here," he said, and patted the side of the bed, his wedding ring clicking the metal side rail. I nudged in close and leaned down to his chest.

"My son," he said, rubbing my head. "My son, Delton."

"Whatever happens, dad, don't worry. I'll take care of things. But you're going to be fine. Everything's going to be fine."

"Proud of you," he said, eyes focused on me, in no hurry to address anyone but me. We sat this way, with each other, perhaps for the first time. This was a taste of the love I'd always craved.

Back at the bungalow, the first order of business was to clean up the mess I'd made. I was a bit taken aback at my forceful reaction. After dumping out the last shards of glass, it seemed like there was nothing left to do. I sat back on the couch, staring at the ceiling. The phone interrupted my space-out.

"Delton! Oh my God! Is everything alright, how's your father?"

It was Carmen.

"He's okay, it was just a bad episode. The doctor says he's going to be fine."

"I couldn't—when I got your message it was such a shock, I was so worried about you. How are you feeling? You should have called me earlier, you know, I would've come over."

"No, it's okay, thanks babe. It just means a lot that you care. My dad is a bull, nothing can stop him, and my mom is super-relieved, so I'm grateful."

"Me too," she said, softly.

She had to get off the phone, as she was gearing up for elections and working longer hours, but promised to see me the following weekend.

Chapter 18

It was an unseasonably warm winter morning. It felt good to break out the sunglasses and ditch the layers of clothes. Carmen had called *telling* me we were spending the day together, causing a sweet rush in my head. Sure, I'd been thrown by her abrupt declaration of love, but we'd had plenty of phone chats and hung out a couple times since the summer, though it had been a while since I'd seen her. Still, in the midst of this excitement, I couldn't shake my concern for my father's health. Fortunately, he was now out of the hospital, recuperating at home. This comforted my mother, and she insisted that I stay away at school, and let my father rest.

Carmen and I planned to meet under the clock atop the information booth in Grand Central Station. When I arrived, it was bedlam, the great hall's legion of commuters rushing to different tracks. It took a little tap dancing to avoid bumping into people and arrive at the clock, but its large hands confirmed my timeliness. Circling the booth, I spotted Carmen, and before I could get two words in, she tugged at my sleeve and hurried us out, through the melee.

"I have the best day planned," she said outside, loud enough for me to hear over car horns and construction jack hammering. "You'll be dizzy inside of two hours."

"I'm already dizzy. Are we going to Great Adventure?"

"You'll see."

We took a cab through the bustling streets and were soon standing in front of the Metropolitan Museum of Art.

"I just love the collection they're showing. You're not hungry, are you? I have a plan for that too, but not until later, okay?"

I watched her climb the wide steps to the museum's entrance. People were spread out reading, eating, feeding pigeons; the air was thick with the smell of fried pretzels from a nearby cart. Carmen sashayed through it all in tight jeans and a short leather jacket that hugged her hips.

Inside the museum, sky-high vaulted ceilings smothered the day's light, and a deep quiet enveloped the cavernous space. We wandered down halls with European prints. It was inspiring to see that on a canvas, a talented artist could strip away all that was not essential.

"Del, c'mon," Carmen cooed, dragging me by the hand. Then she dropped it and skipped down a long hall, and just as I'd reach her, she'd again slip away. But if she came upon a painting she really liked, she'd pause and wait for me, ready to describe the details of its composition. She liked to finish these scholarly descriptions by blowing softly in my ear.

"You like that," she whispered, her hand snaking along my thigh, and as I moved to put my mouth on hers, she'd spin away and skip ahead to the next room. It was a maddening little game, but aside from this tantalization, her knowledge of art was very attractive. It was as if she'd memorized the placards. But she hadn't. She studied art history in college.

We left after a couple hours and walked along Fifth Avenue until we stumbled upon an entrance to Central Park. The frigid spell of winter was momentarily lifted, and activity in the park was reminiscent of springtime with roller skaters, frisbee throwers, walkers, runners, bikers, cops on horses, people playing with dogs and picking up dog shit, sunbathers and picnickers. A trumpet lick, as if from a secret enclave, floated through the air. We held hands. When we reached the other side of the park, Carmen mentioned a restaurant she wanted to take me to, a bring your own bottle place.

I'd had other adventures near the park over the years, so I knew a great little wine store on Columbus Avenue. The old Slavik owner with the mustache and brown vest greeted me. Stacks of wooden crates with wines from all over the world filled the sawdust-covered aisles. I almost grabbed a Malbec, only to remember a time when I'd done so with another girl. But what wine would complement Carmen? I spotted a Pinot, and while no connoisseur, I knew this particular bottle was not known for its subtlety; in fact, it was considered especially bold. I bought two of them and the little Slavik man wished me luck with a lopsided smile. All plans fell into place.

In the restaurant, we were seated at a corner table with a wide glass window, where we admired the last of the sun's fading light. The waiter uncorked the first bottle and poured two glasses. We tasted the wine slowly, letting its flavor settle on our tongues.

"You're the first circumcised guy I've been with in a while. I've missed it," she said, giggling nervously, her teeth around the rim of the already near empty glass. I poured her another.

"Boy, one glass and you're off to the races, aren't you?"

"Let me see it."

"See what?"

"Y'know."

I took a quick look around with a nervous smirk.

"It's feeling a little shy at the moment. It's not used to public speaking. Besides, and I'm not sure I want to explore this, but what kind of guy do you normally go for?" Her bad-girl talk aroused and repulsed me all at once.

"I usually like Italian guys. They're so aggressive. If they see something they like, they go for it."

"Like Norris?"

It just came out. Hadn't occurred to me until then that he was Italian.

"Let's get back to your circumcision."

"You do realize how horrifying that sounds?"

She laughed. The waiter returned and we ordered fried calamari, Caesar salad, and an entree of linguini to share.

"Did you have a thing with Norris?" A wad of distress like wet tar settled in my mind.

"Excuse me, Mr. Trial Lawyer, but I'll have to object. What is it? Oh yeah, irrelevant. Really, Delton, who cares? Speaking of," she went on, "tell me about the trial class. How is it so far?"

She reached over and took my hand. I don't know if it was the wine, the mellowing effect of the lovely day, the stubborn bump in my trousers, or all of it altogether, but I didn't want to feel upset. I chose to focus on the good and simply poured more wine.

"The class is great. I feel a sense of direction."

"I'm sure you're a natural, babe, powerful in your little Sunday suit. You must look so cute up there!"

"I'll definitely take that trial workshop you mentioned, once I'm licensed. Thanks for your encouragement."

The appetizers were served and I felt myself slipping into an inebriated state. I only saw the pretty face in front of me. Life was good.

"Actually, when I was a kid, my old man would drag me into his office. That's the only time we ever really spent together. It was a real blue-collar scene in there. His workers were muddy from head to toe. Can you imagine? All these surly tough guys loading and unpacking boxes of inventory, and I come whistling in wearing a little jacket and tie? The irony is, back then, all I wanted to do was be like my father and do what he did. Maybe all sons do, I don't know, but to me, that dirty warehouse was the most glamorous place in the world."

"Can you describe it?"

"First of all, it was the mid-eighties, so there may have been one computer, not that my father would know how to turn one on anyway. The office had wood-paneling, a musty carpet, blackened tiles, brown-tinted mirrors, metal filing cabinets, glass ashtrays, cloth samples, lots of heavy binders and catalogues and stacks of paper, and phones with thick plastic cords that rang nonstop. My favorite part was my father's private office—with a leather loveseat against a mirrored wall, and an antique globe whose top opened to store bottles of whiskey."

"How very Hollywood."

"I couldn't grow up fast enough to be allowed in, and now that I'm almost ready, I can't imagine anywhere less I'd like to be."

"That doesn't sound so surprising. A lot of boys probably go through this when they grow up."

"Could be, but the problem isn't that I don't want to go there, the problem is that my father is convinced I am going there."

"How's he doing, health-wise?"

"He's recovering."

The main course came and the waiter uncorked the second bottle of wine.

"Your dad is quite the character. He seems to know everybody, politicians, subway turnstile workers, whoever, plus I know how much he's helped businessmen starting out, particularly immigrants."

"Can I tell you another quick story?"

"I'd love a not-so-quick story," she said, smiling with those big eyes that corrupted all my judgment.

"Wait, we haven't talked about you, other than your penchant for uncircumcised Italians."

"Shut up and tell the story."

"So I'm maybe ten years old, playing in a soccer game on a Sunday afternoon. My father showed up, which was unusual and a really big deal. I played my little heart out and he stood on the sidelines, puffing a big stogie in the sun, and I felt like he was actually proud of me. After the game, we got in his Caddie and picked up pizza to take home to share with my mom. We lived in an old apartment complex, but it had a gated entry with a guard. My father had lived there forever, so everyone knew him.

"On that day, the regular guard wasn't there. Normally my father would roll right through, but this time the gate stayed down. The new kid rapped on his window and asked for license, ID, apartment number, even checked the plates. My father revved the engine and yelled at the kid to open the gate, but he wouldn't do it. He just kept asking questions.

"Mind you, the old man didn't produce a license or answer any of the questions, so there's this sense of impasse. Suddenly, he drives the Caddie through the gate. Broken wood splayed all over the windshield. We parked in his spot and headed upstairs. As expected, the cops weren't too far behind."

"You're lucky to have a father like that."

"Think so? Exciting as that was, seeing the cops cuff him in our living room, not so much."

"Sure, but I think his zeal is what's great, and that's what I see in you."

"I'm not looking forward to his zeal, when he finds out I'm not working for him."

"I think you should consider taking him up on the opportunity, but either way, I'm sure he'll respect the decision you make as the son he raised."

"It's easy to say that, isn't it? But, you're outside looking in. The truth is, we're never in someone else's shoes, so we don't actually know what they're facing. We may mean well, but it's like we're all grownup children, insisting things are what we think they are."

"I am a child," she said, sticking her tongue out at me.

Chapter 19

I enlisted Darby and Herc to join Finkle and me for the much-anticipated visit to The Palace. I was going for a festive vibe, and besides, with the approaching pressures of the bar and finding a job, this was a chance to spend a little downtime with these guys. It was hard to imagine daily life without them. This must be how ex-cons feel about friends they made in cell block. The relationships have a bittersweet quality because the time spent together was unpleasant, but they went through it with you and understand your experience. In the beginning of school it was hard to accept that these guys were going to be my law school buds; nearing the end, it was hard to accept they'd soon be gone.

I set it up to meet at a bar around the corner from the club, figuring a drink beforehand was a good way to get into the spirit of things. It was filled with tourists decked out in New York sports team regalia, and a ballgame blared on about six television screens. Herc soon appeared in a black Members Only jacket, trusty umbrella by his side on this cloudless night. His Unabomber rims had been traded in for mirrored sunglasses, the sort worn by motorcycle cops who track down outlaws in late-night skin flicks. Finkle arrived shortly after in a Dokken t-shirt and faded stonewash jeans, his goatee clipped, the hoop earring swapped for a stud. One glance at him was proof that not *all* things change in life. Darby was right behind him—though I feared he had his engagements confused—in a naval pea coat with brass buttons, and brown docksiders. Then again, if any of these strippers were runaway WASPs from Connecticut, it would be kismet.

"So glad you could all escape for a gentlemen's night out," I said. "What're you all having? This one's on me."

"I believe the best course of action would be to see the strippers, expeditiously," Darby said, picking his nose.

"Dancers," Finkle said, suddenly politically correct. "But I agree, Darby needs to see some titties."

"You boys want to skip the pleasantries and get straight to the nastiness?" I said.

Without another word, we shuffled out of the tourist bar, crossed the busy boulevard and walked down 46th street. In another half block we came upon the pearly gates and entered The Palace, all in the name of masculine joy and legal research.

The establishment may have been fighting the city for its survival in the courts, but that was no excuse for its careless appearance.

"Look, how unprofessional!" I bellowed. "The music isn't even on while a dedicated artist works the pole. And don't tell me that's leftover food!"

"I think I'm going to puke," Darby said.

"C'mon," Finkle carted Darby off to sit at the foot of the main stage.

"Everybody take a seat," I said, extending chairs around its circumference. "Darby, you bring a stack of dollar bills like I told you?"

"What?" he said. The poor fellow was in a daze.

"Madame," Herc yelled to the cocktail waitress in lingerie. "Shots. Whiskey."

The Palace wasn't busy. The cocktail waitress returned with the shots. I immediately sent her back for a second round. It was important to get properly intoxicated for this assignment, plus I needed that truth serum cooking in Darby.

Meanwhile, a somewhat chunky Asian girl danced in front of us. She was a long way from memorable, but it felt good to get those first drinks in the system and settle into the place.

"How you feelin' tonight, baby?" A stripper working the floor had spotted me as chum in the water.

"I'm feeling well and frankly, touched by your concern."

"You won't forget me then, sugar?"

"Not a chance," I said, winking at her, already buzzed.

The music came back on, a nightmarish remix of Christina Aguilera and a god-awful rapper. Give me old school hip-hop or give me death. It didn't help matters that the club's speakers sounded blown-out, their heavy bass rattling with static. The chunky Asian dancer finished her set and a blonde with pixie hair took the stage. She was a marked improvement and all four of us pulled out fat stacks of bills. I flung a couple singles at the undressing, twirling pixie and turned to Darby.

"Okay my friend, spill it. Something you lose lately?"

"I'm not sure what your question is in reference to."

"First, drink that shot!"

Darby gave one last look of apprehension, took his glasses off, and downed the liquor. He tucked his little head into his chin, wrinkled up his nose, and proceeded to cough up a hairball. Herc and I slapped him on the back repeatedly.

"Thataboy! Just went down the wrong pipe!" I said.

He nodded, drool dangling from his lips.

"Fuck that, it went right where it belongs! Now another!" Finkle shouted so all of Times Square could hear him.

"Drink some water." I slid Darby a glass of strip club tap. He drank it and put his glasses back on. "Now, tell me what happened with Ramona," I said.

The pixie girl had lean white legs and could spin like an acrobat on the pole.

"What do you mean?" Darby reached for the part in his hair with a furtive look.

"I have it on good authority that you two are now more than friends."

"We've always been, I like to think, more than friends."

"What I mean is, you are now a man in every sense of the word."

"What sense of the word?"

"The sense of the word that you fucked her," Herc shouted over my shoulder.

Darby shifted nervously. Our eyes locked. He started to giggle.

"Yes! We did it!" He shaded his eyes with his hand. "How did you know?"

"Finkle probably heard it from Amy, who got it out of your girl," I said.

"I suppose a thank you is in order. Thank you, Delton," Darby said.

"I just gave you a couple tips, but I feel like a proud parent!"

"How'd that little ass-rubbing on you feel, Darb?" Finkle interjected, while coaxing the pixie toward him. He was papering the stage at her feet in dollar bills with the competence of a man with Malcom Gladwell's ten-thousand hours under his belt. He saved a couple for her G-string and, honoring the timeless principle of quid pro quo, she spread her butt cheeks open in his face.

"Bet you didn't think Darby nailing Ramona was possible, Lowe," Herc said.

I looked at him in those mirrored sunglasses that bore my reflection.

"Seeing Girardi's hairy ass on top of Angelina in my own bed redefined my definition of what's possible."

We ordered another round and the stripper from earlier came back to claim me. This time I had no chance of exercising sound judgment. A rush of boozy, throbbing lust flooded my system. I was drunk. These half-naked women were transforming before my eyes from grubby sex workers into majestic sirens. But I still managed to keep my head in the game with respect to our legal research. She escorted me to a dark corner for a lap dance, during which I yelled, "I support your First Amendment right to grind on my package!" She looked over her shoulder at me like I was nuts. "Never mind, carry on, tiny dancer," I said.

I returned to my seat in front of the stage. Finkle was away getting his own lap dance. Darby had excused himself for the restroom. I sat next to Herc and we toasted to our future.

"Herc, you want a dance?" I said.

"I'm always dancing."

"Ohh-kay. So what are you planning to do after graduation and the bar?"

"You want to get into that?" he said, throwing a couple bucks at a dark Latina who was jiggling her fat butt in front of him. Finkle and Darby reappeared and took their seats.

"Welcome back, gentlemen. Herc and I were about to explore the uncomfortable topic of what we're all going to do after we graduate and pass the bar," I said.

"Who says we're passing the bar?" Finkle questioned.

"I am!" Darby raised his hand.

"Piss off," Finkle said.

"All right, Finkle, that's enough. I would've thought after daddy got his medicine, he'd be nice to people. So, c'mon, it'll be our own little group therapy. I can't think of a better place, Herc, can you?"

Herc's mirrored glasses were now bent off his face as his nose burrowed into the cavernous backside of the Latina.

"Herc, you in there?"

He pulled his face out, adjusted his glasses, and gave a curt little nod to the Latina as if humbled and honored by her contribution.

"Abu Dhabi. United Emirates. That's where I'm going," he said.

"What the fuck is in Abu Dhabi?" Finkle said.

"Good question, so I'll repeat it. Herc, what the fuck is in Abu Dhabi?" I said.

"I've been following the political upheaval in the region and the US stratagems for enforcing its policies amidst the unrest there. I sense an opportunity."

"With the State Department?" Darby asked.

Herc laughed. "That's not something I'm free to discuss, but it could be of a political nature," he said.

"Sorry I started this little Q&A with Herc. How about you, Darby?" I said.

Darby sipped at the same beer he'd nursed for the last half-hour. "I have a tentative slot with Proskaur as a first-year associate." It was a prestigious white-shoe law firm in the city.

"Oh yeah. You had your internship there after second year. I'm glad they liked you," I said.

"I have to pass the bar, and they put you on a probationary period to start so I'm a little nervous about that," Darby said.

"Finkle, what about you? You've been quiet on the subject whenever I've brought it up."

"I think if Herc has an extra ticket and lets me borrow his Members Only jacket, I might end up in the Arab Emirates."

"Dude, it's a banner evening for you. First, an unexpected career opportunity, and now we'll investigate the legal issues for our paper. Speaking of which, where's this connection of yours?" After all, we were here on assignment!

"Don't worry, Del, she's just late. We'll check again in a couple minutes," Finkle said.

"What about you, Delton?" Darby said.

"I have no idea. I'm worried about my father's health and business, plus I have a defense attorney close to the family. The bar freaks me out. I really don't know much after all this time and that scares me."

Finkle suddenly motioned for me to come with him. A large Latino man with a bandana guided us through a curtain. We emerged in a dark little hallway, where a girl in a bikini appeared. She took Finkle's hand and led us into a room. We were now officially backstage at The Palace. Once inside what appeared to be the girls' dressing room, Finkle's AOL chat girl closed the door and called to the Latino bouncer that she'd be about ten minutes.

"You'll have to ask me whatever you want right here. I'm late, ran over here from Queens—had to drop my kid off at his asshole father's place," she said.

"No problem," Finkle reassured her.

I must admit this domestic teaser was a bit of a turnoff.

"What do you wanna know?" She blew a little bubble and clacked her gum. She was young and cute, pale and fleshy, but the tattoo of a sword on her right thigh was unattractive. The dressing room was almost empty. There were large oblong mirrors with a row of bulbs above them, mostly burned, with stripper thongs slung over barbershop-style chairs. Blotted tissues, nail polish, and blow dryers crowded the countertops. Only one other girl was present, the chunky Asian, doing her makeup in the mirror. She noticed me out of the corner of her eye.

"Hey baby," she said.

"Hi," I said.

What's with strippers always calling me baby? It really ruins an otherwise pleasant term of endearment.

"Whatcha doin' back here?" she said.

Finkle was busy getting the information we needed and I thought it easier to stay out of his way. I was distracted anyway, grimly fascinated by this dressing area like it was a harem's quarters in a medieval palace.

"I'm just waiting for my friend. He's talking with one of your colleagues."

The chunky Asian stripper slid her green thong around her large buttocks. I caught a whiff of stale perfume and unclean flesh.

"You want a fluffer, baby?" She cut her best sideways figure for me.

"Finkle, how we doing?" I don't think he heard me, focused as he was on the job. "That's a generous offer, but I'm okay. We're actually in the middle of a business meeting at the moment."

"Oh yeah? For what, baby?"

"We're law students and we're interviewing a witness."

"You lawyers? My boyfriend got himself a drug case right now, and he's not happy with his public defender. I got cash for a lawyer. You interested, baby?"

She had taken a seat in her chair and threw a sash around her neck like a showgirl. It was hard to believe a G-string full of dollar bills could finance a proper legal defense.

"Did the cops find the drugs on him?" I dove in.

"Yeah, but they ain't had no warrant or nothin'."

"Right, right." I nodded. "Listen, I'm sorry, we're not lawyers. We're law students. I can't handle that case, but I wish your boyfriend good luck with it."

"Why you even ask me then?" She made a popping noise with her mouth.

"Finkle, how we doing?"

"Done in a sec here."

He handed me the notes he'd taken regarding AOL-girl's dance work, which essentially amounted to her statement, and he snapped a couple photos of her. The man in the bandana returned and escorted us back to the floor, where we rejoined Darby and Herc, both of whom wanted to know about our Palace connections.

"How'd it go?" Herc said.

"Finkle got what we needed. One other little tidbit did catch my attention," I said.

"What's that?"

"Remember the chunky Asian from before?" He nodded. "She thought we were lawyers so she told me about this criminal case her boyfriend had and how she wanted to pay a lawyer to handle it. Of course, I told her I couldn't, being a student and all, but it got me thinking. Getting cash for cases would be cool. In fact, I could carve my own niche repping strippers." I imagined myself hoisted triumphantly atop thong-clad working girls. "But you wouldn't benefit from any of this insight, Herc. I don't think this sort of opportunity exists in the Arab Emirates."

The dancers switched and another Latina was replaced with a poorly aging, strung-out looking white woman. Our group let out a collective groan.

"How about one last round and we'll wrap up the hunting expedition?" Herc said, summoning the cocktail waitress.

"Back to the topic of the future. I'm terrified," I said. "I think it helps to say it out loud. Isn't that the first step in recovery?"

"I still wet the bed sometimes," Darby volunteered.

The last beers and shots came. We were all loaded.

"I'm that guy who's bat-shit crazy 'cause I got nothing to lose," Finkle said, knocking back his shot.

"That's probably a heavy metal lyric," Herc said.

"I think she likes you, Del," Finkle observed.

The toothless stripper was bending to the floor right in front of me. It was the oldest ploy in the book to goad the customer for dollar bills. She took it a step further by opening her shaven crotch.

"Herc, I'm sending her to you," I said, my thumb pointing at him.

But she inched closer to me, her thighs threatening to envelop my head.

Sure enough, my head got trapped between her knees and she wouldn't budge. To my unspeakable relief, she released me, tucking her long legs back into a seated crouch. I could breathe again! But without warning, and the force of a cannon, both her legs shot out and gripped my ears tight in a scissor lock. Again deprived of oxygen, I was forced to inhale her odorous, fur-less bush, which she thrust into my mouth in a rhythmic humping motion. Mercifully, she unclipped her heels from my ears and receded away, out of sight.

The first thing I heard—once hearing was restored—was Herc's maniacal laugh and his umbrella pounding the stage. Finkle actually teared up, and I wondered if Darby's bedwetting extended to times of great amusement.

"You got wrapped up like a chicken wing!" Darby shouted.

We finished our beers and left The Palace, drunkenly wandering the nighttime streets, shouting chicken wing all the way to the train.

Chapter 20

After much labor, Finkle and I finished writing the re-search paper and argued the lawful merits of pole-dancing to an astonished moosehead. In stride now, we did a shorter preparation for finals, just enough to keep up our hard-earned, disreputable class standing. Thankfully, they came and went without catastrophe, and we sailed into last semester.

Third year went by in a blur. The courses were largely a formality at that point, though an insight I had in the civil ligation course reinforced my evolving perception of law. It was clear this bow tie couldn't litigate his way out of a bathroom stall; he had no spine, no vision, no nerve, only information. I began to feel more strongly that with the right training, I could do better, not in school, but in life.

Finkle didn't come over for the last round of finals. We simply winged it. At this end point, we had the hang of the tests, and besides, they were no longer the boogie man under the bed. Now we feared the Bar Exam. It promised to be the mother of all tests. We had that treat to look forward to following graduation.

After the last final, I slept through the afternoon. It was already balmy and hot with the first wave of summer. The town would soon be filled with vacationers. I decided to take a leisurely stroll to the beach. It was the twilight hour, the moon's shadow set back in layers of fading purple light. A changing of the guard. The shore would soon be busy, its houses lit up with voices and laughter. The waves were rising and falling, never quite the same, splashing on the shore. I whispered into the salty air—I did it. I finished law school.

I made preparations for graduation. Carmen politely declined attending due to a work obligation, but said she'd celebrate with me in the city the following weekend. I privately speculated she might not feel ready to meet my folks. We actually saw less of each other throughout my last semester, though I didn't really know why.

"Delton, it's your Uncle Nate." It was rare for Nate to call me on the phone. Protocol was typically for me to call him, so I braced myself for bad news. "I'm going to be out of town for your graduation. Couldn't be helped. Flying to Nevada on a federal case."

"Sure, I understand," I said, relieved this was his reason.

"Remember, your education starts the day after you graduate."

"That's what I'm afraid of. Who's going to hire me with my C-plus average?"

"You really don't know anything, do you? The law grads with A's work for the ones with C's. It's a fact, like criminal lawyers becoming kings in the afterlife."

"I like the sound of that."

"Well, you know your father still expects you in his office. Nobody, not even me, can change his mind about that."

"Yeah, about that—I wanted to talk more with you—"

"Gotta run, kid, good work." And he hung up.

On the morning of graduation, I fixed myself a vodka cocktail and rolled a joint. Bob Dylan played softly. The effects of the drink and smoke calmed me, and I slid deeply into the couch, listening, letting the tension melt away. I drifted off, musing with satisfaction that the day had finally come when my relatives and friends would greet me at the ceremony. This prompted me to glance at the clock.

It was time to dress in the elaborate gown. It would look nothing short of regal if only I could get the sash to lay flat. It stubbornly sat contorted like a dead quail around my neck. This look was not acceptable. I was a graduate!

There was a downpour outside. I'd misplaced my umbrella again, something I could never keep track of, which is perhaps why Herc always carried one. I had to give it to the guy—say what you will about his eccentricity, he understood preparation. A flannel shirt over my head would have to do. My feet were soaked by the time I reached Jaspr's front door. After I repeatedly rang the bell, his new girlfriend, Alice, answered and invited me inside. She said Jaspr was downstairs working out. He hadn't shown me that part of the house before, but then again, I hadn't seen his sex swing either. Alice straightened out the sash for me and opened the door to the basement.

A blaring radio warned that to go any further was to take it right into the Danger Zone, a' la Top Gun. Jaspr's bald head shone under a bench press holding several huge plates of weight. His spandexed, muscular legs were shaking as he pushed up the bar. Standing quietly in the doorway, I took stock of his private pump room until he finished his set.

"Del, how ya doing?"

He toweled sweat from his face and Take My Breath Away came on. Good lord, this must be the whole soundtrack.

"Hey Jaspr, sorry to disturb you. I haven't seen you lately and I'm graduating today. I told you the date last time."

"Ya," he said, springing off the bench to lower the music. He looked confused. "Vant try squat thrust?" He gestured to another workout apparatus where he began to load weight.

"No, I'm good. I don't think you heard me. I'm not just trying this gown on. I actually graduate from law school today."

He took stock of my outfit. "Oh shit. This is beautiful shit."

"I'm moving out too, my lease is up."

"I vant you come here, man and man." He extended his arms out to embrace me.

"That sounds a little funny when Take My Breath Away is playing."

"Ha! I vill miss this, ya?" He hugged me to his sweaty, hairless chest.

"When I no with her," he jabbed a thumb upward, "you make it so I keep house?"

"Your girlfriend?"

"Ya, ve marry soon, divorce after."

"I don't know what that means. Congratulations?"

"Ya. You in Carmen's pants?"

"I am."

"Good, but still you look like problem. Ass no hard?" He did his famous pantomime of his hands squeezing imaginary parts. He and Finkle had this in common.

"No, nice butt, in fact. That's not the problem."

"Sit," he said, motioning to the bench. I complied. He stopped the cassette tape, which was good, since I was afraid we hadn't quite bottomed out musically.

"Tell Jaspr."

"I don't know, man. I thought things were great between us. I'm really into her, but it's like, one minute she's close, even too close, then suddenly she's distant."

It was weird to have an honest moment with a deviant in spandex planning his divorce before marriage.

"Vatch her."

"You mean spy?"

"Ya."

"Hmm, I don't know if I agree with your methods, but you raise a real option. We never really had the talk, but I figured, perhaps naively, I was still her number one."

"Ya, but smell like number two." He wiped fresh sweat from his face, the room feeling hot and dank. "Must know if the vomans care for you."

Did Carmen really care for me? I thought so. But Jaspr had a point. I needed to know.

"Well, that's good advice, maybe not the spying part, but helpful. Actually, I've got another issue for you that's been weighing on me. The whole time I've been in law school my father has been waiting for me to work at his office. It would be more than that—I'd belong to his world. That frightens me almost as much as telling him I don't want to do it." He watched me closely, with more depth than I'd ever seen from him before. "And the pisser of it is at the same time, I've wanted nothing more than his acceptance of me." Jaspr raised an eyebrow. "I'm sorry, it's just that it's been circling in my head for a long time."

The impact of saying this out loud, in my graduation gown, hit me unexpectedly. I wasn't aware of the warm tears on my cheeks until I felt the squeeze of muscular arms around me, and my head resting against Jaspr's hard chest.

"It's been very cool being your neighbor. We'll be in touch, and I'll represent you down the road—possibly in your divorce proceedings. See if you can make it today. The ceremony starts in two hours at the law school. I'll leave directions."

At the ceremony, I lined up on stage next to Finkle. My folks were in the audience, along with Jaspr and his girlfriend, a couple undergraduate buddies, and even Bilkees had accepted my invitation. I caught sight of the old Indian professor in the front row, who gave me a little wave. I was grateful for this eccentric little man's kindness, particularly during that dark hour during 1L.

The trouble was, when my name was called and I approached the podium to collect my diploma, as soon as it was in my hands, my head started to spin. I somehow veered off the line, and instead of backpedaling, I took a sailing leap off the stage. This prompted raised eyebrows among the bow ties, but it was too late. They had already unleashed me on the real world.

The graduates stood together on the campus great lawn after the ceremony. Here it all began, three years ago on orientation day. Unfortunately, the dean, with his peach schnapps and swollen calves, could not be here, as he'd been indicted in a savings and loan scandal. As for the raisin-bunch gang, they were all now graduates too, save poor allergic Alicia, who never did return to school following her hospitalization.

"Okay, Larry, Delton, get close together, I'll snap a photo."

My mother pulled a brick-sized camera out of her purse. It was evident that women, as a species, were more prepared for special occasions than the men they married.

"Take the shot and we'll get one with you, Joanna," my old man said.

I stretched my arm around his shorter, thicker frame, my black gown spilling over his sports coat.

"This one will go up in your office at the shop. I'm getting it all cleaned up for you," he said.

My mother snapped a couple shots and I could see on the camera screen how lit up he was under the brim of his fedora. This rare expression of joy on his face brought home the significance of this moment. I was now and forever a law school graduate.

I waved off my folks' help with packing, but was treated to a surprise visit from Finkle the next day.

"Y'know, I'm no expert, but I think all your shit is supposed to go inside things called boxes."

"I know, but it feels so right laying all over the floor, doesn't it?"

In the end, it was such a beautiful late afternoon that he convinced me to blow off packing and shoot some hoops instead. When we got there, we had the court to ourselves. It was near dusk as we started throwing shots and goofing around. Finkle talked about his latest conquests.

"Have you actually gone out with any of these girls?"

"I did. This one chick is so hot, Del. She calls herself vulva. She has this piercing . . ."

"I don't want to know. Where'd you meet, what's her name, vagina?"

"Vulva. AOL chat room, about a week ago."

"Like I had to ask. There are other ways to meet women, y'know."

"You're right. I miss sorority chicks, but I can't afford quality binoculars, an unmarked van and a fake moustache right now. To be a proper stalker is too expensive. I'm just a humble student."

"My mistake. It appears you have thought this through."

Finkle threw me the ball and lit a cigarette. "How's the Carmen thing going? I could have Vulva set you up instead."

"I don't think I need to meet her bestie, Anal."

He laughed, putting his arms up for me to pass him the ball. He had beastly pits.

"Actually, Carmen and I are hanging out this weekend. She wants to celebrate my graduation," I said.

"Cool. But you know what I say. Hit her and quit her."

I clanged a jump shot off the metal backboard. It made a hell of a racket, but it was almost dark and nobody was at the park.

"Is that how you really felt about Amy?" I said. "I know you cared about her. I mean, look how upset you were about the whole abortion fiasco."

"I'm exercising my fifth amendment right against self-incrimination."

"C'mon."

"Look, she was funny and great in the sack. Happy now?"

"So, what was the problem?" I said.

"We were never going to be the power couple she wanted." He grunted, dribbling the ball around me. "What really pissed me off was that she made me feel like I meant something to her, then once I showed her I was into it, she pushed me away. The abortion problem didn't help, but once she got on law review and things started to change for her, that's when *she* changed, too."

"Yeah, I get it. This isn't something I'd be dying to talk about either. But let me make one last point. Your approach to law and a career was always different from hers."

"She never got that a career in law to me," he said, taking a wild hook shot that air-balled, "was gonna be about winning cases. In other words, gettin' paid and gettin' laid."

"That could be your firm's slogan."

"We should make it our firm's slogan."

"No shit?" I said, taken aback.

"We could sue deep pockets and make a ton of dough. We could rent a little space in Brooklyn. Start marketing as soon as we're sworn in. You could do the trials."

"A little space to rent? Our office would be as big a mess as the bungalow during finals."

"Yeah, and?"

"Well, I am going to that trial workshop at the start of next year, if I ever pass the bar. You are aware I've got the issue with my dad and maybe my uncle's office."

"Just think about it."

"I will. We've certainly come a long way from the library basement," I said, taking a fast run at the hoop and jumping for a layup over Finkle's head. When I landed, he was still looking up at the hoop.

"Where's the goddamn ball?"

"It's up there, you idiot," he said.

"What the hell?" Sure enough, the ball hadn't come down from my shot. It was stuck between the rim and backboard. "With a million bucks and all the AOL girls in the world, I couldn't do that again."

"Fuck it, let's go." Finkle gathered his things.

"I can't. Even though my landlord's ball is worth about two cents, I'm leaving the bungalow today, for chrissakes, and I want my deposit back."

"Got a ladder?" he said.

"Nope."

"There's nobody around and nothing within walking distance."

"Get on your hands and knees under the hoop," I said.

"Excuse me?"

"Just do it," I said, back-walking to about half-court. "I'll show you white men can jump."

There was no light now, save for a distant streetlamp, which showed Finkle's form and roughly where the ball was wedged. He got down on all fours under the hoop.

"You got into that position a little too easily," I said. "Looks like you've had some practice."

"Fuck you."

"Here I come."

I took a long running start and jumped off Finkle's back, my outstretched hand just reaching the bottom of the backboard.

"Shit! I was so close!"

"I'll get up there," he said.

"You'll get up there? You aren't tall enough to go on rides at the fun park."

We switched places and predictably, he failed to even touch the backboard. We emptied our pockets and desperately threw our lighters and keys at the ball. We tried once more with Finkle's hands providing liftoff, and I still couldn't reach it.

"How many Jews does it take . . ." Finkle cracked, sitting on the pavement, while I repeatedly kicked and shook the basket's pole, to no avail.

"Let's just get outta here," I said, offering Finkle a hand to get back to his feet. We slowly gathered the contents of our pockets in the dark, and just as we turned to leave, I heard the ball bounce back onto the court.

After Finkle drove off, I decided to spend one final night in the bungalow and soak it all in. I ordered some of the familiar shitty takeout and lounged on the couch, blowing smoke rings and staring up at the ceiling. It was hard to imagine that I would not come back. During my stay, I met Jaspr, romanced Carmen, and saw Finkle do unspeakable things to inanimate objects. Above all, it was the place where I first overcame real challenges.

I remembered those early days with Finkle and Amy, feeling so lost, like I couldn't cut it; the treacherous times dodging Galler's venom; getting the boot from Moosehead's Property class, only to discover an actual appreciation for all his courses; the endless nights outlining with Finkle at my dining room table, surely headed for the hangman's noose. If it weren't for the misery I'd lived through, I wouldn't be here now, ready to move on, and instead would have been relegated to delivering pizza and living with my parents. In a funny way, the brutal struggle I endured was not the end of the world. It was the start of one. As I stubbed out the last smoke in the pack, the light of dawn broke through the blinds, and I realized I would miss it all.

Chapter 21

I was enrolled in a different bar exam prep course than the majority of graduates, Finkle included, and relocated to a boarder's room in the house of a family friend. The good news was I had my own space to study. The bad news was the family friend, Denny Reilly, a parole officer since the 70's, ran his place like a halfway house.

"Flunk the bar and look where you'll end up," he said, milk dripping down the side of his mustache, as he slurped the remains of his cereal bowl. "I took it back in 74', 75' and 76', then gave up on the damn thing. I was good at spelling my name right. Got points for that, but that was about it."

"You went to law school?"

"No, counselor, I went to dental school. It was a big mix-up. Where are the fucking molars? That's what I shouted in the test room before they carted me off to the nuthouse." He wiped his mouth. "You ever want a study partner, somebody to bounce questions off, I'm right here."

"Thanks, I'll keep that in mind when I get to root canals." I smiled. He didn't.

"I gotta bail-jumper to deal with. Gonna violate his ass. I'll give you ten to one he's on the corner sippin' Colt with other young bloods." He coughed in disgust. "They'll all get to know me soon enough."

"You were trying to give this guy a break before sending him back to prison?" I said, only too happy to learn this man's life story. I would have de-clawed feral cats if it distracted me from studying.

"Daddy, you ate my Lucky Charms!" A little girl in a pink tutu and shiny blonde curls bounded into the kitchen.

"I'm sorry, baby, you know that's daddy's weakness. Counselor, meet Christie, my beautiful daughter. She's off to a recital this afternoon. First, I'll go see the ballet, then I'll go bust balls."

"Nice to meet you, Christie." She gave me her little hand. Her eyes shined her innocence.

"My daddy busts balls better than anybody," she said, doing a little twirl.

"I bet he does." I laughed.

"So listen, Delton. Your father and me go back. That's why a stinking lawyer is welcome at my home. Couple house rules. You can use this kitchen phone. Any other phone in the house is off limits. The most important rule – don't forget it— no cussing in front of Christie. I don't give two shits what she hears from me. But you, you keep it Dial soap clean around here, capiche?"

"Absolutely."

"And don't touch my damn cereal. Now, good luck studying. If it doesn't work out, we can always—" he pointed to his parole uniform— "use a few good men."

"Yes, sir. Thank you." I threw away the rest of the banana that was disintegrating in my hand. "Have fun today, Christie." She headed out and didn't look back. I heard Denny fire up the car. I was left alone with my books.

"I know you have civ pro mastered. I can't believe they want to stick us with corporations, too. That one's a bear," I said.

"Yeah, between corporations and con law we're totally flunking," Finkle said.

"Thanks for the pick-me-up." I was on the yellow rotary kitchen phone with Finkle. It felt nostalgic to drag the grimy plastic cord as far as it would stretch and sit down on the linoleum kitchen tile, my back against Denny's wood paneling. It was in reality, however, a dreary predicament. The entirety of my life boiled down to sleep, study, and bar class. It was altogether overwhelming, but immensely helpful to bullshit with Finkle.

"How are your essays coming?"

"Really well. I'm on top of it," he said.

"No kidding. Maybe I should've taken the regular course with you."

"Nah, it's not the course. I brew this black-death coffee, it's not even street legal—I get it from this Arab dude in Brooklyn. I found this shop when I was following this hot chick from Prospect Park—I was on a study break at my cousin's place a couple weekends ago—and she went into the store."

"Was she Middle-Eastern-looking?" I said, putting aside the felony stalking for the moment.

"No, white as snow, but the shop had those handmade pashminas and shit—she was trying them on. Anyway, they took me into this backroom with hookahs and paraphernalia, and I smelled this coffee they were drinking. I told the Arab guy it smelled good and the next thing I knew, I was sitting in a plush chair with little pillows everywhere, in front of this copper pot he uses to brew the stuff. He gave me a demonstration on boiling the ground beans, and then we had a cup together. I gotta tell you, I felt relaxed like I'd gotten a hummer, but also amped-up, like I'd snorted a couple pills. So while I'm relaxing in the leisure room, we started to play a game of dominoes and the guy tells me about the hardship his family endured, that they came from Turkey mostly on blind faith, and that relatives in Brooklyn helped him get on his feet with this store. We played the game and I just hung out for a while, but strangely, I felt better about law, the bar, the future, everything. Obviously, I couldn't help buying a bag of the beans and a copper pot to make it myself."

"That's quite a story, but believe me, I think I can relate. It's weird how a shift in perspective can come from the strangest, most unexpected places." After a pause, "And what about the girl?" I asked.

"Forget the girl. I just needed a distraction."

"Well, now you'll be busy brewing coffee all day," I said, laughing. "Amazing that you found a better hobby than hot ass."

"I'm a renaissance man. My palate is exquisite in pussy, as well as beverages."

"Davinci couldn't hold a candle."

"I'm drinking a mug right now. You ought to try some. It's a new experience."

"What I'd really like is a new experience of pussy," I said.

"Bad word! I'm telling daddy!"

"Pussycats! I said pussycats, Christie." I cupped my hand to the receiver. "Shit, Finkle, I'm fucked."

"Those are bad words, too." She stood over me, her tiny face contorted in a scowl.

"Listen, honey, can you tell me what your most favorite thing to eat in the whole wide world is?" I nervously clutched the phone to my shoulder, ready to flee before Denny came downstairs.

"Cheeseburger and mcnuggets and vanilla ice cream." She giggled.

"McD's? The golden arches? No problemo, go ask your father if I can pick some up for you as a special treat." She jumped up and down. "But then you have to forget about those words you think you heard, okay?" I put my hand out. She shook it.

"I only heard two words. Happy meal." She ran off to make her plea to the parole officer.

"Sorry about that, Finkle."

"Yeah, whatever. Good job. You've been there like three days and you're already guilty of child abuse. So look, I figured out the best way to memorize and argue both sides of any issue. First thing, I drink a mug to get pumped. Then I take a practice essay and stand in front of the mirror. I read it twice, slowly, spotting all the potential issues. Then I duck and move and throw little jabs and uppercuts, arguing both sides of the facts, until I'm out of breath. By then, I've answered the entire question."

"You're answering correctly?"

"Of course. The physicality helps me focus, but the key is that I pretend the question is part of a real case. I have to argue for my client, but I also anticipate opposing counsel's arguments, and I wanna knock that fucker out. That's how I answer essays. Then I sit with another fresh mug and write it all down."

"Sounds like it's working for you, though I can't tell if you also have hypertension," I said.

I studied the dry, lifeless material all day, employing Finkle's rather ingenious strategy of pretending the issues were in a real case, for real clients. I didn't, however, shadow-box myself in the mirror under the influence of Arabic coffee. As Bananarama once famously said, it was a cruel summer, and I had precious little contact with the outside world. At least in the bad old days, Finkle and I, and sometimes Amy, would go through this madness together. I wasn't sure why I took this other course, except that it was on a tip from a family friend who swore by it. There were others from my graduating class in the course, though nobody I really knew, until I ran into Girardi the following evening during the break.

"Hey bub, long time." Girardi coughed into the nape of my neck. It was an odd relief to see him.

"You're the man with all the theories. You think we're in the right place?"

"Oh, I know we are," he said, wiping dirty hands on his windbreaker.

In light of the Angelina coup, if he were right about this, I'd be forced to concede the man was some kind of an oracle genius. This unlikely prophet had me rethinking my whole life. He made me keenly aware of how little I truly knew about anything—relationships, family, fulfillment, or how to record television shows without commercials.

"I'd ask you how you know, but you wouldn't answer me anyway."

"This course focuses on areas that'll definitely be tested, while the other course mostly ignores 'em," he said, sucking on his cigarette.

"How do you know what will or won't be tested?"

"Look at the bar essays of the last few years. There's a pattern. This year there'll be no torts, property, or criminal. But you'd better know contracts and corporations backwards and forwards. Also, you don't necessarily want to argue both sides of every issue. The essay will tip you off on where they want elaboration. Otherwise you're wasting time and not hitting all the points."

"You could probably tell me who shot JFK, Girardi."

I lived to see another day at Denny's, as the old Ronald McDonald trick was a success. But I was concerned about Girardi's prophecy.

"Finkle, he thinks he cracked some kind of code." I filled him in on everything Girardi said. "It sounds, as usual, unconventional. But he does tend to know the answers in class, and he has been right before."

"He doesn't know jackshit," Finkle said. "I get that you don't want to lose faith in your bar course, but he's a crackpot. There is no fucking code. Maybe during first or second year we might have thought that was possible, but what's the one thing we've learned after three years?"

"Expect the unexpected," I said.

"Exactly. We have to prepare for every course equally, especially torts, property and criminal. Girardi just likes to screw with you. You're gullible. I've told you before, your biggest problem is you believe people too easily." He paused.

"And as for arguing both sides of every issue, the bar grader wants the answers spoon-fed a certain way, so while the time crunch means we'll probably miss some points, we have been taught to argue both sides."

"Yeah, right, regardless of what we miss, at least we'll be thorough with what we do argue from both sides."

"You got it."

"The hell with Girardi," I said.

"Stay away from him. That shouldn't be too hard, given his stench."

The bar was given in a monstrous, space shuttle-esqe structure ordinarily reserved for giant trade shows. Thousands of folding chairs were set up along endless rows of tables. The pressure was strangling, the clock marched at a rapid clip, and my overstuffed brain just spit out content. After two days of nonstop testing, by the end, I hadn't a clue about my performance. According to many lawyers, that sort of bewilderment was exactly the best one could hope for. If such was the case, I was in good shape.

Denny wished me well before leaving for work, with the comforting reminder that if I flunked, I'd always have a place to study.

I received a package in the mail from Nate. It was a Startac cell phone, with a post-it sticker instructing me to call him.

"Hi Nate, I'm calling you from the cell phone you sent me."

"That's right, kid. Now that you're a graduate and took the bar, you're practically in the club. Once you're a licensed attorney, wherever you end up, you'll need a phone for all your business contacts."

"This is so cool. Thank you, Uncle Nate."

"Don't thank me. I'm the jerk who missed seeing you graduate. But I don't want you to miss any opportunities."

The first order of business was to get the hell out of my current residence, which I made good on, resisting the urge to incinerate my materials in a yard fire. Denny didn't deserve that.

Finkle was crashing at his college buddy's apartment in the city, and he arranged it so I could stay. We quickly adopted a routine of smoking high-grade marijuana delivered to our door in sealed plastic cases. The dealer, who called himself Skywalker, appeared shortly after he was summoned by pager. He looked like a fusion of raver and pedophile, in black cap and shades, but with pants the color of skittles. We enjoyed Skywalker's product for several days, basking in the pleasure of not having our brains beaten by law study. It was a reprieve from the mental strain we'd suffered.

The other piece of welcome news was that Carmen was phoning me off the hook. She said that unlike last semester, when she was consumed with work and travel, my absence during bar prep was too much to bear. We got together a couple nights in the city, and between her and Finkle's crash pad, I was in a constant state of illicit pleasure. She did, however, have to catch a plane for a business trip.

My last day welcome at Finkle's crash pad had come. It was a bright, sunshine-filled Saturday afternoon in New York City. I'd brunched with Finkle down in the West Village, but afterward he had an appointment so I took a long walk uptown, stopping to sit on a park bench. The pigeons there pecked at the ground, oblivious to the massive trees and many humans that loomed above them. Sunlight streamed through the great oaks, their leaves undulating in the breeze. The light foot traffic was steady. My flip-phone buzzed.

"Hey babe!" Carmen sounded flush with excitement. "I'm back early!"

"Really! How—"

"Oh, they didn't need me as much as they thought they did, for a change. So here I am!"

The pigeons bobbled their necks with joy. The people passing by were smiling. I felt on top of the world. "We're going out tonight. Put something pretty on," I said.

"Ohh, I like this idea."

"Finkle, you sure that's enough gel? There won't be any left for all the bridge and tunnel guidos."

We pushed each other out of the way in front of the bathroom mirror.

"Very funny. So tell me about this chick."

I'd persuaded Carmen to find a friend for Finkle. Perhaps I should have asked Denny Reilly to arrange for a nice parolee.

"I know nothing, dude. Let's just get going."

There was a bar I liked in Chinatown with an entrance through an open grate that descended underground. I went to college with one of the bartenders. We arrived before the girls, and my college buddy, Randy, poured us a couple jack and cokes. We lit cigarettes and chilled out to the trance beat. It was still fairly quiet near the small dance floor, with its little stage.

"Hey Randy, what are these?" I pointed to the large binders on the bar.

"The songs, bro. It's karaoke night. Feel free to find a duet for you two homos."

As if on cue, the sound system kicked on and a small Asian man walked out with a microphone. The customary screen with song lyrics lit up, and he belted out Journey's Don't Stop Believing. It was awful. Fortunately, Carmen joined us with her friend.

"Guys, this is Neesha."

We exchanged pleasantries. She was a lovely Indian girl with long brown hair. Finkle's lazy eye raised into an arch.

"Shots for the ladies?" Randy was on the scene, arm muscles popping out of his shirt. I gave him a stern look. Carmen and Neesha demurred.

"Set us up with shots of Patrón," Finkle ordered. "You guys like tequila?"

"I want extra salt," Neesha said.

"I'll bet you do," Finkle quipped.

Randy ordered three straight rounds. We stood in a row, slamming our shot glasses down hard on the wood bar, hollering at the Asian man, who was presently butchering Kid Rock's Cowboy.

"I'm next!" Finkle shouted. "Neesha, come back me up!" He grabbed her by the hand and they made for the stage.

"You look great tonight, baby," I slurred. "I'm so glad you're here." I summoned Randy. "One more for me and the lady!" Carmen and I knocked the shots back and instead of the lemon squeeze, I pulled her toward me and we kissed. She tasted so sweet with the liquor flavoring her lips.

"I'm proud of you, Delton. You took the bar. You did it!" Her cheeks looked so soft, I couldn't help grazing them with my fingers.

"I don't know if I passed."

"So what! Even if you didn't, that's beside the point. You made it through hell, and are sitting here, with me, drinking tequila. The toughest challenge, and you conquered it! Just thinking about it gets me hot."

She was right! This was *it*. My moment. This longed-for joy, finally here.

"Motorin', what's your price for flight? In finding Mr. Right! Sister Christian oh the time has come . . ."

Finkle was rocking out at full karaoke blast to Night Ranger's Sister Christian. Neesha was right there with him on backup vocals— "We'll be alright tonight . . . you're motorin' . . ."

They rode it home to applause and whistles from the Asian man's party.

"Come back to Finkle's with me," I said to Carmen.

"Okay," she said, sliding her arm around my shoulder.

Finkle and Neesha jumped into the cab with us. Back at his place I lit a joint and poured some cheap rosé Finkle had stashed in the cabinet. All four of us were lit, blurry-eyed, in a fit of laughter, dancing to David Bowie's China Girl. Carmen and I stumbled into my room, undressed in a sloppy fervor, her skin suckled in my mouth, my face buried in her hair. We fell onto the air mattress and had hard, fast sex. When it was through she curled up at my side, cradled in my arms, the sound of her breath lulling me into peaceful sleep.

"Goodnight, baby," Carmen whispered.

"Goodnight babe," I whispered back.

Then, the sound of persistent buzzing.

"What is that?" she asked.

"Shit, it's my phone."

"That better not be a booty call," she muffled into my chest.

"Of course not."

Buzzing.

"I'd better get that." I rolled off the mattress and flipped open the phone.

"Hello."

"Delton." It was my mother. "Your father . . . has passed away."

Chapter 22

The funeral was held two days later. Jews bury the dead quick. After many phone calls and abrupt explanations, a panorama of people in my father's life assembled at the service. It was curious that in a room with so many voices, the pews and high ceiling conspired to mute any noise. With every step of the new shoes my father had bought me, an echo quietly sounded, and faded away.

"I loved him, Delton." An older man in coke-bottle glasses and brown suit patted me on the shoulder. He went to sit with other men I recognized, from the times I visited my father's office as a boy. There were several groups like this, those I knew from when I was dragged to business and political functions, where my father spoke and was often honored. These plaques now filled several cardboard boxes I had to put into storage.

There were women in hats whispering to one another, including those from my father's staff. In a pew behind them were my own friends, trying to contain themselves after one of them cracked a joke. Thin sunlight broke through the hall's stained-glass windows, but the room remained cast in darkness.

"Delton, are you ready?"

The rabbi, a short man with a thick beard and stubby legs, grabbed my arm and pulled me aside. He had soft eyes but they betrayed an uneasiness; he was more a political operator who represented the interests of a Jewish section of the Bronx, rather than the leader of any congregation. He was still the natural choice to handle the proceedings, being a long-time friend of my father's, but I had the sense he was overwhelmed by the standing-room-only attendance.

"I'll say a few introductory remarks, then Nate, and you will give the closing eulogy."

The rabbi strode up the high stage to the lectern. I took my place between my mother and grandmother in the wings. My mother peered out at the crowd. She trembled slightly, but calmed when I wrapped my arm firmly around her. Her eyeliner ran a little but she dabbed at it with a tissue, and then she stood up straight.

"Good morning, ladies and gentlemen. Kindly take your seats and settle down, please. We shall begin, please . . ."

The clamor died down and soon there was silence.

"I would like to invite the immediate family of Larry Lowe to enter and take their seats."

I walked arm in arm with my mother and grandmother, along with my two uncles, and we sat in the front row.

"We are here to honor the life of a great man," the rabbi continued. "Larry was a close personal friend of mine. He was always giving, to his family, his business associates, those in his community, and anyone with whom he came in contact. By the look of today's turnout, it is obvious he has touched a great many lives. Most of all, even beyond his tremendous contributions to charitable organizations and devotion to his lifework, was the love he had for his family, brother, brother-in law, mother-in law, and his wife and son. I do not think it's an overestimation to say that he lived for Joanna and Delton. They were his greatest blessings. Delton was the apple of his eye. He would often share with me how he raised this boy, along with Joanna, to grow up to be a man worthy to step into his shoes, and continue his legacy of contribution. He was particularly overjoyed at Delton's recent graduation from law school and his having taken the bar exam. Having known Delton since he was a small boy, and seen him become the man he is today, let me say I have no doubt whatsoever that, as Larry was fond of saying, the apple does not fall far from the tree!" The rabbi paused to wipe sweat from his forehead with a handkerchief. "You will hear from this terrific young man shortly, but first, I would like to invite to the podium a longtime, dear friend of Larry's, Nate Cohen."

Nate stood and made his way to the stage. His grey hair was slicked back into perfect place, his black suit immaculate.

"I'll keep this short, because Larry never liked long speeches, and brevity is the most apt reflection of life itself. I never knew a man as able as he, who could overcome obstacles as swiftly. We met several decades ago in a Bronx that was on fire; but where average eyes saw the flames of decay, he saw the renewal of its spirit. He threw himself into both business and service from first having nothing. Before long, he was the voice and agent of progress for countless civic boards and business groups, particularly those of hard-working immigrants, like himself. He is directly responsible for the prosperity of many families in this city. He created opportunity not only for himself, but many others.

"Oftentimes, I would counsel him to proceed with caution, but that is precisely when he would throw caution to the wind, and elevate his plans to even greater heights. I can say it was his inspiration to push me harder in my own law practice, as well as to grow my belly with many pastrami sandwiches, in order to manage the rising stress levels." Laughter rose from the congregants.

"Even in life, we are in the midst of death, and Larry Lowe personified this message. He lived fully for today, ever mindful of tomorrow, for his beautiful wife Joanna, and remarkable son Delton, as well as every human being with whom he came in contact. He took the shirt off his own back to give it to another in need. That is the Larry Lowe I will always remember."

Nate collected his notes and stepped down. The rabbi scampered back up to take his place. A funeral hall is the only place where a rousing speech is followed by thunderous silence.

"I now have the pleasure of inviting Larry's son, Delton Lowe, to the podium."

My legs were shaky, but from a place deep within I felt a strength I'd not known before. I could have eaten through barb-wire. At the lectern, I sought the eyes of the mourners before me. They silently pleaded, let us see Larry's spirit alive in you.

"Dad, I stand here today prouder than ever to be your blood, to be your son, and to be a Lowe. For even in death, you continue to give me life . . ."

My ears were stuffy and my voice shook. A swell of raw grief filled my chest and pinched at my throat. Before I could continue, tears spasmed out from my eyes, nose and mouth, onto the speech I'd written. I wiped my face with a tissue and persisted on to the end.

After the ceremony, the mourners scattered in separate directions.

"Nicky, Jeff, let's go," I heard my father's friend from high school tell his kids. He gave me a hug and then was off, this service already a memory. In a way, it seemed my father's supposed impact had scarcely mattered at all.

I was also under immediate assault from a head-spinning variety of his associates, who demanded I address their individual business transactions.

"Hey kid, don't forget we need to have a talk. Your old man and I have a long relationship, and I'll bring you up to speed on things. We'll get it straightened out."

I didn't even know who this guy was. Then I overheard two of his current office associates having a private exchange, and casting furtive glances over at me. When they noticed I saw them, one approached.

"How're you holding up, champ? Very nice speech you gave your old man. He would've been proud."

"Thanks, John. I appreciate that."

"Of course. Listen, if there's anything I can do. One other thing, we need to get together as soon as you're able, we have a lot to talk about. Larry and I had an agreement you need to be made aware of, and it would be very helpful."

I put my sunglasses on. It was bright outside in front of the funeral parlor. "What kind of agreement?"

"We don't have to get into it right now, but there's a note that's come due that he was going to make good on this week. Anyway, listen, this is not the time. We'll all be by the house with some food and we'll talk then, or whenever you get the chance. Sound good?"

He took off his suit jacket and twirled it over his shoulder. It was like a school dance when you're the pretty girl in town and all these guys are casually trying to fuck you.

"Sure thing," I said, shaking his hand.

Back at the house, people brought refreshments while the family sat shiva – the Jewish week-long period of mourning. Nate showed up with tons of deli meat, and every time I went to the kitchen for a breather from the throng of visitors, Nate was piling a fresh plate from the refrigerator. He commented that the leftovers wouldn't eat themselves, then headed back downstairs to mingle.

Carmen was unable to attend the funeral, but once back in town, she proved to be an extraordinarily comforting presence during shiva. She helped direct the traffic of people and food, which relieved my grieving mother from the logistics. She even ran interference on some of those business vultures. It was the first time I had an inkling of what an asset she must be to her clients.

My mother and I sat in the kitchen smoking cigarettes, with food platters, flower arrangements and boxes of my father's relics laid out all around us.

"Well, we made it this far," I said.

"I never knew peace and quiet could be so peaceful," my mom said, and we laughed.

"It won't last, don't worry. I was thinking of all the bullshit I heard from these associates all week."

"You'll handle it. They'll circle like sharks with blood in the water, without realizing the shark is you. I'll find some clothes for you to wear to the office." She stubbed out her smoke. "Just promise me that we'll discuss everything when you get home every day."

"Of course, mom. I mean, first off, I'm going to live here with you for the foreseeable future. And I'm going to need your help. We'll deal with it together. I don't want to actually run the business going forward, as a career. I just want to salvage as much of the assets as I can, for you."

"I know you don't, and as much as your father wanted you to join him in the office as an attorney, he would understand your decision to go your own way, with him gone." My mother took a deep breath. "Let's get some rest and then we'll start organizing all this crap. I need my kitchen back."

Sitting in my father's huge chair at the office, it became painfully clear I didn't have the benefit of his guidance to help me wade through the files. In a quiet moment, I let myself feel the weight of his absence. He would never again sit in this chair, inhabit this space. It was odd to think that whatever opinion he had of me would be his last; he would never get to know me better, nor whom I might become.

The office used to be a maelstrom of loud voices and intercoms, beeps from trucks, and most of all, his booming commands, but now only distant voices could be heard on a phone or in the warehouse. The collective chorus of a healthy, thriving business had disappeared virtually overnight. I had movers empty the premises of most of the desks and cabinets, leaving the halls bare, and the remaining employees settling accounts. I was determined to make good on the promise I gave my father at the hospital, though it might look differently than he envisioned. The mission now was to preserve his legacy by finishing the deals he started, and earn their maximum value. But it was not going to be easy.

"Delton, line eight." It was Dolores, the elderly lady who'd answered phones and typed letters for my father for twenty years.

"Who is it?" I was buried under a pile of contracts that dealt with two different deals my father had made.

"It's Robert Nimble from Soles Superstore."

"Put him through." I stuck a paper clip into each packet as a placeholder.

"Yes, Robert."

"Delton, I'm going to come in and see you. The lender is leaning on me to pay down the note now, they're calling it in. What do you—"

"They're accelerating the note because there's a default, which had nothing to do with my father when he was—"

"It had a lot to do with him, he chose to put this storefront on Leffitz Ave., and he took a piece of it. That was his choice and now he's locked in."

"He is not locked in to any of it, Robert, because first of all, he's not here, and second of all, he had no liability in this matter. There is nothing in writing that substantiates any of your claims. If you can produce any documentation I'll be glad to take a look at it. But otherwise, if you'll excuse me, I have other matters to address."

"Hey listen, we had a handshake when he promised six grand on the first of each month for the next eleven—"

"Once again, according to my records, none of that is so. Show me otherwise. Until then, best to you."

My new cell phone buzzed on my father's desk and hadn't stopped for three weeks. There was a backlog of people making all sorts of claims.

In the months that followed, I confronted all the issues in this manner; people would leave my father's office and say to the next man in line, 'watch out, the kid's a lawyer.' I concluded all current deals, progressively let the staff go, and liquidated the inventory.

All of the important people he'd introduced me to, whether at a fundraiser, vendors, through Norris, whoever—not one picked up a phone to offer me any help. That was the reality.

Several months later, about the time I'd finished settling my father's affairs, a letter with the State Bar of New York's embossed letterhead came for me. I passed the bar.

"Delton, I am so proud of you! My lawyer son! I knew you would do it."

"Do you think I should practice law, mom? What should I do?"

"Well first, I think you should practice being happy. Look how far you've come and what you've achieved. You're a steamroller! You took care of the business, and now you have this trial lawyer thing coming up, so just keep at it and we'll see."

The swearing-in ceremony to formally license new attorneys was held in a courthouse in the city. At dinner with my mother afterward, I wrote my name with the word 'esquire' in black ink on the white linen. My father would've liked that. He waited a long time to see it in writing. As much as I dreaded this point, when his idea of my future faced me, I missed him. Despite our sharp disagreements, he was the only man that never wavered from one thing: wanting the best for me.

Chapter 23

It was an especially bitter winter. New Yorkers labored under the weight of heavy coats and plodded through the considerable snow in boots. A man wearing a fedora and beard exited a city diner and I stopped in my tracks. In that instant, memories of my father flooded my mind, and it was all I could do not to embrace this stranger in a hug.

At the start of the year, not long after the admission ceremony, I attended the Trial Lawyer Institute's national workshop. Many criminal defense attorneys, prosecutors, judges, professors, and civil litigators were there to give instruction.

I took a seat with the rest of the lawyers and a man with wispy white hair stepped forward in a bright green plaid suit. He resembled a short and stout leprechaun, and to complete the picture of lore, was about 100 years old. The poor fellow needed the mic stand lowered nearly to the floor to make his opening remarks.

"As many of you know, I am Brian O'Shaugnessy. For those of you whom I have the pleasure of meeting for the first time, I apologize for my accent! I now have a terrible lisp, as part of my tongue has recently been cut out from surgery. On the bright side, I've discovered that's the only way to shut a trial lawyer up!"

In the spirit of fraternal appreciation, everyone hooted and whistled.

"Thank you. I know it is impossible to stop the brilliant mouthpieces in this room from speaking out on behalf of their clients. I can say that in my life, being a trial lawyer has given me a place to call home in the professional world for fifty years."

He choked up a little and wiped his eyes with his sleeve.

"To those of you new to courtroom practice, remember, there is no shame in stumbling. I recall puking up my breakfast in a courthouse bathroom before my first court appearance." He cleared his throat. "Monitors are handing out packets of case information. This workshop's case will deal with an alleged rape, where the defendant is charged with multiple felony counts. At the end of the week, we will bus in high school kids to act as jurors in this mock criminal trial. Any questions?"

A man behind me raised his hand. "Will there be any pretrial work?"

"No," O'Shaugnessy answered. "You just worry about the examinations of witnesses and closing arguments before the jury. There will be no investigation, discovery process, motion practice, pre-trial hearings or jury selection. Anything else?"

No hands.

"Well, in that case, I welcome you to the finest trial lawyer training institute in the country. Thank you all."

My assigned prosecution partner was a mousy little woman named Maggie. She was a practicing estate attorney. I learned that her husband had been severely disfigured in an automobile crash. They were very unhappy with how their personal injury attorney had handled the case. Apparently, this experience had prompted her to try courtroom litigation.

We were grabbing lunch between sessions of direct and cross-examination drills. I noticed Maggie slumped over, nibbling a sandwich. She was middle-aged, the slip showed at the hem of her dress, and makeup smeared her homely face. She might be, I thought with disgust, something of an eyesore to the jury.

"So how's your estate practice, Maggie?"

"Oh, estate work is fine. I don't want to say it's the most thrilling ride of your life, but I like it."

She chewed her alfalfa sprout sandwich and kept her eyes low to the table.

"Well, I bet you would scare the grim reaper himself after all the wills you've handled."

This was apparently not the right thing to say, as little Maggie started to cry.

"Maggie? Forgive me, what did I say?" Lawyers at a nearby table overheard the comment and glowered at me.

She sobbed quietly (why were women always crying around me?) and pulled a stray sprout from her front teeth.

"It's okay, Delton. You're a sweet boy. It's just, since my husband's car wreck, he can't walk. He's always in pain. And the lawyer that handled the case made all these promises, and none of them came true." She started to sob again. I placed a hand on her shoulder. "I swore I would learn to do it myself, maybe even switch my practice to personal injury to help people get justice."

"What happened with your husband's case?" I said.

"Our lawyer pressured us to settle for way less so he could take his cut. Then when we didn't cave to the pressure, he blew off the trial. And the Judge thought he was a dirtbag, too, you could tell. Not that money would bring my husband's health back, but it would take this awful taste out of my mouth."

"Maggie, the awful taste in your mouth is from that alfalfa sandwich with no spread you're eating."

"You're funny," she said, chuckling, her eyes a bit wet. "It's just, my husband never let me down, and I hate the thought that I didn't do everything I could."

"It sounds like you truly did all you could. Please don't be hard on yourself. I don't know your husband, but he sounds like a lucky man."

"Thank you," she said, brushing a crumb from my tie.

"So listen, let's learn everything we can this week and prosecute the shit out of this fake rapist, okay?"

She blinked up at me. "Okay."

Each instructor had his or her own style, and it soon became evident that no matter what approach I took in a given drill, according to somebody, it was incorrect. Maggie and I worked on direct examination, cross-examination, the introduction of items into evidence, opening statements, and closing arguments.

By day three, Maggie began to resemble a single mother on welfare. The constant stream of objections from opposing counsel, her inability to remember the correct litany for admitting a piece of evidence, and her overall fear of public speaking had left her rattled. On day four, with the mock trial approaching, I pulled her aside.

"Listen, Maggie. These lawyers remind me of the creeps who hide their faces on the evening news." She looked at me like I was an alien from a flying saucer. "What I'm trying to say is that they're bullies. They act big until challenged. Guess what—we're going to fail—but we'll do it spectacularly."

"What if I don't know what to say?" she said.

"You ask to consult with co-counsel. Even if I'm just as clueless, we'll get through it together. So let's take the next two days to make mistakes, except now we'll not worry about these dipshit attorneys, okay?"

"Okay, but what if . . ."

"Eye of the tiger, Maggie!"

Her face lit up and she threw a fist in the air. "Eye of the tiger!"

We took meticulous notes of each other's performances and spent our time poring over the materials, slowly developing our theory of the case and questions for the witnesses.

The last day had come, the day of the trial. I'd knocked back three cups of coffee and my bowels rumbled in protest. Hell, this case wasn't even real; there was no actual victim or defendant, yet somehow none of that mattered.

Maggie was outside our 'courtroom' and predictably she looked like she needed smelling salts and a bucket. She was, however, dressed smartly in a brass-buttoned suit, her face made-up and hair whipped into a no-nonsense bun. She carried an accordion file half her size that threatened to topple her. In spite of our mutual panic, a part of me was getting a Robert Redford-Debra Winger vibe a' la Legal Eagles.

My phone vibrated. It was Carmen. My clammy hand flipped it open.

"Hello?"

"Hey baby. How's Perry Mason?" The lilt of her voice was a balm to my nerves.

"We're starting in just a couple minutes. I don't know why I'm so nervous. Maybe 'cuz it feels like I'm in a Men's Wearhouse for lawyers here, with all the grey suits."

"None of them look good naked, I'd bet the house on it."

"I honestly hadn't pictured that."

I could hear her breathe.

"You are going to have fun convicting this fake rapist. Go with it and have a good time. Look at it as an adventure. We know you've already been through a lot worse and you handled it. Then we'll see if you can come over and handle me."

I started to smile. "When you put it that way, this lawyer thing is a piece of cake. Nobody could ever handle you."

"So call me after, k?"

"I'm really glad we—yeah, I definitely will."

I clicked off and fed a coffee machine a couple quarters. I hurried back to the courtroom and slurped down yet another cup.

"Maggie, how you doing?"

"Not great."

"It'll get better once we start." My stomach shifted with a horrible coffee-induced bowel shake. She didn't seem to notice my pained face.

"You think?"

"Yep. I do. Everybody is nervous. Look at that guy over there." I pointed to one of our opponents, while squeezing my sphincter as tightly as possible.

"He does look pale," she admitted.

"You kidding? The man sees dead people!"

"Okay, I feel better."

"Good. So like we agreed, you give the opening statement, we split up the witnesses, and I do the closing. Am I missing anything?"

"Your fly is open, so nobody here is missing anything."

I looked down.

"Got you," she said. We smiled at each other.

"Let's go size up this jury."

The high schoolers loitered around the hall, then filed into the room. It felt a little silly to lavish such close attention on this 'jury pool,' but Maggie and I decided to take everything seriously. The jurors were laconic, slovenly dressed, and likely stoned. In a way it was ideal practice, since the great majority of adults detested jury duty and would be just as distracted.

One of the instructors sat in front to serve as judge. He could have been any middle-aged white guy. The two defense attorneys looked like a young Hall & Oates; one sported bleached hair and an earring, the other black curls and a '70s 'stache. These guys might also be a good option if you were after a pimp who violated parole.

"Prosecution, your opening statement."

Maggie got up, shuffled some papers, and stood in front of the jury.

"Ladies and gentlemen of the j-jury, the prosecution is here today t-to prove to you, beyond a reasonable doubt, that the defendant, Jimmy Miller, assaulted and raped a woman, Minnie Kingsley. You will hear from Ms. Kingsley, and the evidence will show the defendant knew her, went out on a so-called date with her, and forced her to have non-consensual sex with him. The prosecution will prove, based on the evidence, that Ms. Kingsley was assaulted and raped, and at the close of the evidence, our burden of proof will be met and you will find the defendant guilty on all counts . . . "

She laid it out, using the key phrases we'd practiced to avoid objection. In many ways, the prosecution has a more straightforward job, to construct a house of evidence, while the defense must think of creative ways to tear it down. But the prosecution has the pesky burden of providing proof beyond a reasonable doubt, while the defense has zero burden to do anything at all.

I fist-bumped Maggie, who radiated relief. She had come through on her first task, and I was proud of her.

The defense gave a brief opening statement designed to undermine the narrative Maggie had just delivered. We put on an air of cool aloofness for the jury. Jurors noticed body language. It was clear that the art of the trial had much to do with choreography and presentation.

Maggie then walked the victim through direct examination. The witness really played it up, even tearing as she recounted the incident of a man forcing her into sexual copulation. We put on our expert witness and he provided an explanation as to why there could still be a rape without evidence of actual bruising in the victim's private area.

We rested our case and the defense was now free to put on a case (in real cases the defense often puts on very little or no case at all).

They questioned their client, who admitted he knew the girl and that they indeed had consensual sex. Maggie took her shot at the defendant on cross-exam. Perhaps a bit emboldened by her smooth opening statement and direct exam of the victim, she unlatched her shell and all but cracked it open. A pertinent excerpt:

"Mr. Miller, you met Ms. Kingsley shortly before the incident, correct?"

"Yeah, a few days before I invited her to this party."

"You drank at this party?"

"Yes."

"What did you drink?"

"I don't know, a few beers, maybe a shot or two of vodka."

"Well, how many beers? How many shots?"

"I just told you, I don't know the exact—what do you want from me?"

"I want the truth!" Maggie yelled, and pounded on the table, to a round of chuckles from the lawyers.

I cross-examined the defense's expert. It was a tough row to hoe, as the evidence we were looking for, forced entry of the victim, simply wasn't there.

I was ready to cross-examine the defense's last witness, a friend of the defendant's, who saw something that night. He was a key witness for us, actually, as our theory of prosecution depended on extracting damaging admissions from him. The defense would have him say he was present and didn't see or hear any sign of struggle.

"This is the big one, Delton. You up for it?" Maggie said, taking my hand as we waited for the witness to enter.

"Shit, yeah. I'm not afraid anymore."

In stepped a short older man in a bow tie, frenetic limbs betraying an amphetamine habit. It was Professor Galler! The original ball-breaker was my witness! I hadn't seen the son of a bitch since school—certainly not during the workshop—though I was vaguely aware he'd had a career as a trial lawyer. He took his seat on the witness stand to give his direct testimony.

I asked for a moment from the judge and sprinted to the nearest bathroom. The stall was filled with perverted etchings, crudely drawn penises mostly, along with the gift of an unflushed log in the toilet. I wondered if Finkle hadn't mysteriously passed through here, to haunt me. Bile surged into my throat and expelled into the battered toilet. Between heaves, an image of a leprechaun without a tongue danced across my mind. The anecdote of puking his guts out before his first court appearance now had real resonance. This was now my unofficial inaugural.

On my return, the defense began their questioning of Galler and finished in moments.

"Counsel, cross-examination?" The judge prompted me.

My first inclination was to toss the rest of my cookies right there on the lectern, but fortunately a mental image of Jaspr doing a heroic squat thrust came to the rescue. There was no way out but through it.

I faced Galler on the stand. His nose and eyes were red and twitchy, but his expression was one of bemusement, goading me to take him on. I won't be humiliated here, I told myself, not by the man who crushed my spirit in the classroom.

"A moment to consult with co-counsel, Your Honor?"

"Ok, Mr. Lowe, but make it fast. You haven't even started your cross and the jury has a bus to catch right after closing arguments."

"Yes, Your Honor," I croaked, sweat heating up my neck and arms. I sat next to Maggie.

"Delton, what did you tell me?" She hissed. "Eye of the tiger. You're prepared. Now trust your instincts and go after this shifty midget."

I'd created a monster.

"May I proceed, Your Honor?"

"You may."

The whole room was still. The bow tie loomed enormous, hostile.

"It was a dark night, the night in question, correct?" I started.

"No darker than any other night."

"You didn't find it suspicious that they were in the woods, alone, at night?"

"Not particularly."

"They were alone, with the exception of your presence?"

"As far as I know."

"Alone and in an unlit area, correct?"

"It was lit from cars going by on a nearby street."

"That's it?"

"Yes."

"So you couldn't see if the defendant had a knife, or held a weapon to the victim, right?"

"No."

"You couldn't see if the defendant had his hand over the victim's mouth, right?"

"No."

"You couldn't see if the defendant was in fact restraining the victim with his body?"

"No."

"You testified on direct examination that you only heard the defendant's grunts and moans. You didn't hear any sounds definitively coming from the victim, did you?"

"No."

"You couldn't see her mouth, correct?"

"No."

"Sir, what were you doing there?"

"Getting some air."

"You were at the party earlier?"

"Yes."

"Well sir, the party was some two blocks away. This was off in the woods where nobody else went."

"Objection. Counsel's testifying," the defense attorney said.

"Sustained."

"You expect this jury to believe you wandered over to the one totally out-of-the-way place where your friend happened to be having sex? Is that your testimony?"

"I live around there. It's a nice place to walk when I want to be alone."

"But you saw you weren't alone, right?"

"At a point."

"Isn't it true your friend instructed you to keep a lookout while he forced a girl to have sex with him?"

"No."

"So no pedestrian or passing car would hear or see anything?"

"No."

"To protect him from authorities?"

"Objection! Argumentative," the defense attorney said.

"Overruled. This is cross. But watch it, counsel," the judge admonished. "You may answer the question."

"No."

"But you stood near enough to see them for more than two minutes?"

"Best estimate."

"I have nothing further, Your Honor."

Maggie leapt up, jubilant, and wrapped her arms around me. I noticed a grin on Galler's face. The defense rested, but before I could process this monumental exchange, I had to cobble together my closing argument.

I argued it to the jury, dancing for them like a young Liza Minnelli. All the points Maggie and I wanted to make came to mind and spilled from my mouth in as cohesive a way as possible. It was a little difficult to ignore the jurors' death stares, but I would not be deterred. I finished with a dramatic call for a guilty verdict and sat down at counsel table.

"You killed it," Maggie whispered.

I needed a towel for my sweaty face, but felt elated.

"I don't know if they heard a thing," I said to Maggie, motioning toward the jury box.

"Oh, they heard, all right," she said, smiling.

"The jury will now deliberate," the Judge said.

The jurors left the room and were back in ten minutes.

"Has the jury reached a verdict?"

The foreperson stood. "Not Guilty, Your Honor. On all counts."

"Oh shit," Maggie said under her breath.

"I think there's been jury tampering," I said.

"Thank you to both sides for arguing an excellent case," the Judge said.

I actually believed those words, and that was good enough.

"You know what, Maggie? We did."

Chapter 24

"When are you going to the bank today?" Mom asked, as we sat at the breakfast table. Her eggs were untouched. It was about a week since the workshop ended. It had been several months since my father passed and I'd moved in with my mother. It was time to go; she was doing well and I would still live nearby. I planned to see a couple apartments later in the day, though I'd been trolling ads for weeks and was already weary with the city rental market. The last place I checked out still had chalk lines from the previous tenant's crime scene.

"I need to straighten up the account with the latest deposits and bills. But this local branch has totally annoying hours, like nine-thirty to eleven, and then it's closed until two in the afternoon. And the wait is worse than the DMV."

"After that," she said, ignoring my complaint and rifling through the paper, "there's a sale at Epstein's. You could use some new shirts and pants."

Epstein's was where manhood went to die. The store had clothing for boys and adolescents, mostly, but because of my tiny frame, I could still slip into any outfit they had on display. In earlier years, I'd scurry under the bed like a terrified kitten at first whiff of an Epstein's visit. I was traumatized from when I showed up for third grade at my new school in a cardigan sweater and penny loafers.

In the store, I'd spend the cumulative run time of the Star Wars trilogy marching dutifully between dressing rooms and aisles, trying on endless clothing my mother ferreted for me. The last time I wore a new Epstein's outfit, in high school, after dodging the popular girl clique all day with a series of cunning detours, I bumped into them. They promptly burst out laughing at me, and I made a solemn vow to never step foot in an Epstein's again.

"Mom, has it escaped your attention that I'm twenty-five?"

"If you don't want to shop for yourself, come with me to Bloomingdale's. I might like a new dress and purse. We'll use part of the deposit, after you drop the check off at the bank."

"Mom, I wanted to relax a little, maybe meet up with some friends."

"Sure honey, but come spend the afternoon and we'll get shakes and grilled cheese sandwiches at Lannen's Deli after. Sound good?"

"Well, okay but—"

She turned my head and picked at my neckline.

"I think it's time you got a haircut. We can stop there after we shop and get a bite."

It was all the motivation I needed to find my own place. I continued to scour the ads with a vengeance, and eventually found a small studio on the Lower East Side, one that could be considered affordable by Manhattan's standards. I moved the last of my things on a Friday afternoon in early spring. It was an exhausting pain in the ass, but I already felt a sense of relief and the taste of freedom that comes with being on your own.

Carmen called my cell the next day.

"How'd the move go?"

She'd been lobbying me to do it, eager to have me closer.

"I'm done. I just wanna sit on this fat sofa, watch TV, and stuff my face with ribs."

"Yeah, scratch that. Pack a bag. I'm scooping you up in 45 minutes."

"Where are we going?"

"Don't worry about it."

She was at my door in forty-five-flat. The girl kept a schedule with military precision. When I hit the sidewalk, parked in front of my building was a sandy-brown '77 Datsun convertible. A feral beauty sat in the driver's seat.

The sight of this classic funkmobile made me picture Bilkees as a young fox on the town, a '45 in the deck, cruising under the city moonlight. But I needn't concern myself with faraway, dreamy images; right in front of my nose Carmen sat behind the wheel, top down, engine purring, headlights aglow.

"Get in or stay out!" Carmen called.

I tossed my bag in the back and threw a leg over the front door, Dukes of Hazzard style, almost squashing my gonads on the tranny stick, and we drove off. A soft pack of Winston cigarettes sat up on the brown-finished dash and I lit one, contented, bathed in the warm yellow light of the radio dials. I loved that riding in the convertible felt more like flying, breezing through the air, the sky itself not distant at all.

Carmen remained mum on where we were going, but I soon recognized the trajectory toward Upstate New York. We drove at length on a quiet highway, headed for the Catskill Mountains. She took an exit into a sleepy town that reminded me of my old bungalow.

"So, I hope you're up for meeting my parents."

"Come again?"

"They used to run a hotel up here during the summer, and even though it closed, they kept their house. It's been our summer home since I was a little girl. You'll like it, trust me. And they're here just for tonight. We'll have the whole place to ourselves by tomorrow evening."

"Any more surprises?"

We parked in a long driveway with a giant Tudor on a hill, that could have been the house from Psycho. Carmen put her hand on mine and gave it a little squeeze. We hopped out with our bags and headed up to the house. Carmen opened the front door.

A big hound dog bolted out and leapt at me with tongue kisses. The house smelled of an odd blend of cooked brisket and stale perfume. Mr. and Mrs. Barrington sat on chaise lounges in a study.

Mrs. Barrington held a martini glass and embraced Carmen with no fuss, simply uttering, "Hello, dear," and advising her husband that his daughter was in residence. Mr. Barrington emerged, setting down a yellow pad and manila file on the foyer table. His cutting blue eyes had a hint of sorcerer in them, and indeed, one glance immediately silenced the barking dog.

"Pleased to meet you, Mrs. Barrington," I said, going in for a hug, but she pivoted away. I recovered with an awkward pat on her shoulder.

"Yes, you too, Delton."

"Mr. Barrington." I extended my hand and he gripped it firmly as one would an ax handle. I learned that he managed finance deals over a long and successful career. I assumed the hotel was a pet project he'd given his wife for social gravitas. I later learned the place went belly up without his care, and its consequent financial drain unexpectedly forced him out of retirement.

"Why doesn't everyone wash up for dinner," Mrs. Barrington suggested.

I retreated to the bathroom, shut the door and collected myself at the sink. My forehead was a little sweaty, so I splashed my face with cool water, though the only 'towel' was a neat stack of paper-thin napkins. It took three of them to absorb all the water, and of course, some dripped onto the rest of the stack.

After washing up, I found Mr. Barrington alone in the study.

"The girls are fixing dinner. Tell you what, maybe you can help me with something."

"Sure, anything."

He went to an upholstered chair in the corner, a beastly thing with red velour padding and golden rivets.

"Ever worked a staple gun?" he asked.

"I haven't, no."

I couldn't disappoint the man, but I had a terrible fear of mechanical devices. The mere thought of walking into Home Depot brought on a panic attack.

"You see, this touch-up is a two-man job, on account of the material and angle of the seat. It's not for sitting."

"A chair that has transcended its basic functionality. How regal," I said.

He ignored my comment. "Take this. Hold here. I'm going to flatten the material and when I say, squeeze. Be careful, it's manual and the staple comes out quickly. Let's do this in three places. Can you handle it?"

I nodded. He gave a brief demonstration and then placed it in my hand. The seat stood up so high he barely had to bend, and from this awkward position he stretched the fabric over the side of the cushion.

"Now!"

I squeezed the sucker and sure enough a staple popped out.

"Good. You hit it. Not so hard, right? Let's do number two."

He resumed his stance over the chair. I felt like a gunslinger, already swelling with manly pride.

"Now!"

I squeezed again.

"Good! Last one."

I was starting to enjoy this. Maybe I could do little odds and ends around my place.

"Now!"

"Oh—whoops." It was Carmen. She'd entered the study.

"Ahh shit!"

I shot into my index finger. A gush of blood ran down my hand.

"Oh my God! Dad! Why'd you give him a project, he hasn't been here five minutes!" She ran to the kitchen and returned with ice and paper towels. "It looks worse than it is," she said, instructing me to put pressure on the finger and dragging me back to the kitchen.

"Oh, dear," Mrs. Barrington said. "Carmen, there are tweezers in my sewing kit in the drawer next to the pots."

"Will I lose the finger?" I said.

Carmen laughed. "Maybe for about an hour." She performed triage, excising the staple and dressing the wound with a bandage.

"We ready to eat?" Mr. Barrington stuck his head in the kitchen like nothing happened.

Carmen exchanged the bloody towel for a sack of frozen peas to ice my poor hand, and we convened in the dining room. A steaming pot of brisket with Brussels sprouts and a jug of milk were passed to Carmen's father at the head of the table, then to the women, and lastly to me. When everybody's plates and glasses were full, Carmen noticed my glass still empty.

"Mother, Delton doesn't drink milk."

"Oh dear," she said, hand over her mouth. "Are you kosher?"

"I'm not religious, Mrs. Barrington, but you're right, any Jew who keeps kosher—does not eat milk and meat together. I just don't particularly care for milk," I said. "Could I trouble you for a glass of water?"

"Milk gives you strong bones," Mr. Barrington said.

I let that comment go. His wife went into the kitchen and brought a glass of water. She also turned on a transistor and a Wagner movement danced in the background.

"Has either of you spoken with Margaret recently?" Carmen said.

Mr. Barrington slugged an entire glass of milk down and wiped his mouth with a linen napkin. He covered a tiny burp with his liver-spotted hand and looked at Carmen.

"Ask your mother."

"Yes, dear, she's finishing up sophomore year with high marks, and she's on the university's student government. I believe she's vice president."

"Oh, how nice," I said.

"Why haven't you applied your degree to something more reliable than these silly PR places?" Carmen's father said, while stripping meat off the bone with his teeth.

"Dad, we go through this every time. I like my work and clients always ask for me."

"That's all well and good, but it's not as solid as an ad firm that's been around, and knows how to take care of its people. I could still make a call to Al Lemming," he said.

For some reason, the Brussels sprouts were hard as a rock and tasted like yard grass, but civility mandated I not spit them out.

"So, Mr. and Mrs. Barrington, I understand you once operated a hotel up here?"

A hue the color of her milk came over Carmen's face. It was foolish of me to bring up such a touchy subject.

"We did at one time," Mr. Barrington said.

"Perhaps we should have left it for the Jews," Mrs. Barrington chimed.

"Mother!" Carmen yelped. "That's a terrible thing to say."

"I didn't mean anything by it, dear. There was a large Jewish demographic that used to vacation up here. Isn't that right, Delton?" Mrs. Barrington said.

"According to the movie Dirty Dancing, the Catskills were indeed a Borscht Belt for vacationing Jews."

The table fell into a low murmur of eating and drinking. Mrs. Barrington and Carmen then collected the plates and invited me to join Mr. Barrington in the study. At this point, I was ready to swear off surprises as a life event, desperately wishing I was back at home in the city. I daydreamed of running out of the house and jumping in the car.

"Dad, can I trust you alone with Delton?" Carmen said.

"He's in good hands, honey. No pun intended," he chuckled.

"Very funny, dad," she trailed.

Mr. Barrington stuck a pipe in his mouth and released his hound dog from captivity, which immediately made another beeline for my face. He pointed to a chessboard on a little table and lit his pipe.

"It's been a really long time, but sure, I know how to play," I said.

Mr. Barrington corralled the dog beside his recliner. The pipe smoke smelled pungent and rich, which somewhat relaxed me. The chessboard pieces were handmade animal figurines. Actually, a stuffed deer head was mounted on the wall behind the fireplace.

He motioned for me to make the first move to start the game. I pushed a pawn forward (half-expecting to hear checkmate!). It was silent in the study, save for the dog's whimpers and the labored protrusions of smoke from Barrington's mouth.

"I see you have a stuffed deer head. Are you a hunter?"

He scratched at his gray stubble and made his first move on the board.

"I was. Used to take down game, large as antelopes. I rarely get out these days, but every so often I oil up my barrels."

"Can I ask you what that's like? Kind of a man versus nature thing?"

I nervously moved another pawn.

"It's hard to describe. If you've ever really succeeded at something, you would know what I mean. There's a sense of power. The fact that the setting is the woods makes victory all the more unpredictable, and therefore more satisfying."

"I can appreciate that. I think I'd rather get that feeling from writing a poem, but I understand what you're saying."

"I'm sure you do."

The dog's big gums blubbered, the animal now in dreamland. Mr. Barrington replenished his pipe. A momentary stillness gripped the room.

"My daughter tells me you're a lawyer," he said.

"I am. I was admitted recently, and now I'm trying to figure out what's next."

"You're not applying to firms?"

"I'm not too interested in that."

He leaned forward. "Well, what are you interested in?"

"I'd like to make use of the degree, find a way to help people and enjoy what I'm doing. I also would like to spend time in court, I think."

Mr. Barrington didn't respond. We moved more quickly now, until I found my figurines woefully outgunned. Carmen came into the study to join us, in time to watch her father hand me my ass in two finishing moves. He took the dog and excused himself for bed.

"Uh, where am I staying, babe?"

Carmen looked at me funny, grabbed my bag and plopped it in her room. We closed the door and started to undress.

"Didn't you learn not to say more than necessary?"

"What are you talking about?" I said.

"With my father. Why did you tell him your life story, that you're not interested in making money and being successful?"

"I didn't say that."

"You told him you weren't interested in a firm."

"Listen, you didn't even tell me I was about to meet your parents. You were listening at the door?"

She sighed. "Okay, let's forget it. It's just that he can be really judgmental. Didn't you hear him at dinner?"

"It's no big deal."

"I still think you need to be punished," she said, dropping her bra on the floor and removing her panties.

"Babe, I don't think that's such a hot idea."

"You know it's hot." She crawled over the bed, naked, and rubbed against me. I always felt she could turn anything around, real-quick.

"I know the door's closed, but I don't need your father's barrels busting it down any second."

I pushed away her writhing body. She pouted and slid under the covers, facing the other way. I got in bed and watched her fall asleep, leaving me to wrestle insomnia on my own. After a time, the ceiling became a blurry backdrop for my thoughts on what to do with my life. It wasn't always easy to ignore the influence of so-called authority figures.

"Del, you up?"

Carmen was already washed and dressed.

"Uh, technically."

She opened the curtains and a blast of sunshine ended any hope for more shuteye.

"It's almost ten. We really slept in. Anyway, my parents have decided to take an earlier train, so I need to drive them into town. Why don't you put something on and come say goodbye?"

"Gimme a sec," I said, pulling the blanket back over my head. I heard her scamper out of the room. This was good news, I told myself, finally rolling off the bed. I brushed my teeth and rummaged for the clothes I discarded last night. I got it together and found the troupe all packed and ready for departure near the kitchen.

"Mr. and Mrs. Barrington, thank you so much for your hospitality. This was better than a five-star hotel."

Carmen shot me a look.

"Thank you, dear, you're welcome any time," Mrs. Barrington said, her husband pushing the luggage toward the door.

"Work on your chess game, young man, and good luck to you," he said, with scarcely a look in my direction, taking the dog by its leash.

"I'll be right back, Delton, okay? In about a half-hour, forty minutes tops. There's food in the kitchen. Go make yourself an English muffin and some coffee."

They were out the door and I was suddenly alone in the Barrington house.

I dawdled around the kitchen, stirring some shitty instant coffee and toasting the muffin. The little transistor radio played Tchaikovsky and when the piece ended, the disc jockey announced the time. I noted that it was now ten, and they'd left maybe ten minutes ago. I took my clothes off and sat on the little stool in the kitchen in my underwear, munching the muffin and slurping the mud. It definitely said a lot that Carmen wanted me to meet her parents. I found myself reflecting on her support after I lost my dad, as well as the soft feel of her hand in mine.

By the time I polished off another cup of coffee, the DJ announced it was fifteen after ten. I put the dirty dishes in the sink and went to our bedroom for a proper shower.

I dried my hair and wrapped the towel around my waist. I wandered the hall, enjoying the solitude, the comfort of it. I came upon the master bedroom. They had neglected to give me a proper tour last night, a wrong I could surely remedy now that I stood in the doorway. It may have been a fear of unearthing Mr. Barrington's secret gimp gear, or simple decorum, but in the end, I chose not to cross its threshold.

A moment ago, a calm pervaded the house, but now a certain dread crept into my psyche. Where was Carmen? It had been longer than she said. I went back to our room, dug through my jean pockets and flipped open my cell phone. *Six* new messages! All in the last twenty minutes! What the hell?

The first message was from Skywalker, asking if I wanted him to drop by my apartment with new product. I deleted that one. The next four were quick hang-ups, but with a lot of noise in the background. The last one was a loud, frantic voice: "This message is for Delton. Carmen Barrington has been in a car accident in the town of Liberty, at the corner of Main and Honeysuckle. She's receiving medical attention. Thank you."

I clasped the phone shut, choking on a breath, slid commando-style into my jeans, pulled on a shirt and ran out of the room. How would I get to wherever the hell Honeysuckle was? The Datsun must be the car in the accident. Maybe the Barrington's had a car? There was a garage off the kitchen, but the only thing in there was covered by a tarp. Did the Barringtons have Doc Brown's time-traveling DeLorean in their garage? I didn't want to find out.

Right on the refrigerator door was the number for a taxi service. I waited for thirty minutes—without Carmen answering her cell—until the damn taxi finally pulled into the driveway. I hopped in and barked the coordinates, and the cabbie let out a slow whistle.

"What is it?"

"Bad accident over there, my friend. Just came up that way."

"Can you hurry? I think my girlfriend was in it."

"Alright, we'll take Algonquin and skip the traffic coming off I-16."

"I don't give a shit if you take Thunder Road, just get us there."

"You got it, chief."

He backed out of the long, snaking driveway, head turned over his shoulder, little pencil in his mouth. It never failed. Every taxi in history, outside New York City, was somebody's old Chrysler or Buick, with crushed tissue boxes and germ-ridden magazines all over the back seat. If it weren't for the exterior color and working windows, it would've been a dead ringer for Darby's piece of shit.

"What was your girlfriend driving?"

"A Datsun convertible. '70s make."

"Yeah, I seen that one. Fuckin' thing was on its side, man."

He peered at me through the rearview and saw my face blanch.

"Sorry. Maybe she's okay."

We sped along an endlessly curving road with tall trees and ramshackle row houses. I checked my phone. Nothing. A line of stores finally came into view. It was a one-horse town so it didn't take much to find the site of the crash. It was chaos out there, gawkers on the sidewalks, a fire truck, two ambulances with EMTs, three cop cars, and broken glass all over the road. In the center of it all was a flipped station wagon, its front window blown out, and the Datsun nearby, turned on its side. In the commotion, I saw a stretcher being loaded onto the back of one of the ambulances.

I threw a wad of dollar bills at the driver and jumped out of the car. My eyes were bleary with confusion, the unfamiliar surroundings and shitstorm of activity short-circuiting my thinking. The first thing I did was run over to where the stretcher was loaded. It wasn't Carmen. A heavyset man lay flat on his back, a gash across his forehead. A gaggle of little kids in orthodox Jewish garb ran in circles around the back of the ambulance. I asked an EMT where I could find the driver of the other car. He pointed off to the far side of the street and there Carmen stood, two EMTs around her.

As I drew closer, she appeared to be miraculously untouched.

"Carmen!"

She gazed at me, not quite registering my presence, obviously in a kind of paralysis.

"What's your relationship to Ms. Barrington?" An EMT in baggy pants with neon strips asked me.

"I'm—she's my girlfriend."

"I need you to stand back, sir."

"Excuse me, I have a right to—"

"Wait." A little sound from Carmen. Her eyes darted, over-whelmed by the clamor, and she spread her arms out toward me. I stepped past the EMT and embraced her. She trembled and laid her head on my shoulder.

"You're okay, baby." I mouthed to the other EMT behind her, 'Is she okay?'

"She seems okay to us, especially after a wreck like that. She's very lucky to walk away from it. Her blood pressure and pulse are a little high, but hell, that'll happen if you're late for work. So, based on our cursory examination, she didn't break anything or sustain a concussion. But when we're through, she should go to the hospital to be checked more thoroughly."

"I'm okay," Carmen whispered in my ear. We pulled apart and I studied her face. She seemed to be more with it, her color returning.

"Her car looks pretty well fucked-up though," the other EMT added.

"It's a loaner," Carmen said with a smirk.

I let some air out. She was okay.

"We'll just be a few more minutes," the EMT said. "Sorry for my profanity, Miss."

I left Carmen in their care and took the opportunity to put my newly minted lawyer hat on. While I didn't have a camera, there were several locals standing on both sides of the street. Witnesses. I sauntered up to a friendly looking one holding a little girl's hand.

"Excuse me, sir, did you happen to see the accident?"

"Matter of fact, I did. Who's asking?"

"I'm the boyfriend of the girl who was in the Datsun over there," I said. "Would you mind telling me what you saw?"

"That crazy guy in the hat and beard shot right through a red light coming down the hill into the intersection. Your girlfriend was making a left turn with the green light, and then whammo! He hit her right on the passenger side of her car. She'd would've been toast if hit on the driver side. Then her car tipped over but somehow didn't flip, damn cars were real heaps of metal back then. This guy's station wagon, with all those kids in it, swerved out of control and hit that fence over there. Unbelievable that all those kids crammed in the backseat weren't hurt. Just this idiot."

Thank God, she had the convertible top up.

"That's very helpful, sir. Do you mind if I take down your name and contact info?"

That's how it went. I interviewed two other witnesses before the cops shooed me away—and all their accounts were consistent. This orthodox guy in a station wagon ran the red light and hit her. We took the ambulance to the hospital and after several hours waiting in the ER, she checked out fine, with a little whiplash and a referral to a chiropractor.

We settled back in at the house.

"Would you like a little wine or something?"

"Sure, that's a good idea," she said.

I uncorked a bottle of Chardonnay from the refrigerator and poured two glasses.

"What a day. Maybe you can see it as an opportunity. Surviving the accident, I mean."

She sipped her glass, looking pensive.

"I'm so relieved you're okay," I said, wrapping my arms around her.

"Well, my boyfriend came to my rescue."

It was the first time I heard her say the word.

"I always wanted to ride in on a horse and save the day."

"Well, your being there made me feel a little less crazy. Even safe."

We kissed and held each other. After another glass, we fell into a deep sleep, and caught the morning train back to the city.

Chapter 25

The birds gathered along the streetlights outside my apartment window. A car honk prompted them to clap their wings in unison and scatter. My eyes were slow to open. It was a Tuesday morning and I had nowhere to be. Nonetheless, the day wouldn't start itself; I forced my legs to swing off the bed and ran the water in the shower. The phone in the living room rang.

"Get on the train and meet me at court this afternoon. Two o' clock, Department O, Bronx Supreme."

"Okay." He clicked off. Nate was especially busy in the mornings.

The subway uptown was packed with bodies. Two men in suits were discussing strategy for a robbery trial they had coming up. I understood a lot of the legal particulars they mentioned. There was something about this conversation that brought to light the terrifying clarity of my situation. I needed Nate. No other firm would offer me a job. Moreover, I'd neglected to apply to the District Attorney or Public Defender offices, where top grades were not as prioritized as litigation prowess.

The train surfaced from its tunnel. Above ground, the decay of boarded tenements and busted fire hydrants rushed by. The train ground to a halt at the appointed stop, and once walking these streets again, I felt a sense of familiarity return. The windblown dirt, smells from a Russian bakery, the bang and rattle of other trains, and city dwellers scuttling about reminded me of when I ran errands for Norris. I hadn't received as much as a phone call from him since my father died.

The courthouse's massive steps and sculpted justice scales brought to mind the museum outing with Carmen. Would she feel excited for me? I was on the verge of entering court for the first time as an admitted attorney. At the top of the steps I heard metal detectors beeping in the entry. That sound, like a warning, brought a critical fact to my awareness: empty weed canisters from Skywalker were still in my bag!

Traipsing back down the steps to an adjacent park, furtively looking over my shoulder, I quietly deposited the contraband into a trashcan. I left the reeking bag open, praying for a gust of wind. I realized this habit, moving forward, was an untenable one; if I persisted, I would need my own attorney.

The lobby boasted a high ceiling and wide hallway that echoed with the sound of heels clicking its marble floor. It was a grand old structure, adorned with copper-plated elevator doors and lavish clocks. It felt like Grand Central on an off-peak hour, as steady foot traffic passed through its cavernous space.

I couldn't find a directory, so I asked a bespectacled woman in a pantsuit by the elevator bank where to find Department O. She sent me to a floor where the hallway was empty, and I circled around until I came upon it. Nate and another man exited just then, laughing together. He finished up his conversation, introduced me quickly, and we left, my first foray into court already over.

His driver waited at curbside in a sporty BMW. He was an ex-boxer who wore a leather jacket, had a shaved head, and spoke with a thick New York accent.

"Nate, youse already defend the guy? It ain't even five o'clock and your guy is free?"

"Now Joe, I wouldn't make my client wait another minute to get out of that pesky twenty-year sentence. I was worried he wouldn't beat the rush-hour traffic."

Nate's office was crammed with brown accordion case files, boxes of documents, mountainous filing cabinets, and a wall of courtroom sketches of him on trial. An assistant sat out front, an older woman named Betty, who spoke softly and giggled at Nate's jokes. There were two other offices for his associates. It was rather threadbare decor for one of the city's premier criminal defense attorneys, with the exception of Nate's private office. It was an opulent arrangement with plush couch, big-screen television, an antique desk encased in glass, and a stocked bar. Clippings of his cases and photos with famous clients were framed on every wall. I took a seat across from him, noticing the gold buttons embroidered in the armrests.

"You think you're going to get a pass here?"

"No."

"Is that why your tail is wagging between your legs?"

"Hey Uncle Nate – you called me."

He couldn't help but smile.

"Listen, Nate, I know you're not only my uncle, you're one of the best defense attorneys in town. Where else would I be?"

"One of the best?" He cockeyed me. "Have you seen the clippings?" He gestured to the surrounding walls and lit a thick cigar.

"I certainly have. They're very impressive."

"You don't make friends very easily, do you?" he said.

"I have plenty of friends," I said, aware that the rabbit punch was part of his repertoire.

He eased back in his leather chair and studied me. "You know how much I miss your old man, Delton. But the fact is, you now get to choose what you want to do. I gather you want to practice law?"

"Yes."

"What have you done to get a job?"

"Well, I sent resumes off to firms. Okay, one resume."

"That's it? How do you expect to get anywhere being lazy?"

"I'm not lazy. I took care of my father's whole—"

"I know," he sighed, leaning back in his chair. "You mentioned you're interested in trial work. Have you applied to the District Attorney's office, or the Public Defender's office?"

"I have not. Not yet, I'm getting my options together."

"Now you know that's not going to cut it."

"Yeah, I know." I cleared my throat, "What kind of volume does this office get at a given time?"

"It's not the volume. It's the client and size of the retainer."

"I see. And turnover? Settling cases?"

"We don't turnover. We try cases here."

"Well, I want to try cases."

"What if your guy tells you he did it?"

"He could be half-mad and not know what he's saying."

"What if he's competent to stand trial and he tells you he did the shooting?"

"It's not my job to judge him, that's for a jury to do. I'm there to do everything within my legal power to represent him zealously."

"Do you want him to spill his guts to you?"

"If I don't anticipate his taking the witness stand. This way I have all the facts from his side, but if it's likely he'll testify, I may not want to know."

"Why not?"

"I can't suborn perjury, like if he wants me to elicit a bunch of shit from him under oath that contradicts what he already told me, or it clearly doesn't add up."

Nate's eyes softened. "You remember what I told you about your license, never to risk it for a client?"

"I do, Uncle Nate. Can I ask you something else, a bit off-topic?"

"Yes." He twirled the cigar in his lips until it lit.

"You're a pretty observant Jew, aren't you?"

"I keep kosher. Where did that come from?" His eyes narrowed.

"Nowhere. I know asking a defense attorney how he morally represents people that lie, kill, and steal is sort of taboo . . ."

"Maybe it's not in you to do this work after all."

"That's not what I'm saying—I'm pretty sure it is—it's just the clients on your wall make up a kind of criminal hall of fame. Don't misread me, but didn't you win these cases when there was strong evidence against your guy, because you talked the jury out of convicting?"

"That's the art, kid, raising reasonable doubt and tearing down the government's case. But the government can be a vengeful machine bent on destroying a life when it's not warranted. That is what we do. We are a necessary check against this power. Plus, it's business, and when you're the best, business is good, especially repeat business."

"I doubt the Talmud talks about repeat business."

"Don't be so naive. The Talmud talks about life serving the highest good, and what may appear harmful can actually be beneficial, in a larger sense. There are plenty of biblical tales that point to one fundamental truth in human existence; we each have a role to play, and we are entrusted to fulfill it with strength and faith, despite the perceived outcome, for the highest good."

"I didn't mean to get into a theological roundtable with you. Look, I eat bacon, I don't go to synagogue, and I still miss the nerve endings taken at my bris. But I am a Jew that honors tradition, and that tends to include a fair amount of guilt. So, I was curious about your take on defense work, which is complex and morally ambiguous, and how it relates to your religious observance."

"There are no answers, Delton. And I promise you one thing, if there are, you don't have them, and neither do I." Nate shifted around in his huge leather chair and set his cigar down. "You want to question my faith and doubt the honor of this work, that's up to you. Whether this work is for you, that too is up to you. Whether or not you work here, that is up to me."

"I want to work here, Uncle Nate. I want to rip the government's head off and stuff it down their neck."

"Good. That's what I want to hear." He gave me a sly smile. "I'm going to put you with Ken. He's one of my two full-time associates. He'll show you what he and Anna, my other associate, will expect from you. Just do what they say unless a problem comes up, then bring it to me."

I threw myself into the work, doing twelve-hour days for a minimum of seventy hours per week. The first two weeks were especially grueling, given the steep learning curve of adjusting to life in the office.

Ken was a pencil-thin, manic collection of limbs that never seemed to stop moving. He worked the phone, reviewed a file, wrote a motion, and heated his vegetable soup all at once, explaining that the family recipe kept him calm. Nate said Ken was a top trial lawyer with a mind like a diamond, able to come up with inventive arguments on the fly. Ken assigned me research for his various motions.

"Lowe, I need you to photocopy every case you find on warrantless trunk searches in car stops, highlight the relevant finding and facts, organize it into a folder, and have it on my desk by tomorrow morning."

"Ken, an hour ago you asked me to draft two speedy trial motions and a motion to controvert the search warrant on the *Blanco* matter for court on Wednesday," I said.

"Yes, and? Is there a problem?" His office stank of Chef-Boyardee.

"No, of course not, it's just that I need time to research this motion, and the research on the car stop is an entirely different matter."

"Lowe, there's at least forty-three hours between now and my Wednesday morning court appearance. Stop jabbering in my doorjamb and solve your problem."

That was it. His attention veered to his computer screen, and all I could do was follow orders. It did not take long to taste the life of a young lawyer.

Anna, Nate's other colleague, used to do freelance work for the firm and recently joined as a full-time associate. She handled federal work with Nate, even pitching in on the latest Nicky indictment for racketeering. She was a good deal friendlier than Ken and less restless, too, which was ironic, given Anna sipped Diet Coke and chewed Nicorette gum nonstop. She showed me the ropes, as Nate was never around and Ken was in his own world. One afternoon, as we sat together in her office, I noticed the empty Diet Coke cans spilling out of the wastebasket.

"Yes, my habit has ballooned to twelve cans a day since I stopped drinking coffee." Anna smiled.

"Maybe just a little coffee might ease you off the soda," I offered.

"Listen, Delton, there's always a ton of work. You have to do a good job because I can tell you have a heart, and you want to sleep at night, don't you? So who cares if your client did it or not? You're still the only thing standing between the conviction-hungry government and a human being rotting in prison. This is a lot to accept, it's not for everyone. But hey, take a guy like Ken. He couldn't give a crap. He gets off on the craft of it, the battle, the duel of wits with the prosecution. I really want to win, but because it's legally important to win, to keep the system honest, y'know?"

Three months passed quickly and I'd developed a routine. I scarcely saw Nate; he was either on trial or schmoozing clients, but I got used to his absence. I'd alternate from Anna to

Ken, doing all the tasks they didn't want to do. Anna continued to be cool, but Ken was a tyrant who relished shitting on an underling. No matter whom I worked for, the assignments were always done in the office. I never saw the inside of a courtroom.

One night I left the office late at night totally burned out. Ken was a monkey on my back; I had to be behind my desk again in six short hours. After I got off the train and bought takeout, I dialed Carmen. She picked up after several rings, just before it slid to voicemail.

"Hey."

"Hey. How are you?"

"Fine." Her voice sounded distant.

"What's the matter?"

"Nothing's the matter. Why would you ask that?" She snapped.

"Listen, Carm, it's not my fault I work long hours that probably break every child labor law. That's just how it is for new lawyers."

"But you don't call much. You don't really want to see me."

"What on earth are you talking about? You think I want to see Ken's face at 1:00 a.m. on a Friday night? Besides, you've always been the busy one. Don't make this out like it's only me."

"I never avoided seeing you." I heard her exhale smoke. There were voices in her backdrop.

"That's so ridiculous, I absolutely want to see you. Where are you, a bar?" I made it to the stoop of my apartment building, tie undone, shirt tails out, takeout food in my lap.

"Yeah, with a client."

"So what the hell are you upset with me for!"

She chuckled. "Maybe you're right. I just—when I don't see you, or hear from you, I start imagining things."

"It's not gonna be this crazy all the time. Don't you miss me?"

"Yeah." Her voice grew quiet. "I really do."

"I promise we'll spend more time together. Maybe this Sunday. But I have to be in the office all day tomorrow. Okay?"

"Okay. See you."

She hung up.

Chapter 26

I had the feeling that anything I said would not be what Carmen wanted to hear. To my surprise, on our next call, she alluded to my moving in with her. It was difficult to compute. Meanwhile, Ken was gearing up for trial, so I was tied up all weekend and worked right through the week. I tried calling her a couple nights later, but got no answer.

She called me back Friday night and said I had to visit her new place right away. This was a relief, as I really wanted us to have some quality time together, and be back on the same page.

The doorman of the luxury building checked my credentials and wouldn't let me up. He told me he was not notified of any visitor pass and would have to confirm with the resident. I stood in the lobby, staring into this giant mirror behind the front desk, while he called Carmen for permission. He then showed me to the space-age elevator, which shot to the twenty-first floor. Carmen greeted me at the door, very tipsy, cheeks flushed and eyes glassy.

"Sexy pants, get in here!" She threw her arms wildly around me.

"I'm here, babe. You seem pretty lit. Did you go out already?"

I set a hand on her lower back and ushered her inside. A woman about our age was on the couch sipping a drink.

"Oh, I didn't know you had company. Hi, I'm Delton."

She was high-fashion, in black boots, black dress, hair pulled tight in a ponytail.

"I'm Jane," she said in a low decibel, her lavender-colored nails scraping against my palm as we shook. It was the way she looked at me, a slow burning energy that made me think of only one thing.

"So you girls started without me. How naughty."

I went to the kitchen. There was an uncorked bottle of champagne chilling on ice. Carmen's new place was quite minimalist, only black film stills on the wall, and a white couch with a black Formica-top table.

"We were a little prematurely excited," Carmen said. "I had an early bite with Jane, and then I figured, why send her home when she's so much fun?"

"It's true, Delton. I'm so much fun."

It wasn't amusing. "So how do you two know each other?"

"Oh, as kids," Jane said. "We grew up in the city and went to high school together."

"Have a drink already!" Carmen thrust a flute of bubbly into my hand. "Let's toast to Delton. He graduated law school and passed the bar! My big lawyer-man."

We all clinked glasses.

"So you're an attorney?" Jane asked. She pulled a long cigarette out, and I wondered how her pink lipstick would look smeared on its tip.

"I am, not that I'm capable of keeping you two out of trouble."

"You'll need a lot more than legal skills for that, honey," Carmen quipped.

"I think you two had a lot to drink over dinner. That's when Carmen starts spouting corny lines." I took her in my arms and ran a hand down to her hip, kissing her on the mouth. "But you do taste good."

I turned back to Jane and released Carmen.

"So how about you, Jane, now that you know my life story. And do you have any music in this place, Carm?"

"I'm a makeup artist, but very specific and sought-after," she said, crossing her legs in that short black dress.

"What is it you do?"

"Well, I used to work for runway models in New York and Paris, and for high-end magazine glossies. But I found a niche much more my speed."

"Which is?" I asked, finishing off my flute. Carmen immediately swiped the empty from my hand. She also put on some low-key electronic beat.

"I'm a makeup artist for adult film stars, mostly out in LA."

"If you did runway work, you must have walked away from a fortune."

"The change of lifestyle and its perks are so worth it," Jane said, with a flutter of blue eyes.

"She's in town visiting, Del!" Carmen called from the kitchen.

"Of course, I lived in New York City forever, so it's always a real indulgence to visit, but I like my kidney pools and hot springs," Jane said.

"Like in Palm Springs?"

"Yes, but it's all so wonderful! The thing about living out west are all the attractions. Do you go out there?"

"Not enough, apparently. Anyway, I guess in a sense, as one quite familiar with adult film, I'm an admirer of your work."

"Can I tell you something?" She uncrossed her legs and leaned forward.

"Anything."

"There are girls who spent a little too much time on the farm, their faces kicked in by donkeys. But honestly, I crave that challenge. Once I come on set, more than any other artist—I send little Cinderella to the ball," she said, licking her lips in a self-satisfied grin.

"Sure," I said. I was losing my composure, and trying not to show it. Carmen emerged from the kitchen with a fresh flute for me.

"I have strawberries too, lady and gentleman," she announced. "Anyone?"

I couldn't tell if I was the patsy in some kind of wicked, predatory sex game, but whatever was going on here, I just wanted to be alone with Carmen.

"Yes, I'd like some strawberries. In fact, I'll help you get them ready," I said, taking Carmen by the elbow and escorting her to the kitchen. "Be right back, Jane. Need a drink?"

"I'm okay, but you should catch up. I'm so glad Carmen finally brought you by, Delton. We haven't seen Norris in ages."

The champagne bottle sat on the counter, so I quickly drained my drink and poured another.

"What do you think of Jane?" she whispered, pulling a little bowl out of the otherwise empty fridge. She must be living on champagne and strawberries, I thought.

"She's an attractive girl. Not as much as you, though."

"Aww, that's sweet," she said, running water over the bowl. Our eyes met. What the hell had Jane just said? *We haven't seen Norris in ages.*

"Have you been up here with Jane before?"

Carmen ran a hand through her hair. "We're friends. Sure."

I didn't answer.

"Like my new place?" She giggled.

"I thought you were my girl, Carmen."

"Del, we never . . ."

"Aha! So you and this bimbo-"

"Shhh. Keep your voice down. Jane can hear."

"I'm sorry if the porn star can hear us!"

"Artist for porn stars," Carmen corrected.

"Adult actors," Jane called from the couch.

"Sorry, Jane," I said, not sure why I was apologizing. "Look Carmen, trying to include me in a three-way is very thoughtful of you. I mean, the last gift I got was a new sweater, but I need to know. What's the deal with you and Norris?"

"We ended it before you and me, but we started working closely again for elections . . ."

"So you pursued him."

"Nobody pursued anybody. Can we stop this?"

"How long?"

"There's no-"

"Are you seeing him now? Don't lie."

"It was very on and off, mostly off . . ."

"On enough that he saw you and Jane together, right? Because you're both doing him."

"It's not like that."

"What's it like, Carmen? What's it like to be so avant-garde? I absolutely must hire Jane for my next get together. I just love what she can do with hair and costuming."

"Stop it, Delton." Her hands covered her face. "You didn't want to see me. Or live with me."

"I'd just got back on my feet. I'd lost my dad, moved into the city, and started a whole new career. How is that a reason?"

"I didn't say it was."

"You've been acting strangely since the car accident. I don't understand. You say you want *me*, but really, you just want. . . somebody."

Through mascara-smudged tears, and after a long pause, she addressed me evenly.

"I love you, Del, whether or not you believe that. But you should go. "

I didn't have anything more to say, and yet, as soon as I was in the empty hallway, the door shut behind me, all I wanted was to be let back in. For my heart, foolish muscle that it was, nothing could reverse this bottoming-out, this sense of failure; not time, not if Norris disappeared, not even Carmen herself.

I took the stairs one flight at a time, twenty-one floors, until reaching the lobby. Its shiny polish looked fake. I glanced in the wide mirror behind the concierge's desk. The face I saw was creased with pain. I slid the ring with the Indian carvings off my finger and fired it at the mirror. I heard glass shatter, and shouts behind me, but soon the city air was all there was.

Chapter 27

A couple days later, back at my desk, I could scarcely touch the stack of files in front of me. The work blurred, running together, and yet time seemed to slow to a dead stop. Nate phoned the office from court and invited me for a late lunch at an Italian restaurant in Harlem. I was only too happy for a reprieve. The place was dark, even for an already cloudy afternoon. Nate was not alone.

"Nicky, this is my friend Larry Lowe's kid, Delton Lowe. He's a new attorney in my office. You actually met him years ago at his law school celebration dinner."

He was grayer in his hair and mustache now. Leaning in to shake the man's hand, I inhaled a medley of spit polish, worn leather, dry cologne, and aged Scotch.

"Pleasure to see you again, kid. You gonna be in court soon?" he said.

"I hope to."

"I ordered the chicken with peppers, is that okay with you?" Nate said.

"Absolutely, Uncle Nate."

"Hear about my latest win, Nick?" Nate asked.

"Can't say that I have."

"Jury came back not guilty. Bad rape case, but the jury bought my defense—the woman got her bruises from an unrelated assault. It was my client's second not-guilty with me on a rape at trial." Nate dabbed his lips with the sauce-encrusted napkin tucked at his chin. "He said he's always going to use me."

"That's great, counselor, but we was gonna talk about *my* case."

"Of course."

Nicky snapped his fingers and a rotund man emerged from the shadows and handed Nate a briefcase. Nicky then dismissed him.

"All right, look, I'm not on them government tapes. They tapped the wrong line. Better yet, they recorded talk from guys I don't even know. So I ask you, what does any of this got to do with me?"

Nicky wiped his chin and folded his arms, a totally innocuous move, but it had such menace. It was the first I'd heard a mob client talk about his case.

"They haven't turned over all the tapes yet, Nick. It's a discovery process—and don't worry. If they can't prove your involvement, and if nobody flips, you'll be fine. I'm assuming you won't want a plea offer."

"An offer? Please." He ripped a piece of bread and slathered it with butter, shaking his head. Every movement put me on edge.

"All right, you and the kid enjoy. I need to drop a few anyways," he said and got up, rubbing his belly and smiling with a mouthful of chewed bread. I wondered if he was a real killer and if so, how he could appear so amiable. When he walked away, the air in my chest escaped through my nostrils, as if I'd held it the whole time.

"That was quite a story on your rape case," I said.

"A satisfying win, because . . ." Nate saw me scowl. "Look, Del, it's good to let the clients know you're winning. It's business. Also, the hell with it, you know how many lives I've saved from overzealous prosecutors? C'mon, let's finish up and get back to the office." Nate grabbed the case.

"What's in the briefcase, Nate?"

"The bottom line, kid. There's no justice until Mr. Green shows up, like I once told you." He popped it open, revealing bundles of cash, tightly sealed. "More work means more legal fees, and you heard the man—he doesn't want a deal. This case is headed to trial."

Nate gave me the rest of the day off. There was a light drizzle as I walked uptown without any destination in mind. The direction seemed to unfold by itself, with New Yorkers passing on the sidewalk, yellow taxis changing lanes, and an electric saw grinding at a construction site.

I saw a sign hanging on the front of a building to reelect an assemblyman in this district. I figured he might need Carmen's public relations, Willy Rodger's canvassing, my late father's fundraising, and ultimately, even Nate's legal counsel. He likely ate at the same joints and shook all the same hands. Everybody just doing their job.

I looked away and immediately caught sight of another large sign, an advertisement for diamonds. It read—'Open this box and live out your dreams!'—accompanied by the image of a couple walking arm-in-arm into a sunset, a fat diamond on the woman's finger.

It was easy to imagine myself there. And yet, absorbing the sign, I couldn't include Carmen. I didn't want to; the bitter taste in my heart would not allow it.

As I continued to walk the streets, each intersection, with its hurried traffic and busy storefronts, reminded me of my father. I missed him. But I knew I could not live his reality. I needed to live my own.

At the next crosswalk the light was red, and so I stood on the corner, waiting. A man came out of a kosher deli wearing a tan brown fedora. It hung low enough to cast the man's eyes in shadow. I had seen this before.

My father would always be here.

The rain finally broke after another couple blocks. The clouds drifted apart, and faint hues of purple and orange became visible, like fresh strokes across the sky. The memory of Finkle and me hiding in Galler's evidence class came to mind—his unicorn sex tryst was hard to forget—and I realized how much I missed him.

We hadn't spoken much of late—both of us workingmen now—but I called him on the spot.

"How's the criminal defense practice?" he said.

"Fine, but I want to be in court and try cases. How's the insurance defense firm?"

"Oh, I'm living the dream – writing nonstop motions—but hey, they cover my carpal tunnel."

"Is there still a place on the marquee for Lowe & Finkle, P.C.?" I asked.

"Finkle & Lowe? You mean it?"

"Hell yes," I laughed, "but you handle the family law cases."

"I can do that," he said.

"Good, you can start with Jaspr's divorce."

"Oh shit, he's getting divorced? I didn't even know he was married!"

"He's not," I said, smiling. "Forget it."

THE END

About the Author

Erik Lewin is a former criminal defense attorney turned writer and stand-up comedian. For more information, visit www.eriklewincomedy.com.

CPSIA information can be obtained
at www.ICGtesting.com
Printed in the USA
FSHW010727040219
55459FS